TWO

WEEK

'TIL

Christmas

Laura Greaves is an award-winning author, journalist and editor who announced her intention to be a writer at the age of seven, largely because of her dual obsessions with *Anne of Green Gables* and *Murder, She Wrote*.

Two Weeks 'til Christmas is her third novel. She is also the author of *Be My Baby* and *The Ex-Factor*, as well as two non-fiction collections of dog stories, *Dogs with Jobs* and *Incredible Dog Journeys*.

Laura lives in NSW's stunning Blue Mountains with her family and two incorrigible (but seriously adorable) dogs. Her enduring *Anne of Green Gables* fixation is matched only by her dog obsession, which is why you will always find at least one four-legged-friend in Laura's books.

Connect with Laura:
lauragreaves.com
facebook.com/lauragreaveswritesbooks
instagram.com/lauragreavesauthor
twitter.com/Laura_Greaves

TWO

WEEKS

'TIL

Christmas

LAURA GREAVES

MICHAEL JOSEPH
an imprint of
PENGUIN BOOKS

MICHAEL JOSEPH

UK | USA | Canada | Ireland | Australia
India | New Zealand | South Africa | China

Penguin Books is part of the Penguin Random House group of companies
whose addresses can be found at global.penguinrandomhouse.com.

Penguin
Random House
Australia

First published by Penguin Random House Australia Pty Ltd, 2017

1 3 5 7 9 10 8 6 4 2

Cover design by Louisa Maggio © Penguin Random House Australia Pty Ltd
Text design by Samantha Jayaweera © Penguin Random House Australia Pty Ltd
Cover photographs: couple by courtneyk/Getty Images; Christmas decoration by
Karen Katrjyan/Shutterstock; lights by Studio Peace/Shutterstock
Typeset in 12/18 pt Sabon by Midland Typesetters, Australia
Colour separation by Splitting Image Colour Studio, Clayton, Victoria
Printed and bound in Australia by Griffin Press, an accredited ISO AS/NZS 14001
Environmental Management Systems printer.

National Library of Australia
Cataloguing-in-Publication data:

Greaves, Laura, author.
Two weeks 'til Christmas/Laura Greaves.
9780143787709 (paperback)
Subjects: Christmas--Australia--Fiction.
Romance fiction.

penguin.com.au

To the ones we can't forget

PROLOGUE

On the rare occasions Claire allowed herself a stroll down memory lane, Scotty Shannon was always her destination. She would find him in the recesses of her mind, waiting for her, still wearing the crooked smile that always surprised her because it made his serious face look so different. She would visit with him for a while, deep inside the thoughts she kept hidden away for safekeeping: those brittle moments whose replays she rationed for fear of wearing them out and losing them forever.

Claire always took care to return to one of the happy days. Sometimes it was the first time Scotty told her he loved her, in the grotty kitchen of the dilapidated house he shared with three other veterinary science students. Sometimes it was earlier than that, the night of the beer-soaked O-Week party, the first time she'd seen him in the three years since she'd left Bindallarah. He'd walked into the bar, wearing a Santa hat even though it was almost Easter, and a tiny voice inside her head had exhaled and said, *It's you. At last.*

But most often she went back to Bindallarah and back to the start. Back to the Shannon family's property, Cape Ashe Stud. Back to the stable roof late one Christmas Eve, when she was fifteen and Scotty was sixteen and their futures seemed as infinite and unknowable as the velvet blackness above them.

They often climbed up there after one of the many dinners Claire shared with the Shannons that year, when the atmosphere in her own home grew so thick with tension that choking down a meal was impossible. They would lie on their backs, side by side but not quite touching, and listen to the mares nickering and stomping in their pens below. They'd stay there for hours, talking and laughing and watching the moon trace its languid arc across the sky, drunk on the heavy summer heat and the intoxicating nearness of each other.

And then on Christmas Eve he kissed her. From the corner of her eye, Claire had seen her friend make the decision; watched him resolve that it was now or never. Scotty had a terrible poker face. His thoughts played out in his expression, scudding across his features like summer storm clouds. Then he was resolute and his frown relaxed. He had always been that way: most at ease when he knew his purpose.

The sharp angles that made the other girls at school look past him softened. His hooded moss-green eyes widened. He raised himself up on his right elbow and looked down at her. He saw her. He saw *through* her protective layer to the very core of her.

He lowered his face to hers and when their lips met she felt known. It wasn't her first kiss, or his, but it was *theirs*, and its effect on her body was powerful. All of her senses intensified until she was thrumming with energy – and desire. Suddenly she could hear the waves crashing on Bindallarah Beach, five kilometres away. She could smell the spicy scent of the massive pine tree the Shannons festooned with fairy lights every Christmas. As they relaxed into the kiss, she felt the shape of him, felt herself curve to fit. She kept her eyes open, watched his fingers twist through her tawny curls, and knew with certainty that she would never, ever forget this moment.

Claire rolled the memories of Scotty around in her head like boiled sweets on her tongue. He was a treat, her guilty pleasure. She savoured them, tried to make them last, tried to resist biting and shattering. She strove to be gentle with them, because she hadn't been gentle with him.

Other memories bubbled to the surface, but she pushed them back down. The look on Scotty's face when she left Bindallarah for boarding school a month after their kiss. Or the day, five years later, when he offered her everything and she threw it all back at him.

No, when she wanted to remember, Claire cherry-picked the moments that captured the best of Scotty – the best of her. She chose the snapshots that comforted her unquiet soul. It wasn't that she still loved Scotty – she would hardly know what to say to him if she ever saw him again – but he soothed her somehow. On days like today, when her heart felt heavy, she wrapped the ghost of him around her like a security blanket.

But even the memory of Scotty, even recalling the way every cell once burned for him, wasn't doing anything for her mood tonight. The two glasses of wine weren't helping either.

Claire took another deep gulp of her shiraz as she toggled irritably between social media sites on her tablet. It was all babies, birthdays and bleating about the state of the world by people who were doing absolutely nothing to try to change it. Minutiae. None of it was important, not really. It was hardly life and death. None of her virtual friends or acquaintances was making hard decisions, taking big risks. Not one of them knew what it was like to bet it all – and lose.

Claire sighed and scrolled through the recent posts in one of the equine vets groups she was a member of. She toyed with the idea of making a post herself. Maybe one of her esteemed colleagues could explain to her how she'd managed to lose a champion three-year-old thoroughbred to supporting limb laminitis when her surgical repair of his initial fracture just a week ago had been flawless and his recovery seemed to be textbook perfect. She sure as hell didn't have any idea, and the not knowing was eating her up.

She clicked on the search field and typed 'laminitis'. A list of previous posts on the topic unfurled on her screen. Quickly, Claire scanned them, her blue eyes flicking over the names of the posters – mostly colleagues she knew well and some she didn't know at all.

And then a name she'd said more often than she'd uttered her own appeared.

Claire froze. It couldn't be him. She had searched for him before – more than once – but aside from a couple of years-old mentions in the university alumni magazine, Scotty didn't seem to have any kind of online footprint.

But how many Australian equine vets called Scotty Shannon could there possibly be? Perhaps she could imagine there were two Scott Shannons in their field. But *Scotty*? It had to be him. Her Scotty.

She clicked on the name and the mystery doctor's profile filled the screen. The profile picture was a stallion in full flight – handsome, but of no use to her whatsoever. There were no other photographs. She clicked on the 'About' tab.

Hometown: Bindallarah, New South Wales.

Claire's mouth went dry.

It *was* Scotty. Right here, right in front of her. Eight years since they'd had any contact and he was in her living room, uninvited and undoing her the way he always had.

Her stomach twisted uncomfortably. How long had he been using the site? Had he looked for her? Seen her profile?

Her index finger hovered over the 'Add friend' icon.

Why hasn't he reached out?

Claire swallowed another mouthful of wine. She knew why. She had asked him to stay away. Told him she couldn't be in his life any more.

She had begged him to forget about her and Scotty had obliged.

But everything had been different then. They were so young. She was only twenty; Scotty was twenty-one. They hadn't even finished university. Her life, as ever, was in chaos, while he was diligently carving out the path he had long intended to tread. He had been devastated when she turned their world on its head. But they had grown up since then. Maybe now he would understand. Maybe he would even be happy to hear from her after all this time.

Claire's index finger trembled. She tipped her wineglass to her lips once more. If Scotty was still angry with her, she thought she could bear it; she deserved it. But if he really had forgotten her? She couldn't decide which was worse.

She took a deep breath and tapped the button.

CHAPTER ONE

'Seriously, Claire, just pick one. While we're young?'

Jackie tapped her foot on the café's worn linoleum floor. Actually, tapping was putting it mildly. In the clunky black lace-ups she insisted on wearing with her scrubs, Jackie's impatient *pat-pat-pat* thudded like a kick drum.

'Give a girl a minute, will you?' Claire tossed a mock-peeved glare over her shoulder. 'It's a hard decision.'

Under her breath Jackie muttered, 'It really isn't.'

Claire pretended she hadn't heard. Jackie had only joined her for the trip to the café to escape the astringent clinic smell for a few minutes. She brought the exact same lunch from home every single day: a tiny tin of tuna, six green olives, two Ryvitas with hummus and a single Babybel cheese. It was really no wonder Jackie always seemed so brusque and irritable – she must have been starving.

Claire returned her full attention to the chiller cabinet in front of her and weighed up her options. An unusually busy day meant she hadn't had a moment to eat; now it was nearly four o'clock and she was ravenous. Was she in a chicken-and-avocado-on-wholemeal mood? Perhaps a panini with salami and chargrilled vegetables would hit the spot. Or was it an old-school ham-and-salad-roll kind of day?

'You might have been absent when they covered this at uni, but the ability to make quick decisions is generally something most people expect of an emergency veterinarian,' Jackie said as her staccato on the lino approached machine-gunfire proportions.

'But that's just medicine, Jac. This is way more important. This is *sandwiches*.'

'Ugh!' Jackie threw her hands in the air. 'I'll be out the front. Try not to let me grow old and die there.' She marched outside.

Claire plucked the panini from the shelf and took it to the counter, placing a bottle of apple juice beside it. She'd known it was what she wanted the moment she'd laid eyes on it, but she wasn't about to let Jackie Ryman force her decisions. Beneath her snippy exterior, Jackie was friendly and fun, but she could be demanding – it was part of what made her such a brilliant vet – and Claire didn't do demanding.

She paid for her lunch and pushed through the plastic strips that hung in the café doorway into the sultry December heat. It was like stepping into a furnace. The oppressively hot and humid Sydney summer was already in full swing and there were still two weeks until Christmas. She could drive from the clinic to Coogee Beach in under fifteen minutes, but there was no hint of a sea breeze here on the fringe of Centennial Park. The branches of the enormous Moreton Bay fig trees barely stirred. The air was like soup.

'What are you doing for Christmas?' Jackie asked as they plodded towards the clinic. The street was nearly deserted. Even the passing cars seemed listless.

'Sitting inside with the curtains closed and the air conditioner on if this insane heat continues,' Claire replied.

'How festive.' Jackie made a face. 'Are you working?'

She wasn't. Claire always volunteered to work over Christmas, as well as at Easter and on public holidays. After all, she reasoned, she was single and didn't have children – it was better that her colleagues with families were able to spend the holidays with them. The cases were invariably more interesting on days when most other vet clinics were closed too. On Labour Day back in October, one of the sweet old geldings from the riding stables at nearby Moore Park had presented with severe colic and Claire had saved his life with emergency abdominal surgery.

And, besides, if she was working she had a legitimate reason to say no to Vanessa every time she begged Claire to go back to Bindallarah. She thought guiltily about the unreturned messages from her aunt on her voicemail, the unopened emails in her inbox. She would get to them. Soon.

But this year, James, the practice manager, had ruined her plans by insisting she take three weeks off.

'Actually, no,' Claire said. 'James won't let me. Something about having accrued too much annual leave. Today's my last day until the new year.'

Jackie gave a low whistle. 'Wow. I would have liked to be a fly on the wall for *that* conversation,' she said with a chuckle.

Claire shot her friend a sharp look. 'What's that supposed to mean?'

'Nothing, nothing,' Jackie said, holding up her hands in a gesture of surrender. 'It's just . . . you're not especially fond of being told what to do, Claire. You were that kid who was always backchatting the teachers, right?'

Jackie was smiling, but Claire's chest tightened as in her mind's eye she suddenly saw herself as a skinny sixteen-year-old, cowering in the gloomy, oak-panelled principal's office at St Columba's. Her skin prickled at the memory of the thick wool dress and matching blazer, which had to be worn on even the hottest days. Sister Hilaria's shrill admonitions still echoed in her ears.

'Anyway,' Jackie said slowly when Claire didn't respond, 'you're not seriously telling me you're going to spend your entire Christmas break sitting in your sad little unit?'

'Excuse me, my apartment is not —'

'Your bedroom window looks out over the bins.' Jackie cut her off. 'It smells like three-day-old Chinese takeaway in there.'

'It does not smell —'

'Why don't you go back to Blendawilla and see your boyfriend?'

They reached the clinic and Claire jerked the door open with more force than was strictly necessary, making the red-and-gold Christmas bells the receptionists had strung up jingle wildly. The blast of refrigerated air that enveloped her as she stepped inside did little to cool her rising temperature – but it was no longer the afternoon heat that was causing her cheeks to flush.

'It's *Bindallarah*,' she hissed, causing several clients sitting in the waiting room to turn and stare. 'And Scotty Shannon is *not* my boyfriend.'

Claire stalked away and used her shoulder to shove through the double doors that led into the clinic's hospital. She considered hiding in a stall to eat her lunch in peace, but sick horses could be irate at the best of times and weren't likely to be thrilled to have to share their quarters with an agitated vet and a smelly sandwich. She went to her office instead.

So did Jackie. 'You do realise,' she said, 'that your reaction just now makes me *more* inclined to keep bugging you about your alleged non-boyfriend, not less?' She perched on the edge of Claire's desk. 'So you might as well just tell me. What's the deal?'

Claire took a too-large bite of her panini and chewed slowly. She knew Jackie wouldn't leave her alone until she told her something but, damn it, at least she could make her wait.

'There's no deal,' Claire said at last.

Jackie rolled her eyes.

'I mean it,' she said firmly. 'We're just friends. Old friends who are back in touch after a few years apart and who chat every now and then.'

'I think you mean "starcross'd lovers who were mad about each other for five years".' Jackie crossed her arms and smirked. 'It's been six months since you reconnected online. Why don't you just ask him out IRL?'

Claire frowned. 'IRL?'

'In real life,' Jackie said slowly, as if explaining the alphabet to a toddler.

'It wasn't five years. We were together in high school, but only for a month or so. Then I didn't see him again until

I was eighteen when we were at university together and it was all over within a couple of years.'

'But you were crazy in love with the guy. That doesn't just disappear.'

Claire paused. She couldn't deny that some of what Jackie said was true. She and Scotty had exchanged a handful of chatty emails since he'd accepted her Facebook 'friend request' minutes after she'd sent it on that bleak night back in June. And they had loved each other once, deeply. But that was a long time ago. It might as well have been a different lifetime. Claire had grown up; she was no longer the frightened twenty-year-old who broke Scotty's heart. He was almost her friend again.

She wasn't sure she deserved it, but when he allowed her back into his life she felt redeemed. She wasn't about to ruin that by imagining there could ever be anything more between them than friendship. There was also the not insignificant fact that Scotty hadn't so much as hinted at anything beyond a friendly interest in her. In six months, he'd never even suggested they meet.

No, that horse had bolted – and Claire had no intention of chasing it. Once upon a time, years ago, there might have been a part of her that hoped they'd get it together again one day. That she would get *herself* together enough to stop messing things up. But life was a tricky thing, and having Scotty Shannon in hers as a friend was better than not having him at all.

She wasn't about to tell Jackie any of that, though. The less her work friends knew about her past mistakes, the better. 'For a start, we live eight hundred kilometres apart,' she said.

'Scotty has his own practice in Bindallarah now. I'm established here. It wouldn't be feasible.'

'Feasible! Claire, this isn't a business plan for a new frozen-yoghurt shop. This is your life,' Jackie said, exasperated. 'It's obvious from the way you talk about this guy – and you talk about him a *lot* – that there's unfinished business between you. You've got three weeks off, so go finish it.'

Once more, Claire felt her skin redden in spite of the frigid temperature in her office. Jackie was always convinced she had all the answers; it was why many of their colleagues found her difficult to work with. Claire usually appreciated – or at least tolerated – Jackie's bull-headedness. She preferred to examine a problem from every angle and assess all her options before committing to a course of action, so she found Jackie's confident, rapid-fire decision-making process refreshing. Most of the time.

At other times, it was presumptuous, arrogant and infuriating. Like right now.

'You're right, Jac,' Claire said. She finished her sandwich and tossed the wrapper in the bin under her desk. She stood up and gripped Jackie's shoulders. 'It is my life. And I'll be the one who decides what to do with it.'

Jackie opened her mouth to protest, to have the last word as always. But her rebuttal was drowned out by the sound of the clinic's PA system crackling to life.

'All available vets to critical care, please. Emergency on approach.'

Jackie's eyes widened; Claire was sure they mirrored her own. In neighbouring offices, she could hear muttering and grumbling from her fellow day-shift vets. A critical case late on a Friday was the last thing they wanted, especially when many of them were about to depart on their Christmas holidays.

Claire didn't mind so much. She loved the challenge of emergency medicine, but more than that she loved that science was finite. In most cases, there were only a handful of possibilities – a small number of potential causes and corresponding treatments. The answer that seemed correct usually was. She could consider all the likely outcomes in a matter of minutes and know with some degree of certainty that she was making the best decision. Sometimes she was wrong – the laminitis case from last winter still bothered her – but most of the time she got it right.

If only she could say the same about the rest of her life.

Anyway, what did it matter if she worked late? As Jackie had kindly pointed out, all that awaited her at home was the stench of sun-baked rubbish. She hadn't even bothered to put up her Christmas tree this year.

Claire spun on her heel and raced down the hall to the critical-care unit, with Jackie close behind. She arrived to find a top-of-the-range float being reversed into the yard by a sleek black four-wheel drive. From inside the float came the unmistakable snorts and squeals of a horse in deep distress.

Claire barely registered the way the concrete of the yard magnified the heat, which was still fierce even as the shadows lengthened and the sun began its gradual drift towards the horizon. The float rolled to a stop and she stepped forward and unlatched the ramp. She lowered it to the ground and peered into the dim interior.

The horse was a chestnut Arabian mare, heavily pregnant. She was slick with sweat; it flowed from her like rain off a rooftop. She gasped and panted, every breath a mammoth effort. Her tail was clamped down hard and her muscles looked rigid, but she was trembling, as taut as the strings of a violin. Claire couldn't remember the last time she had seen such a terrified animal.

As other vets gathered, Claire climbed into the trailer to escape the hubbub of competing voices. 'Shhh, sweetheart,' she murmured, but the mare didn't seem to notice her. Her ears were stiff and twitching, her eyes darting from side to side, the whites exposed. Her breathing was growing more rapid with each passing minute. Claire placed a hand on her neck, then instinctively snatched it back as though she'd been scalded: the poor horse was burning hot.

Anger gripped Claire's insides. In an instant, she knew what was wrong. *Hyperthermia.* The mare had heat stroke, she was sure of it. She put her stethoscope to the animal's side and heard the hammer of her racing heartbeat. This was a very, very sick horse.

'Jackie,' she said quietly. She was still alone in the float, but she knew Jackie wouldn't be far away.

'Right here,' came the reply from just outside.

'It's heat stroke. Take her temp to confirm, but prep the hydro pool and get a hose on her in the meantime. She also needs IV fluids and nasal oxygen, please. And she's pregnant, so once we've cooled her down let's get one of the theriogenologists to ultrasound the foal.'

Claire heard the scuffle of feet as Jackie relayed Claire's instructions to the other vets.

'You want bloods too?' she said.

'Definitely,' Claire replied. 'I'll do that, but let's get her out first.'

'You sure, Claire? Easier to do it while she's confined.'

'She needs fresh air. She's out of her mind.'

Carefully, Claire freed the lead rope from the float's tie ring and wound it tightly around her hand. She knew horses and this mare was telling her in no uncertain terms that, despite being gravely ill, she wanted out of the float. Claire didn't want to risk her rocketing backwards and injuring herself, but she knew she was no match for a 630-kilogram horse. If the mare did bolt, Claire would at best be a sort of flimsy anchor.

She gave the lead rope a gentle tug and took a step towards the mare. The horse stumbled a little and stomped her front foot but then, mercifully, she began to walk slowly backwards. Gradually, she eased out of the float and into the yard, where three vets immediately surrounded her with hoses and wet towels. Claire unwound the rope and handed it to a vet nurse.

Jackie was standing on the mare's near side, her hands hidden beneath the switching tail. She had somehow drawn the short straw and was taking the horse's temperature. When the electronic thermometer beeped, Jackie looked down at the reading and shook her head.

'Forty-one degrees,' she told Claire, the disgust in her voice palpable.

Again, Claire felt fury twist in her stomach. Though it often had dire consequences, heat stroke wasn't a particularly complex condition. In most cases, it was caused by overexertion – too much work or too much exercise in hot conditions and not enough opportunities for the horse to cool down.

Which meant that some colossal *idiot* had, either by neglect or design, allowed a pregnant mare – a horse that shouldn't have even been out of her stall in these hellish conditions – to nearly kill herself on a day that was hotter than Hades. Claire would put money on the mare belonging to a riding stable trying to keep up with school-holiday demand. Mostly, they treated their horses like royalty, but some cared more about cashing in on rich parents desperate to keep their kids entertained, even if it meant pushing an animal far beyond its limits.

'Where's the owner?' Claire spat. 'Who brought her in?' She eschewed confrontation as a rule, but whoever was responsible for this was going to hear about it.

'That would be me,' said a voice from behind her.

She turned and saw the shape of a person standing next to the four-wheel drive that was hitched to the float. The sonorous tone of the voice told her it was a man, but in the glare of the late-afternoon sun she couldn't make out his face.

'Come with me,' she snarled.

Without confirming that he was following her, Claire stalked across the yard and into the welcome cool of the hospital. If the heat was driving her mad, this man who had left his horse to its mercy was making her positively incandescent.

She heard his footsteps behind her as she went into the walk-in supply cupboard. 'Your horse has heat stroke,' she coldly informed him, not turning around.

'I know,' he replied. Something in the timbre of his voice stirred a flicker of recognition in the back of Claire's mind, but she was too angry to follow the trail.

'You *know*?' She wrenched open drawers and cupboards, assembling the syringes and vials she would need for the mare's blood tests. 'Then you should *know* better than to have exercised her in this weather.'

'Can you test her for MH while you're at it?' he said, ignoring her accusation.

Claire scoffed. Malignant hyperthermia – was this guy serious? 'Wouldn't that be convenient?' she said. 'A genetic disease that makes your mare prone to heat stroke. Nothing to do with forcing her to work on a blistering summer's day.'

'I didn't —'

'And I cannot believe you floated her in that state. You should have called and had us come to you. She could have collapsed and died in that trailer.'

'She was already in —'

Claire grabbed a kidney dish from a shelf and dumped the vials and syringes in it. 'I'll be reporting you to the RSPCA. People like you shouldn't be allowed anywhere near animals.'

'Claire.'

'You'd better hope like hell that poor horse and her foal survive this because —'

'*Claire.*'

She froze. *How does he know my name?* She was damn sure she hadn't bothered to introduce herself to this loser. He must have heard Jackie address her in the yard. Unless . . .

A chill unfurled at the base of her spine and scuttled up to her neck like a spider. *I do know that voice.* Slowly, Claire set the kidney dish on the bench. Even more slowly, she turned to look at the man who seemed to know her.

I know that face, too.

CHAPTER TWO

The power of speech had deserted her. Claire opened her mouth then closed it again, doing her best impression of a goldfish.

Scotty Shannon. In the flesh.

Over the past six months they had kept in touch as often as any far-flung old friends in this new digital age: not that often at all. Their occasional emails were full of easy small talk about work, travel, books, what they were binge-watching on Netflix. They hadn't picked over the carcass of their relationship or rehashed its gut-wrenching conclusion eight years earlier. They didn't discuss significant others – not that there was anything to discuss on her side anyway. That wasn't in the spirit of their tentative new arrangement. They were now, if not quite bona fide mates, then definitely warm acquaintances. Anything else that had once existed between them was long dead. Their banter wasn't serious and neither were they. It suited her. Scotty-and-Claire version 2.0 felt relaxed, uncomplicated, *nice*. She liked just knowing he was out there somewhere – and that he didn't seem to despise her.

The geographical distance between them also meant there was no pressure to take their revived friendship into the real world. He hadn't asked her why she never went back to Bindallarah; she never suggested he pay her a visit in Sydney. She'd mostly managed to avoid imagining what she might say to him if she ever saw him again. Claire hadn't contemplated what it would feel like to come face to face with Scotty because it simply wasn't in the cards.

Except now here he was, wearing that crooked smile that had always surprised her because it made his serious face look so different. Now it made him look . . .

Gorgeous.

The thought alarmed her. She was entirely unprepared for Scotty as a man. When she had last seen him, he had been twenty-one: still an overgrown boy. A little too tall. A little too thin. Features a little too big for his face. He had always been beautiful in her eyes, but now, at twenty-nine, Scotty had grown into himself. All the girls who had ignored him at school would swipe right on his Tinder profile for sure. His height was commanding rather than gangly. He'd filled out: his chest and shoulders were broad and sturdy, his hands tanned and powerful. The lines on his face that he'd had even as a teenager had deepened and given his face a craggy character. In his dark blue jeans, scuffed workboots, fitted casual shirt and wide-brimmed hat, he was the quintessential strapping country guy. He'd let his sandy hair grow and the natural curl softened him, lent him an easygoing air. His green eyes were as arresting as ever.

He was, Claire realised with a sinking sensation in her stomach that felt like dismay, sexy as hell. She certainly hadn't anticipated that. And she was staring at him in stupefied silence.

'What the hell were you thinking?' she said at last.

Scotty blinked, as surprised by the question as she was. 'Sorry?' he said.

'The mare.'

'Oh, of course.' Scotty shook his head as understanding dawned. 'Autumn. She's not mine. She belongs to my little brother. You remember Chris? He runs Cape Ashe now.'

Claire crossed her arms and glared.

'Anyway,' he continued, 'Autumn has been, uh, enjoying some gentlemanly company at a stud farm down on the South Coast for the last few months and Chris wants her brought back to Bindy to give birth. I was in Melbourne for a conference so I offered to pick her up and drive her home. We got as far as Wollongong yesterday and she was absolutely fine, but on our way past Sydney today she just crashed.'

Past Sydney. Not *to* Sydney. So he'd had no intention of stopping off to see her. If Autumn hadn't fallen ill he would have continued on to Bindallarah without a word. Not that she had any right to feel disappointed, Claire sharply reminded herself.

'Of course she crashed, Scotty!' she snapped. Saying his name aloud in his presence felt strange and forbidden after so many years. 'It's nearly forty degrees out there today. It was probably close to twice that in the float. She's *pregnant*. How could you do that to her?'

She saw anger flash across his face. 'The float is air-conditioned, Claire.' He hurled her name at her like a grenade. 'Autumn was in climate-controlled comfort all the way. That's why I want you to test her for MH. You know stress can be a trigger in horses that carry the gene. It must have been the anxiety of the transport that caused it, not the heat.'

Claire frowned. His expression was a mix of irritation and appeal for understanding. If it had been anyone else, she would have picked up the phone and dialled the local RSPCA inspector. But this was Scotty. Aside from the fact that he was an accomplished vet, he had been around horses every day of his life. He knew the majestic beasts better than anyone she'd ever met – even her, and she had close to ten years of study to become an equine specialist under her belt.

And he was a good guy, despite this heated exchange. Scotty was a big-hearted, earnest person, whose instinct was to do the right thing by everyone at all times. Deep down, Claire knew he would never have intentionally risked Autumn's safety.

'I'll run the test,' she said. 'The results will take twenty-four hours.' She picked up her collection of needles and vials.

Scotty's breath came out in a *whoosh*. 'Thanks, Claire. Hey,' he said as she turned to leave. 'Autumn will be fine, but obviously we won't be going anywhere for a day or two. Got any plans tonight?'

Claire dropped the kidney dish with a clatter. Syringes and tubes rolled across the floor. Was he going to suggest she put him up for the night? The idea filled her with panic, which was absurd. What did it matter if Scotty crashed on her couch? They'd known each other forever and – she hoped – were on their way to being real friends again. Friends should offer each other their sofa beds.

But the thought of him in her home, filling the meagre space with this potent masculinity he now possessed, felt dangerous.

Five minutes in his presence and she was already practically catatonic.

She dropped to her knees to gather the spilled equipment, buying time. Scotty squatted beside her. 'Because if you don't,' he said, handing her a hermetically sealed syringe, 'how about meeting me for a drink? I'll book into a hotel in the city. We can catch up properly.'

Relief washed over her. A casual drink she could do. It *was* lovely to see him again, and a catch-up in a public place where there was no chance she'd succumb to the long-buried ache now stirring deep inside her would be fine. Safe.

'That would be great, Scotty,' she said, smiling at last. Saying his name felt a little easier each time.

He knew Claire worked there, but it hadn't occurred to him that she'd *be* there.

He'd been cruising on the freeway on Sydney's outer western fringe when he'd seen on the dash-mounted video monitor that Autumn was becoming distressed in the float. He hadn't wanted to pull over and risk her collapsing, or worse, bolting into four lanes of speeding traffic, so Scotty had simply googled the nearest emergency equine clinic. It was her clinic. He had plugged the address into his phone.

His original plan had been to bypass Sydney altogether. He'd been aiming to spend the night at Tuncurry on the Mid-North Coast. Four and a half hours was about the longest he felt comfortable having the mare confined to the float, and, besides, horses were allowed on Nine Mile Beach. He wouldn't ride Autumn this late in her pregnancy, but he knew she'd love a walk in the surf before they made the final push to Bindallarah the next morning.

He had thought about Claire constantly on the drive north from Wollongong, wondered if he should call and tell her he was in the neighbourhood, suggest they get together for a beer. But he didn't know if she wanted that. In the six months since she'd reached out to him online, Claire hadn't given so much as a whisper of an indication that she had any interest in seeing him. He was keen to catch up with her, but he didn't want to push it. Claire was like the horses she worked with: she spooked easily. Always had.

And then, like magic, there she was in front of him in blue hospital scrubs that matched her ultramarine eyes, her dark curls piled on top of her head in a haphazard bun. Scotty watched her work on Autumn as if in a daze. The heat haze shimmered above the concrete floor of the yard, giving the whole scene an ethereal quality. To have her suddenly materialise like that, like an apparition, shook him.

Asking her to meet him for a drink hadn't been the plan, but Scotty Shannon wasn't one to squander an opportunity. It had taken her eight years to come back to him and another six months to shore up their renewed bond so that it felt like it might stick.

He wanted Claire to stay in his life this time. And that meant she needed to know.

He had to tell her about Nina.

Claire made sure she was late. She hated being the first to arrive at a pub, having to walk in alone, decide where to sit, check her phone every few minutes for the usual excuses from last-minute pikers. And she could never decide whether she should order a drink or wait for everyone else to arrive. It was a social minefield. Better to be slightly tardy and glide in after the groundwork was already done.

Besides, getting to the Hero of Waterloo a few minutes after seven o'clock meant the historic pub in The Rocks was packed with the after-work-drinks crowd; the atmosphere was extra rambunctious on such a hot night so close to Christmas and Claire was able to slip in unnoticed and take a moment just to watch. She wanted to refresh the picture of Scotty that she'd carried in her mind's eye for eight years without the shock and irritation that had coloured their earlier meeting.

She spotted Scotty at the far end of the bar, perched on a stool and sipping a pint of beer. He was chatting to a lithe blonde woman standing next to him. She was stunning and she leaned in close to him, the fingers of her left hand resting lightly on his shoulder as she listened intently to whatever it was he was saying. Claire's suspicion that Scotty's days of being overlooked by gorgeous women were long gone was confirmed: the blonde might as well have been wearing a flashing neon sign that said I-N-T-E-R-E-S-T-E-D.

Suddenly, Scotty threw back his head, laughing, and gifted his companion with the same wonky smile that had floored Claire just a few hours ago. Her stomach responded with a small lurch. *Stupid*, she thought. She could tell with one glance that the woman was nothing more than a way to help Scotty pass the time, but the fleeting jolt of envy made her uncomfortable. It wasn't her business who her friend chose to speak to.

Claire made her way through the dense crowd and tapped Scotty on the shoulder that wasn't occupied by the blonde's scarlet talons. When he turned and saw her, a broad grin lit his face.

'You made it!' he said, a note of surprise in his voice.

'Of course,' Claire replied, confused. 'Didn't you think I would?'

'Well, it's just, you know . . . we kind of got off on the wrong foot earlier.' He offered a slightly sheepish smile.

A giggle bubbled up inside her. 'Scotty, please. After everything we've been through together in the last – what – thirteen years? There's no such thing as the wrong foot with us.' *We've already hurt, frustrated and ruined each other as much as we possibly can*, she silently added.

Sensing she'd been relegated to 'third wheel' position, Scotty's new acquaintance pouted a little and said, 'You two obviously have a lot to catch up on, so I'll leave you to it. It was nice meeting you, Scotty.'

His gaze didn't shift from Claire as he said, 'Nice meeting you too, Helen.'

'It's *Hannah*,' the woman muttered as the crowd swallowed her.

And then it was just the two of them. An island of shared history in a sea of what Claire hoped was water under the bridge. She suddenly realised how important it was that this wasn't their last meeting. She had met up with old friends before – long-lost boarding school girlfriends who'd found her via social media; the college alumni she never heard from until they planned to visit from America and needed a place to stay; even the occasional Bindallarah throwback – but she had never kidded herself that those coffee catch-ups or awk-ward weekends of grudging hospitality would lead to renewed friendships.

But with Scotty she did want that. Looking at him now, she wasn't quite sure how she'd managed without him for the past eight years. There had been a Scotty-shaped hole in her life and somehow she hadn't seen it; she'd con-vinced herself she hadn't felt his absence. Their relationship was different now, of course. It had changed, because they had changed. They would never – *should* never – go back to what they were, but she wanted whatever it was they could become.

'What are you drinking?' Scotty asked. Before Claire could respond, he grasped her forearm with his big hand and said, 'Wait, let me guess. Midori and lemonade?'

She swatted away his paw, laughing. 'Oh my *God*, Scotty!' she said. Thinking about the bile-green, melon-flavoured monstrosity she'd claimed as her 'signature drink' back when she'd believed it was cool to have one made her feel queasy. 'I'm not twenty any more. I'll have a glass of pinot noir, please.'

Scotty gestured to the barman. 'So,' he said when Claire's drink had been delivered, 'I think this momentous occasion deserves a toast.'

Claire arched an eyebrow. 'You do?'

'Absolutely,' he said. 'To us. Scotty and Claire, the dynamic duo, together again. At last.' He clinked his pint against her wineglass.

Scotty raised his glass to his lips and drank deeply, his green eyes regarding her closely over the rim. The way he looked at her, steady and defiant, was unnerving. It was as if his gaze held a question, a challenge.

Claire felt unsteady on her feet, almost drunk, though she'd had only a tiny sip of her wine. *Together again. At last.* What did he mean by that? It sounded like a statement of intent, loaded with possibilities she hadn't let herself think about during the months since they'd found each other again. She deleted his emails after replying to them so that she wouldn't go over and over them, looking for clues that she still mattered to him, conjuring deeper meaning where there wasn't any.

But perhaps she had been too cautious. Jackie insisted that no red-blooded single man spent six months corresponding with a woman he had only friendly feelings for – especially, she said, when that woman had been his first love. Could Jackie be right? Here he was, IRL after eight long years, looking so very good. Should she take a chance and ask him out on a real date?

Claire cleared her throat. *Maybe I'll just test the waters.* 'I wasn't sure you'd be happy to hear from me back in June.'

There was that smile again. 'Why would you worry about that? I missed you,' Scotty said. He slid off his bar stool and took a step towards her. 'C'mere.'

He wrapped her in a tight hug, pulling her into his broad chest and resting his chin on the crown of her head. Claire had always marvelled at how well they fitted together, even though Scotty was so much taller. It wasn't that she had forgotten how good it felt to be held by him; she just hadn't wanted to let herself remember.

Being in Scotty's arms felt like home. For eight years, she had believed she'd never be able to go home again.

'I didn't think we'd ever be back here,' she mumbled into the soft cotton of his T-shirt.

He chuckled and she felt rather than heard it rumble deep within his chest. 'I knew you couldn't keep away from me forever.'

No, just eight years. Reluctantly, she pulled away. 'So, what does this mean?' she said, feeling giddy. 'How is this going to work?'

'Well, actually, there's something I want to ask you,' Scotty said.

Claire's heart rate abruptly tripled. She nodded mutely.

'Claire, will you come to my wedding?'

And in that instant, it felt like her heart stopped beating altogether. A sharp pain sliced through her abdomen, and for a moment she thought she'd been struck. 'Your *what*?'

'I'm getting married! Can you believe it?' His grin split his face from ear to ear.

Claire slowly shook her head. She felt caged and panicky. Her limbs fizzed as if preparing to flee. 'I really can't,' she said, her voice flat.

'And I want you to be there,' Scotty continued, apparently oblivious to her desperation. 'Outside of my family, you're the person who has meant the most to me in my life. I can't imagine you not being there on my wedding day. Will you come? Please?'

She searched for something to say, some words to fill the yawning chasm that had suddenly opened up inside her as she racked her brain for any mention of a fiancée. She couldn't recall Scotty ever so much as hinting at dating.

All she could muster was 'When is it?'

'Christmas Eve,' Scotty replied.

The words jolted her back to the present moment. 'Christmas *Eve*? But that's —'

'In two weeks. I know!' he crowed. 'Isn't it crazy?'

That's one word for it, Claire thought.

CHAPTER THREE

'Christmas Eve?' Jackie said incredulously. 'But that's a Sunday. Who gets married on a Sunday? That's so cheap.'

'Jackie, you're missing the point,' Claire wailed. 'The point is Scotty's getting married. To a woman he's known for a *month*. How can he do this?'

Jackie pursed her lips and twisted her thick red hair into a tight ponytail. She pulled a lurid fuchsia swimming cap over the top. 'I'm sorry, I can't think straight until I cool off,' she said. 'You coming in?'

Claire followed her friend to the pool's edge, suddenly absurdly grateful that Jackie was such an early riser. The swimming pool was virtually deserted at seven a.m., even though the outside temperature was already nudging thirty degrees. The city's roads would be choked with traffic by now as the masses flocked to set up camp on Sydney's iconic beaches for the day. She was glad of the comparative peace of the suburban leisure centre where Jackie swam laps religiously every Saturday morning.

Claire eased into the pool and felt momentarily soothed. It had been a sleepless night – the stifling heat would have been enough to keep her awake even without the roiling thoughts clogging her brain – and the still water was a balm to her agitated soul. Even the Christmas songs playing on repeat over the tinny speakers felt comforting rather than grating.

Jackie began an easy side crawl. 'So,' she said, 'who is she?'

'Her name is Nina,' Claire replied, matching her stroke for stroke. 'She's American.'

'How long has she been in Australia? How did they meet?'

'I don't know, I didn't ask any of that! I was too stunned by the whole marrying-a-stranger thing. All I know is that she's a yoga teacher.' She couldn't help the way Nina's occupation came out sounding like an insult.

'Bondawillop has a yoga studio? I thought you said it was the back of beyond.'

'*Bindallarah*. And it *is* the back of beyond. At least, it used to be. When I left it didn't even have a coffee shop,' she said. 'But, again, that's not the point.'

They reached the end of the pool and kicked off the wall to head back the way they'd come. 'Then what is the point, Claire?' Jackie said, slightly breathless. 'The guy's getting married. So what? You're sort-of-kind-of maybe just friends. You didn't want to date him. Is he not supposed to date anyone else?'

No, he's not!

Claire drew in a sharp breath as the words rushed to the tip of her tongue. Thankfully, she bit them back before they were able to tumble out. She didn't really feel that way. Of course Scotty could date. He *should* date. He should fall madly in love and live blissfully ever after. She wanted him to be happy. After everything she'd put him through over the years, she wanted happiness for Scotty even more than she wanted it for herself.

But how could he be happy with a woman he'd only known for four weeks? And why hadn't he ever mentioned Nina in his emails to Claire? A fiancée was a pretty significant life event to leave out when catching up with a former flame.

'He never said a word about her,' Claire said miserably. 'Not once. He's my friend. He *is*,' she said, when Jackie rolled her eyes, 'and friends are meant to tell each other when they fall head over heels in love.'

Jackie stopped swimming. 'Maybe he didn't know how to tell you,' she said, treading water in the middle of the lane. 'You know what men are like – they're not exactly fans of sharing their feelings. It was probably easier for him to stick his head in the sand than to worry that you'd feel . . . you know.'

Claire didn't know. 'That I'd feel what?'

'Well, stupid.' Jackie switched to freestyle and powered down the lane, leaving Claire staring slack-jawed after her.

'What's that supposed to mean?' she said when she caught up with her friend. 'Why would Scotty worry that I'd feel stupid?'

Jackie sighed. 'I know you say you're not carrying a torch for him —'

'I'm *not*!' Claire interrupted.

Jackie held up her hands in a gesture of surrender. 'Okay, okay, I believe you. But what if Scotty thinks you are?'

Claire suddenly felt like all the air had been sucked out of the room. He couldn't possibly think that. Could he?

'I mean, the guy is hot,' Jackie went on. At Claire's sharp look she added, 'Hey, I might prefer the ladies myself, but that doesn't mean I can't appreciate a fine male specimen when I see one. Men with the sort of magnetism that Scotty Shannon has always assume women are interested in them, because women always *are* interested in them. Especially old girlfriends who track them down out of the blue after eight years.'

Claire groaned as the truth of Jackie's statement crashed over her like a wave. Scotty thought Claire was still in love with him. And because he was kind and considerate and always gentle with her feelings, he hadn't wanted to embarrass her by admitting he was in love with someone else – that he would never want her again – until the last possible moment.

What an idiot she'd been to imagine for even a moment that Scotty might still have feelings for her. Why had she even entertained the thought when all she wanted from him was his friendship? She never should have agreed to meet him. She should have been content with his occasional presence in her inbox. She'd brought this torment on herself.

And it *was* torment. As foolish as she felt, it didn't change the fact that Scotty was about to marry a woman he barely knew. That was what was really bothering her. It was such a reckless decision. When he'd dropped his bombshell in the pub last night, Claire had heard herself offering congratulations, had felt her face contort into a shell-shocked smile. But inside, she was stunned – and horrified. Why would he do something so rash? Scotty had always been decisive, always gone after what he wanted, but not without proper planning and consideration. She didn't need to know this Nina person to know that proposing to someone four weeks after meeting them, and rushing to tie the knot two weeks after that, was just crazy. He couldn't know she was The One yet. Nobody could make such a huge decision so quickly.

Claire had known Scotty her whole life, had loved him for more than five years when he proposed to her, and even then she hadn't been sure.

'Okay, let's say you're right,' Claire said. 'How do I make him see that this wedding is a huge mistake without him thinking I want him for myself?'

'You don't,' said Jackie.

'But he can't marry her, Jac. It will be a disaster!'

She hadn't even told Jackie the worst part: that Scotty actually wanted her at the wedding. There wasn't an ice cube's chance on this sweltering day that she would go. Attend her oldest friend's ill-conceived wedding to a stranger in a town she despised? She would rather take rectal temperature readings from flatulent horses every day of her life.

'How do you know? You haven't met this Nina. Maybe they're meant for each other.'

It was Claire's turn to roll her eyes.

'And even if they're not,' Jackie continued, 'having a terrible, awful, disastrous marriage is their prerogative. Scotty's a grown man, Claire. This wedding might be a mistake, but it's his mistake to make. You've got to let him live his life.'

'I might have known you'd take his side. You won't even give me an appropriate amount of time to decide on a sandwich. You probably think Scotty should have proposed after their first date.' Claire pouted slightly for effect.

Jackie laughed. 'I'm on your side, you nutter,' she said, giving Claire's shoulder a reassuring squeeze. 'Which is why I don't want to see you driving yourself crazy over this. Want to swim a few more laps?'

'Nah. I'm going to grab a juice and head home before it's too hot to set foot outside,' she said. 'I could use a nap, too. Didn't get much sleep last night.'

Jackie smiled and plunged back into the water. Claire climbed out of the pool, towelled off and threw her loose T-shirt dress over her damp swimsuit. *Scotty's a grown man*, Jackie had said. She was right – he was nearly thirty and more than capable of making his own decisions. But he had always been a grown-up, really. Even when they were teenagers, Scotty had seemed older than his years. Decisive to the point of stubbornness – it was almost impossible to unmake Scotty's mind once he'd made it up. He was sensible when Claire was brash, reliable when she was flighty. He unravelled every mess she got herself into. She could always count on him. Scotty was her safe harbour.

Now she felt like she didn't know him at all. This just wasn't the Scotty she knew – and even though they hadn't been in each other's lives for a while, she *did* know him. They knew each other better than anybody. She was missing something, some piece of the puzzle that would explain why he was two weeks away from doing something so completely illogical. If only she could spend some more time with him, talk some sense into him, try to make him see why this wedding was a colossal mistake.

Claire picked up her bag and fumbled inside for her mobile phone. A missed call flashed up on the screen.

Vanessa.

A pang of guilt caused her stomach to clench as she dialled her voicemail and played her aunt's message.

'Hello, darling, it's Vee,' Vanessa's melodious voice said. 'I just called you at work and they said you're off until the new year. I'm sure you already have plans, but sweetheart, if you're free we would *love* to have you come back to Bindy for Christmas. Do give me a tinkle when you can. Love you!'

The excitement in Vanessa's voice was palpable. Her heart felt heavy as she thought of her sweet aunt spending another Christmas in that dustbowl town with her daughter, Claire's cousin Augusta, and nobody else. Since Claire's father had died, Vanessa and Gus were all that remained of the Bindallarah Thornes.

She knew she should go back. It wasn't Vanessa's fault that Claire was an outcast in Bindallarah. But she couldn't spend Christmas in Bindy – she'd told Scotty she couldn't possibly come to his ridiculous wedding because she was working. There was no way she could sneak into town for the holidays without word getting out that she was there, without him finding out that she'd lied.

But if she did go back, maybe she could talk to Scotty, reason with him. Maybe there wouldn't be a wedding at all. She couldn't let him marry a virtual stranger. She just *couldn't.* Maybe she could stop this runaway train before it did some real damage.

Claire dialled Vanessa's number.

CHAPTER FOUR

'Well, if it isn't the groom-to-be. Heard the news?'

Scotty put the four-wheel drive into park and turned off the engine. 'Nuh,' Scotty told his brother. 'Reckon you could let me open the door before you tell me about whatever crisis has unfolded while I've been away?'

Chris stepped back from the driver's side door and Scotty pushed it open. He stepped onto the hard-packed gravel drive-way that wound from the highway up to Cape Ashe Stud's state-of-the-art stables and stretched. Whatever Chris wanted to tell him, it could wait. Scotty was in no mood for small-town drama right now.

It should have been a six-hour drive from Tuncurry, where he'd spent last night, to the Shannons' farm in the hin-terland behind Bindallarah, but Scotty's cautious driving and frequent stops to check on Autumn meant it had been closer to eight. The mare had made a remarkable recovery during her two-night stay in Sydney, where Claire's blood tests had confirmed malignant hyperthermia. She was healthy and relaxed now – especially after her swim on Nine Mile Beach that morning – but Scotty hadn't wanted to take any chances. Autumn had a long road ahead.

'Tough trip,' Chris said as he walked to the rear of the horse float. 'Thanks for bringing her back, big brother. She wouldn't have made it if it'd been anybody else.'

Scotty nodded but didn't reply. He was exhausted, stiff and achy. He'd planned to be back in Bindallarah on Saturday night; Autumn's emergency meant it was now Monday evening and he'd missed a day of work. His nerves were frayed and it wasn't just because he was worried about the horse. He couldn't stop thinking about Claire. He'd spent the long hours behind the wheel replaying their Friday-night meeting. He couldn't shake the feeling that gnawed at him when he thought about the way she had congratulated him on his engagement. He knew what the feeling was.

Guilt.

It was obvious that Claire had been blindsided by his announcement. She'd tried to hide it, but Scotty had seen the stricken look that had crossed her face. It had lasted just a fraction of a second before she'd replaced it with a smile, but it had been like a farrier's knife to his heart. Of course Claire was shocked. He'd felt pretty stunned himself as he heard the words tumble out of his mouth. He shouldn't have told her that way. He shouldn't have told her *at all*. It was insensitive. It was cruel. He was meant to be her friend, but he'd dropped a bomb and hurt her. He was a fraud.

He wished he'd had a chance to see her again, to explain, before he left Sydney on Sunday morning. But Claire had said she was working. He'd called and texted her, but she hadn't replied. He'd asked after her at the clinic when he went to collect Autumn, but her colleague – Jackie, was it? – had looked strangely at him and said she wasn't there.

Scotty sighed and joined Chris at the float. It was too late now. Claire wasn't going to come back to Bindallarah. He'd been crazy to think she would. He guessed they'd go back to emails every now and then. Or maybe they were done. Maybe he'd hear nothing from her for another eight years. The thought made him clench his fists in frustration.

The brothers lowered the ramp and Chris went inside and untethered Autumn. He eased her out; she was steady on her feet again, but the heft of her unborn foal meant any movement was pretty uncomfortable for her.

'She looks great, mate,' Chris said. 'Remind me to thank Claire next time I see her.'

Scotty blinked, confused. 'You mean next time *I* see her,' he replied. 'You haven't seen Claire since you were a kid.'

Chris led Autumn towards her stall. 'Saw her on Saturday night,' he called over his shoulder.

Scotty felt his stomach drop to the soles of his worn work boots. 'What?' he shouted after his brother.

'Yeah, that's what I was going to tell you,' Chris yelled back. 'It's big news. Claire Thorne is back in Bindy.'

Bindallarah looked nothing like Claire remembered. Thirteen years ago she had left a sleepy town whose main street offered a pub, a bakery and a dusty grocery store that closed at noon on Saturday and didn't open at all on Sunday. Now the wide esplanade boasted a hip little café and a Thai restaurant, with a handful of quirky-looking shops dotted among the agricultural businesses – all bustling, even at nine o'clock on a Tuesday morning. Their awnings were festooned with bells, baubles and red-and-green tinsel that glittered in the bright morning sunlight.

The street was bookended by a supermarket and a discount variety store, and the strip of scrubby grass that bordered the beach had been landscaped into a handsome park with a towering Norfolk pine trussed up as a Christmas tree as its centrepiece.

Somehow, Bindallarah had been dragged into the twenty-first century – and just in time for Christmas.

'Wow,' Claire said as she climbed out of Vanessa's compact hatchback and took in the town's lively heart. A wave of nostalgia washed over her. It was silly, really. She hadn't wanted to leave Bindallarah at fifteen, but after everything fell apart when she was sent away to boarding school, she'd vowed she would never come back. Since her father's death eight years ago, she'd felt nothing but antipathy for the town that had turned its back on her. She hadn't counted on there being any trace of that teenager's longing for her former home still lingering within her.

'Things are a little different these days, huh?' her aunt replied. Vanessa smiled at her niece over the roof of the car and looped her handbag over her shoulder. 'Come on, let's have a coffee and I'll fill you in.'

Claire hesitated. She wasn't sure she was ready to dive back into the well of gossip that fed Bindallarah – especially when she knew Scotty's wedding would be the talk of the town. It was the first thing Vanessa mentioned when Claire arrived. She said everyone in Bindallarah was as stunned by the news of his rapid engagement as Claire was. But her aunt hadn't said anything about the marriage being the catastrophe Claire knew it would be. She couldn't possibly be the only person in Scotty's life who thought his crazy decision would lead to heartbreak, could she? She needed to take the town's temperature on the subject, but that would mean facing the people she hadn't seen since her father's funeral – the people who had shunned her. She needed a little more time to psych herself up for that.

Since arriving in Bindallarah late on Saturday night, Claire had lain low at Vanessa's cute weatherboard cottage at the quiet northern end of town. The only person she'd spoken to besides her aunt and her cousin, Gus, was the guy at the petrol station on the highway, where she'd stopped to refuel after driving flat out from Sydney.

But she had seen Chris Shannon, Scotty's younger brother, pulling up at the next pump just as she'd been getting back into her car to leave. Claire knew Chris had recognised her; he'd looked at her like she was a ghost. If she knew anything about small towns, it was that everyone within a twenty-kilometre radius would have heard about the prodigal daughter's return by now. She wasn't sure she was ready for the reproving glares and passive-aggressive remarks quite yet.

Claire wondered if the whispers had reached Scotty. She didn't even know if he'd made it back to Bindallarah himself yet, though Jackie had texted to say that he'd collected Autumn from the clinic on Sunday morning and had asked for her. Claire hadn't spoken to him since she'd left the pub on Friday night. He'd called, but she still felt too bewildered by his news to put proper sentences together. She needed time before she saw him again – time to decide how she was going to convince him to call off his wedding.

'Uh, why don't we make it a takeaway coffee and sit on the beach?' Claire said at length. 'It's been years since I've seen an empty beach. In Sydney there's barely room to swing an esky.' She laughed meekly.

She didn't really want coffee; it was far too warm for a hot drink. The heat she'd left in Sydney was tempered here by the sea breeze, but being further north meant the subtropical air felt sticky and close. What she wanted was a few minutes to herself – some time to process Bindallarah's metamorphosis and where she might fit in this strange new town – and by the look of the queue snaking out of the café opposite, Vanessa would be a while.

Her aunt paused. 'Sure,' she said after a beat. 'But just so you know, sweetheart, you have nothing to be afraid or ashamed of. You and I both know what really happened with your dad. Screw what anyone else in this town thinks.' Vanessa winked and strode across the street, her colourful kimono jacket billowing behind her as it caught the breeze.

Easy for you to say, Claire thought. Vanessa didn't have to live with an entire town believing she'd abandoned her father and sent him to an early grave.

Claire watched as her aunt disappeared into the coffee shop, Bindy Brew, then let her gaze drift down the street. Her breath caught as she spotted Scotty's clinic, the Bindallarah Veterinary Hospital, sandwiched between the post office and a surf shop. And two doors down, above a trendy store selling children's clothes and wooden toys, looping script across wide windows advertised the location of the imaginatively named

Yoga by Nina. The vet clinic didn't appear to be open yet, but Claire could see shadows moving across the yoga studio walls.

So the future Mr and Mrs Shannon would live and work virtually shoulder to shoulder. They must have met when Nina opened her business right on Scotty's doorstep. Claire felt another surge of envy as she imagined being able to see Scotty every day the way Nina would, the way she had when they were teenagers, before she was sent away.

'For God's sake, Thorne. Get a grip,' she muttered under her breath. It was ludicrous to feel envious of a woman she'd never even met.

She swallowed the sick sensation and turned away from the street, walking down the short sandy path to the beach. Growing up, the thing Claire had loved most about Bindallarah was its wide, crescent-shaped beach. She had spent hours there, riding one of the Shannons' gentle ponies in the surf or reading magazines on the sand while Scotty had ploughed through veterinary textbooks way too advanced for a high school student next to her. When she and Scotty had become a couple, the dunes became their meeting spot – the only place they could snatch time together away from their disapproving parents, who thought they were too young to be so serious about each other.

When she'd left for boarding school in Sydney, the beach became a memory. She didn't have many happy ones of Bindallarah, but, Claire suddenly realised, Scotty was in them all. She cursed herself for waiting so long to come back.

Her mood lifted as she emerged from the bush-lined path onto the pristine white sand and saw that the beach hadn't changed at all. She dropped down onto the sand and sat cross-legged, drinking it all in. At the southern end, in the shadow of the jagged rock formation atop Tershen Head, a handful of surfers bobbed like corks on the swell, hoping to catch a wave on the famous right-hand point break. In the middle of the beach, close to where she sat, the local surf lifesaving club had set out the red-and-yellow flags that marked the safest swimming spot. A couple of young kids splashed about in the shallows while their mothers kept close watch from nearby towels. Aside from them, Claire had the entire beach to herself.

Almost to herself, she realised, suddenly irritated as she squinted at the shore's northern end. A tall figure was approaching, accompanied by a dog with a strange bouncing gait. Claire's irritation dissipated in an instant. She knew it was Scotty before she could even make out his face. She'd recognise his purposeful march anywhere.

She stood up and brushed the sand from her backside, wishing she'd taken the time to throw on something a little more elegant than her vintage green sundress and flat brown leather sandals. Then again, she'd packed in such a hurry she doubted she'd actually brought anything that could be considered elegant.

The thoughts that had filled her mind just moments ago – thoughts of wanting to wait a while before she saw him – vanished like sea spray. Claire raised a hand in greeting. 'Hi,' she called out when Scotty was still a good fifty metres away.

Scotty waved back. 'Hey,' he shouted over the roar of the surf. At the sound of his voice, the dog unleashed a barrage of excited barks and sprinted towards Claire. The odd canter she had noticed from a distance disappeared when the animal accelerated and Claire realised the dog only had three legs; his front right had been amputated at the shoulder. The disability that hobbled him at walking pace vanished at speed. She wondered wryly if Scotty had noticed that. The dog obviously shared his master's belief that some things in life were best done as quickly as possible.

'Tank! Stop!' Scotty yelled, but it was no use. Tank barrelled into Claire like a missile, knocking her to her knees and proceeding to cover her in slobbery kisses. She shrieked with laughter at the dog's enthusiastic greeting.

A moment later, Scotty was at her side. 'Tank, get out of it,' he growled, hauling away her three-legged paramour – which Claire could now see was some kind of cattle dog mix – by the collar. 'Sorry, Claire. Are you okay?'

Claire took Scotty's outstretched hand and let him pull her to her feet. 'I'm fine,' she said, still laughing. Tank sat, his wagging tail sweeping broad arcs in the sand. 'That's quite a wingman you've got there.'

'What can I say? He knows my type.' Scotty flashed a rakish grin that made Claire feel light-headed. He looked relaxed and happy in his black jeans and blue checked shirt. A black cap that bore the vet clinic's logo covered his hair; the strands that peeked out were still damp from the shower. 'Anyway, I'm so glad I ran into you.'

'You are?' She felt her palms grow clammy.

He didn't sound surprised to see her in Bindallarah. Word of her arrival had definitely reached him, then. The town's bush telegraph didn't miss a beat.

'I was just over at Vanessa's place looking for you. Gus said you'd come into town. I tried to get hold of you before I left Sydney.'

She thought of the half-a-dozen missed calls and text messages she'd ignored as she had driven grimly to Bindy on Saturday. 'Oh, right. Sorry. I was, um . . .' Claire tried in vain to think of a plausible excuse for ghosting the man mere hours after he'd told her how much her friendship meant to him. Somehow she didn't think 'I couldn't call you back because I was on my way here to stop your wedding' was going to cut it.

'Working, right? Yeah, I figured you must have had to do some fast talking to swing the time off.'

Swing the time off? Claire felt flustered, confused. It must have been the sea air. Then the penny dropped.

'Yes! Because I was supposed to be working right through Christmas,' she said, making a mental note to keep better track of her lies. 'That's right. I had to change some things around, so that I could come here instead. I was going to call you once I'd settled in.'

'Well, I just want to say thank you,' Scotty said. He took her hand and her skin burned within his grasp. 'It means so much to me that you're here, Claire. I know Bindallarah hasn't always been the happiest place for you. I get that coming back here is hard for you, but I'm so glad you decided to do it.'

'I'm glad too,' she replied. And she meant it. She *was* glad – glad to reconnect with Vanessa and Gus, glad to feel the silky sand of Bindallarah Beach between her toes, glad to see the town she had once loved thriving, despite what its inhabitants may think of her. But mostly, glad to be with Scotty again. Not *with* him, she mentally corrected herself. But near him. That was enough.

He cleared his throat. 'I also, um, I want to apologise. For the way I told you about Nina, about my . . . engagement.'

Scotty's green-eyed gaze bored into hers, searching for absolution.

'Scotty, you have nothing to apologise for,' she said. 'You're my friend. I'm happy for you.' It was kind of the truth. She *was* happy he'd found love. That was exactly why she had to make him see that rushing into marriage was a mistake. It was because he was her friend that she had to make sure he protected his heart.

He looked uncertain. 'I shouldn't have just sprung it on you like that. With our history . . . you deserve better from me.'

Without warning, Claire felt her throat tighten. Tears stung the corners of her eyes. *Damn him!* It was just like Scotty to be so generous and understanding when she was there with a dark ulterior motive. She squeezed her eyes shut tight, overwhelmed by a sharp yearning to turn back the clock six months, before she'd forced herself back into his life again. She should have just let him be.

You deserve better from me. No. He deserved better than her. He always had.

She opened her eyes. 'Listen,' she said, swallowing the hard lump in her throat. 'What are you doing tonight? Why don't you come to Vanessa's place for dinner?'

His face lit up. 'Really?'

Claire returned his grin. 'Absolutely. You and Nina. I'd love to meet your one and only.'

Before she pulled out all the stops to prevent Scotty from doing something that she was sure was doomed to failure, she should at least try to get to know the woman who had inspired his impetuousness, she told herself. Deep down, Claire doubted his rush to the altar would ever make sense to her.

But maybe if she could see what Scotty saw she'd start to understand why he felt compelled to yoke his life to Nina's in such a hurry. If there was some way she could abandon her mission in good conscience, she owed it to him to look for it. She didn't want to cause Scotty any more pain than she already had.

For a split second, Scotty's smile seemed to falter. 'Well, of course,' he said. 'That'd be great. I know Nina's keen to meet you, too. I've told her all about us.' He abruptly turned his head and looked out to sea, as if regretting his choice of words.

'So she knows she was your second choice?' Claire said, and immediately regretted hers. 'Sorry, that was meant to be a joke.'

Scotty let go of her hand. She hadn't realised he was still holding it. 'No worries,' he said, not quite sounding like he meant it. He slapped his right hand on his thigh and Tank sprang to his feet. 'So, see you around seven?'

Claire nodded. With his dog at his heels, Scotty walked away.

CHAPTER FIVE

Claire was still staring at Scotty's footprints in the sand when Vanessa appeared minutes later and handed her a tall plastic cup.

'The line at Bindy Brew was ridiculous, and it's too hot for coffee anyway, so I went to the smoothie bar instead,' she said. 'That's carrot, apple and ginger with organic almond milk.'

'Bindallarah has a *smoothie* bar?' Claire said. 'This place is more hipster than Sydney.'

Vanessa chuckled. 'Well, the bakery makes smoothies now. But you'd be surprised how the town has changed. The local council is very pro-development these days. We've got a new, young mayor – you remember Alex Jessop?'

Claire's jaw dropped. 'Alex Jessop? The meathead captain of the footy team? The guy whose favourite hobbies when we were at school were rabbit shooting and getting so drunk he'd pass out in his own vomit? He's the *mayor*?'

'That's the one,' Vanessa said. 'Got himself a business degree and spent some time in New York after university.

Came back bursting with ideas for revitalising the town. He's quite the renaissance man these days.'

'Wow,' she said, shaking her head. 'I had him pegged as the "marry the girl next door, have three kids by the age of twenty-five, work at his dad's ag supply business for the rest of his life" type.'

'People can change, sweetheart,' Vanessa said gently. 'You've been gone a long time.'

Claire ducked her head and took a long sip of her smoothie, feeling chastised. It was obvious that Bindallarah was different. She hadn't really expected it to be the same dreary hamlet she'd left at fifteen, though it didn't seem to have changed much when she returned briefly for her father's funeral five years later. But she couldn't simply forget her past here. Bindy had shattered her family, and that memory wouldn't be so quick to fade.

'So, you saw Scotty?' Vanessa asked.

Claire looked up, startled. 'How did you know that?'

'Don't look so shocked,' her aunt said, laughing. 'I saw him walking up the beach path as I was coming down. And besides' – she nodded towards the deep indentations Scotty's work boots and Tank's paws had left in the sand – 'I can't think of any other owners of size-thirteen feet and a tripod dog that you'd be chatting to.'

'I invited him for dinner tonight,' Claire said. 'Is that okay?'

'Of course,' her aunt replied. 'But what will his wife-to-be think?'

'Oh, I asked Nina, too.'

Vanessa raised her eyebrows. 'Really? That's very magnanimous of you.'

Claire felt a flutter of indignation in her chest. 'What's that supposed to mean? Why would I have a problem with Nina? I haven't even met the woman.'

'It's not supposed to mean anything, darling,' Vanessa said, her tone implying that it meant everything. 'I just imagine it can't be easy knowing Scotty's about to marry someone else.'

The words hit Claire like a punch to the gut. 'Someone *else*? You mean someone other than me? Aunty Vee, you don't think I've been sitting around thinking that one day Scotty and I would get married, do you?'

Vanessa sipped her juice and shrugged.

'That's absurd,' Claire said, not sure whether to laugh or cry. 'We're friends. That's *all*. Until six months ago, Scotty and I hadn't even spoken in eight years. Not since . . .'

'Not since he proposed to you and you ran away to America,' Vanessa said matter-of-factly.

Claire closed her eyes and breathed deeply. Her aunt was the only person she'd told about Scotty's proposal, the only person who knew that Claire's confusion and panic had been the catalyst for her decision to do her postgraduate equine specialisation studies at an American university.

She opened her eyes and regarded Vanessa steadily. 'Right,' she said eventually. 'Not since then. He only asked me to marry him because Dad died and Scotty decided he could fix everything. You know what he's like. We're both different people now. I don't have feelings for Scotty any more.'

'And yet, news of his engagement has brought you racing back to Bindallarah,' Vanessa said quietly. 'Something eight years of invitations from your own family couldn't do.'

Understanding dawned. This wasn't about Scotty at all. It was about Claire having left Vanessa high and dry in a town where their family's name was mud. Jim Thorne had burned a lot of bridges in Bindallarah by the time he died, and Claire had been so consumed by her own grief that she hadn't thought much about how Vanessa had coped with the shocking loss of her brother – or how she had managed to clean up the mess Big Jim had left behind. The community might not have blamed Vanessa for Jim's demise the way they had blamed Claire, but they had wanted someone held responsible for the damage he'd done and, with Claire on her way to the United States, her aunt had been the only Thorne still standing.

Claire's heart thudded painfully in her chest as she contemplated for the first time how lonely her aunt must have been, raising Gus on her own without any sort of support network in town. Vanessa's parents were long dead and Gus's father hadn't ever been in the picture. She had been close to Claire's mother, Emily, but when Emily had finally walked out on Jim and moved across the country to Perth, Vanessa's loyalty to her brother had driven her to cut contact.

The tears that had threatened earlier welled up again. 'I'm so sorry, Vanessa. I never wanted to leave Bindy in the first place. It wasn't my decision,' Claire said. She grasped Vanessa's shoulder with her free hand. 'I wanted to come back when Mum left, but Dad wouldn't let me. He said my education was more important. If I'd known what was going on, I would have been here in a heartbeat. I didn't know about any of it until it was too late, not that anybody in this town believes that.'

'I know that, sweetheart,' Vanessa said, her eyes shining. She placed her own hand over Claire's and squeezed. 'Your father made his own decisions. Not great ones, admittedly, but it's certainly not for you to shoulder the burden of his mistakes. I didn't want you to come back here out of some sense of guilt. I wanted you to come back because I love you and I miss you. Gus and I both do.'

'I love you too, Vee,' she said, wrapping her aunt in a fierce hug. 'And I've missed you more than I think I even realised.'

The mantle of guilt was like an anvil on Claire's shoulders. Despite what her aunt said, Claire felt responsible. Responsible for her father's lonely death, for the people whose money he'd lost, for failing to be there for Vanessa and Gus.

Her history with Bindallarah was littered with mistakes. And Vanessa was right: she had only returned now for Scotty's wedding. But that was only half of the truth. She couldn't tell her aunt that her plan was to stop the marriage before it started, that she was terrified Scotty was about to plunge head-long into a mistake of his own.

If she was ever going to set things right in Bindallarah, she had to start with him.

Nina Rioli was breathtaking. When Claire opened Vanessa's front door on the dot of seven p.m. and saw Scotty standing there with a supermodel by his side, she felt herself deflate like a punctured football.

Nina was everything Claire was not: tall, with yoga-sculpted curves, dark eyes and a plump, bow-shaped mouth. Her glossy auburn hair cascaded to her waist in artful beachy waves and her skin was tanned cocoa brown and impossibly dewy. She wore a camisole top with loose linen pants and thongs, but she might as well have been in a couture evening gown. It was as though Nina had stepped straight out of Central Casting's 'yoga bunny' department. She was a knockout.

Claire simply stared at her, unable to speak. In her battered denim miniskirt and faded David Bowie T-shirt, she felt pale, unkempt and graceless in comparison. She had heard people described as 'stunningly beautiful', but she couldn't recall actually being struck dumb by another woman's appearance before.

'You must be Claire,' Nina said eventually, ending the painful silence. Her voice was warm; her American accent carried a hint of a southern drawl. 'I'm so happy to finally meet you. This one has told me so much about you.' She playfully swatted Scotty's chest.

Scotty smiled wanly. 'This is Nina,' he said in a small voice. He seemed stiff and formal.

'Well, I think she knows that, honey,' Nina said, laughing. 'Thanks so much for inviting us. Can I do anything to help?' She stepped into Vanessa's hallway and handed Claire a chilled bottle of rosé. Claire glanced at Nina's hand and noticed she wasn't wearing an engagement ring.

'Uh, no, just make yourself at home. Vanessa and Gus are out in the garden,' Claire said when she finally regained the power of speech. 'Dinner won't be long. It's just risotto. Nothing fancy.'

'Ooh, yum,' Nina said. She seemed genuinely delighted. 'My favourite.'

Nina glided down the long central hallway of Vanessa's cottage, while Claire silently berated herself for choosing to cook her signature Italian dish. With a name like Rioli, and looking like an extra from a pasta-sauce commercial, Nina was probably a gourmet Mediterranean chef.

She turned back to Scotty, still standing on the verandah. 'Were you planning on coming in?'

He shook his head as if chasing away unpleasant thoughts and stepped inside. 'Listen, Claire,' he said, leaning in close, 'there's something I need to —'

'Nina seems lovely,' she said, cutting him off. Her words were clipped and she was surprised to feel something akin to anger bubbling up within her. It took only a glance at Nina to see why any man would fall for her. Her charms were plentiful. But Scotty wasn't just any man. He was the best man she knew. Claire had never thought of him as someone easily entranced by physical beauty. It was so prosaic. Of all the crazy reasons to marry in haste, lust had to be the craziest. She had thought he was smarter than that.

'Yeah, she's fantastic,' Scotty said, closing the door behind him. 'But the thing is —'

'Has she always been a yoga teacher?' Claire turned and walked down the hall to the kitchen. *Let him try to tell me she's a part-time nuclear physicist*, she thought. She slammed the bottle of wine onto the timber benchtop as she heard Scotty enter the room behind her. Through the open back door, she watched as Nina greeted Vanessa with a familiar peck on the cheek. Claire felt piqued: her aunt hadn't mentioned she knew Nina so well.

'Actually, she's a vet,' Scotty said.

Claire whirled to face him. 'What?' The idea that Nina was Scotty's professional equal – and Claire's, too – was as shocking as the news that she was his fiancée.

'Yeah, in the States she was a specialist ophthalmologist, but the visa she came to Australia on means she can't register as a vet here,' he said.

'But the yoga studio – how is she running a business?'

Scotty looked sheepish. 'It's not technically Nina's business. Alex Jessop owns it. Remember him?'

Claire nodded. 'Mr Mayor.'

Scotty laughed. 'Yeah. Nina just works there as a casual teacher and he put her name on the place because, well, I guess he thought she was a good advertisement for doing yoga.'

'You mean because of her insane bod?' came a voice from the back door. Claire pivoted to see her cousin, Gus, bound into the kitchen from the garden.

'Hey, Scotty,' Gus said, running a hand through her bleached blonde crop. Then, registering Claire's gobsmacked expression, added blithely, 'What? Nina is smoking hot. It's not news.' She slid open a drawer and retrieved a corkscrew, then grabbed the rosé and darted back outside.

'Gus has always had a way with words,' Scotty said, offering an uncertain smile. 'But, yes, I think Alex thought that having Nina as the spokesperson for his business couldn't hurt.'

Claire felt like folding in on herself. She didn't know what she'd expected, but it wasn't this. She felt adrift and she didn't know why.

'I want you to be happy, Scotty,' she said for no other reason than because it was the only true thing she knew in that moment.

Scotty flinched, as though her words had hurt. 'I know,' he said softly. 'We will be.'

He held her gaze and Claire felt exposed. Something hung between them, some meaning she couldn't quite grasp. It felt loaded and dangerous. Claire sensed that she was standing at a precipice. She had to decide whether to commit to her plan to try to stop the wedding or stand by and watch Scotty sign up for possible heartache. No, not possible. Probable.

It would be so much easier if Nina was *just* beautiful. Claire could just about get to grips with beauty. Falling hard and fast for a gorgeous woman was understandable, if annoyingly predictable. And if she was only beautiful, then convincing Scotty to call off the wedding would be the kindest thing for Nina, too – she deserved someone whose love for her was more than skin deep. If it was just about desire, the marriage would be disastrous for both of them.

Brains complicated things. If it wasn't just physical attraction driving Scotty's rush to say 'I do' – if he truly connected with Nina on a deeper level – then Claire had no business interfering. But Nina was a stranger to her. She couldn't say whether or not that connection was there, at least not until she had spent some time with her.

'Scotty, Claire,' Nina called from the garden. 'There's two glasses of pink wine out here with your name on them.'

Claire needed to get to know the woman who had won Scotty's heart. And with only twelve days until Nina was set to marry him, she had to start now.

CHAPTER SIX

Claire ladled another steaming spoonful of risotto onto Nina's plate.

'Oh, I really shouldn't have seconds,' Nina groaned, patting a nonexistent belly. 'But you're such an amazing cook, Claire. How am I ever going to fit into a wedding dress in two weeks' time?'

'I'm sure it wouldn't be too late to have it altered,' Claire replied, feeling oddly gratified that Nina had enjoyed the meal. 'Not that you'll need it.'

'Actually, I don't even have a dress yet.'

Gus's fork clattered dramatically onto her plate. 'Are you *serious*?' she said. 'Give me two minutes.' She pushed back her chair and practically ran from the room.

'It's all happened so fast,' Nina said, almost apologetically. She reached out and grasped Scotty's hand. 'I've been so busy with work – everyone in town wants a "yoga body" in time for Christmas – that I just haven't had time to shop. And I don't really know Bindallarah, so I wanted to wait until Scotty came back from his conference in Melbourne to get started on the wedding preparations. He's been taking care of pretty much all of it, to be honest.'

'I don't mind,' Scotty said, gently extracting his hand and picking up his fork. 'There's not much to do, really. We're having the wedding up at Mum and Dad's place, so it's just a few hay bales and a trestle table.' He flashed a cheeky smile and took a bite of his risotto.

An unexpected guffaw escaped Claire's lips as a look of pure horror crossed Nina's face. 'He's kidding, Nina,' Claire said. 'Trust me.' It was typical of Scotty's sense of humour to say something totally ridiculous, but with such a decisive air that nobody could tell if he was serious or not.

'Although,' Vanessa chimed in, 'Cape Ashe Stud is so beautiful, it really wouldn't take much more than that to transform it for a wedding.'

Nina looked vaguely embarrassed to have missed Scotty's joke. 'I hear it's lovely. I look forward to seeing it,' she said.

Claire frowned. 'You haven't been to Cape Ashe? It's only ten minutes away.'

'Uh-uh.' Nina shook her head and took a sip of her wine. She didn't meet Claire's gaze.

Claire looked at Scotty, but his expression was unreadable. A thick silence descended. All she could hear was the shrieking of the cicadas in the fig trees that surrounded Vanessa's back patio and the distant thunder of the ocean. She didn't know what to make of the uncomfortable exchange. Why wouldn't Scotty have taken the woman he was about to marry to his family home – especially when it was the venue for the wedding?

It occurred to her that she didn't actually know where Scotty lived any more. Claire still pictured him in his bedroom at Cape Ashe Stud, but of course he'd left there at eighteen to go to university in Sydney. At uni he'd lived in the crumbling share house that she'd always joked wasn't fit for human habitation and ought to be condemned. And after that – who knew? When she had rejected his marriage proposal and fled overseas, she told herself she'd forfeited her right to know where Scotty slept each night. He might have lived with another girlfriend. So far she hadn't been able to bring herself to ask if there had been others, but she knew there must have been. He wasn't conventionally handsome, but in the fading evening light Claire was acutely aware that Scotty had something – that indefinable 'it'. What had Jackie called it? Magnetism. That was it. Her heart rate quickened involuntarily as she watched his eyes glitter with the reflection of the bamboo torches Vanessa had lit to keep the mosquitoes at bay. She knew there was no way Scotty would have lacked female company between her departure and Nina's arrival.

'Scotty, are you living at Cape Ashe?' she asked him.

He looked surprised by the question. 'No, I haven't lived there since high school. Chris is in the main house with his wife, Amber, and their little boy, Matty. Mum and Dad built a smaller place up on the ridge a few years back.'

'Chris is *married*? Isn't he, like, twelve?' The idea of Scotty's baby brother having a wife and a baby of his own seemed absurd. All these people she'd once known so well, all living lives she knew nothing about.

'He's twenty-seven. Only a year younger than you,'

Scotty said, chuckling. 'He's been married a couple of years. Remember, we tend to get hitched young in the bush.'

Claire shifted uncomfortably in her seat as Scotty's meaning sank in. If she had accepted his proposal at twenty, they could have been married for eight years by now. What would her life look like as Mrs Shannon? She would have come back to Bindallarah with him after university, that much she knew. It had always been Scotty's plan to have his own clinic in town. But what would she have done? Had kids right away? She couldn't have become an equine specialist, not here. It wasn't until she went to college in America that she even realised horses were her passion.

If she'd stayed here, she might not be working as a vet at all. Claire shuddered at the thought. She may not have much in her life besides work, but she *loved* her work. She couldn't imagine being happy without it.

And in Bindallarah terms, being single at twenty-nine made Scotty the male equivalent of a spinster. Was that why he and Nina had got engaged so quickly? Did she tick most of the boxes on his 'Dream Wife' checklist, so he figured he'd better stop wasting time and lock her down?

Vanessa cleared her throat. 'Scotty and Nina live at Thorne Hill, Claire,' she said.

Without warning, a wave of nausea washed over her. She stared at Scotty, open-mouthed. 'You do *not*.'

He looked down at his plate. 'I was going to tell you,' he mumbled.

Nina's head swivelled between Scotty and Claire as though she was watching a tennis match. 'You know Scotty's farm?' she asked, her eyes as round as horseshoes. 'Sorry, *our* farm?'

'Thorne Hill is *my* place. My family's place. I mean, it was. It's where I grew up.' Claire turned to face her aunt. 'But you said the McGraths next door had bought it,' she accused.

'The McGraths did buy it,' Vanessa said patiently. 'But Annie passed away last year and it was just too much land for Brian to look after on his own, so he sold it to Scotty . . . this past winter, wasn't it?'

Scotty nodded. 'Not long before we reconnected, Claire,' he said, and she heard the note of pleading in his voice. He wanted her to understand. 'I actually thought that might have been why you got in touch again after such a long time. I assumed Vanessa must have told you I'd bought it.'

Claire set her jaw. 'Well, she didn't.'

She felt betrayed, though she knew she had no right to. She hadn't wanted the responsibility of the family's dairy farm when Jim had died. Even Scotty's plan that they marry and run it together couldn't persuade her. Her father's increasingly desperate attempts to make it profitable had pushed his own marriage to the brink, which in turn had been the reason Claire was banished to boarding school. Well, *part* of the reason, she admitted, as from the corner of her eye she watched Scotty watching her. She closed her eyes and was drawn back to her final summer at Thorne Hill, when Scotty had been a frequent visitor under the cover of darkness. She shivered at the memory.

Claire had left Vanessa to arrange for the farm to be sold while she escaped to California after her father's death – one more thing she'd selfishly expected her aunt to just take care of. When she had found out the true extent of Jim's financial woes, Claire had told herself she was doubly glad to be rid of the place. As long as the meagre proceeds of the sale cleared his debts and covered her college tuition, she had decided she didn't care who bought the property. But a small part of her had been glad when she'd learned Jim's neighbours were the farm's new owners, instead of some developer looking to carve up the hundred acres of rolling green hinterland to build holiday cottages or something equally depressing.

'I don't get it, Scotty. *Why* would you buy the place? What are you going to do with it?' That he hadn't thought to mention he and his future wife would be beginning their married life in her childhood home was shocking enough, but what Claire couldn't get her head around was why Scotty would want Thorne Hill at all. Her father had failed to make it profitable and it had proved too much for Brian McGrath. How was Scotty going to run both a farm and his vet clinic?

'I've always liked Thorne Hill,' he said. 'It's a beautiful spot up there in the hills and I don't think its potential has ever been, uh, fully explored.' He was choosing his words carefully, Claire could tell. She knew Scotty didn't want her to think he was criticising her father – as if everyone in town wasn't already well aware of Jim Thorne's shortcomings as a businessman. 'I wasn't really looking to buy such a big property, but when I heard Brian was selling I realised it was too good an opportunity to pass up. I've got a lot of ideas for the place.'

'Like what?' she said, trying to pretend she didn't notice Nina looking increasingly uneasy as her fiancé talked about the farm.

Scotty opened his mouth, but before he could reply Gus reappeared holding a stack of magazines. 'Ta-da!' she said triumphantly, dumping them on the table next to Nina's plate. Nina looked startled. 'Every issue of *Cosmo Bride* since 2010. You're bound to find your dream dress in there, Nina.'

'Gus, why do you have nearly a decade's worth of bridal magazines? You're only eighteen. You don't even have a boyfriend,' Claire said.

'Thank you for pointing that out, Claire.' Gus's reply was tart. 'You are correct. But I do have a very clear picture of what my wedding will look like when I *do* find Mr Right.' She pushed the stack towards Nina. 'Go for your life.'

Nina flicked half-heartedly through the top copy and exhaled, blowing out her cheeks. 'Gosh, I don't even know where to start,' she said. She held up a picture of a ballgown-style dress with a bejewelled bodice and a skirt consisting of acres of gauzy tulle. 'I doubt I'd be able to get anything this . . . *weddingy* in time for Christmas Eve.'

Anxiety clouded Nina's flawless features and Claire felt an unexpected pang of sympathy for Scotty's intended. She was a virtual stranger in a town that was insular at the best of times, marrying one of its favourite sons in just a few days' time, without family or friends to guide her. The poor woman must have been terrified.

She suddenly remembered her resolution to befriend Nina. 'I'll help you. We'll go shopping in Alison Bay tomorrow,' she said decisively. The next town along the coast was ten times larger than Bindallarah. 'I don't think there's any actual bridal boutiques between here and Brisbane, but if

I remember correctly Ally Bay has some nice stores. It'll have to be off the rack, but we'll find you a beautiful dress. You'd look stunning in anything.'

Nina's concerned expression gave way to an elated smile. 'Really?' she said. 'Oh my gosh, Claire, that would be amazing. Thank you *so* much.' She reached across the table and gave Claire's hand a grateful squeeze.

'You know, I could help in other ways, too,' Claire said, turning her attention to Scotty. 'I have all this time on my hands. Why don't you let me help out with the wedding plans? Make life a little easier for you both.'

In her peripheral vision, Claire saw Vanessa shoot a sharp look in her direction. Scotty looked faintly alarmed too. 'Oh, well, I don't really —'

'That's a wonderful idea,' Nina exclaimed at the same time. 'Scotty, you've been saying how busy you are. Claire knows Bindallarah so much better than I do. You *know* you could use the help.'

Scotty paused for what felt like an eternity. His emerald eyes grew dark in the flickering torchlight. 'Okay,' he said at last. 'Thanks, Claire.'

She shrugged in what she hoped was a nonchalant way. 'Sure,' she said. 'Happy to lend a hand for an old friend.'

Claire didn't know why Scotty had bought Thorne Hill or why he was intent on living in it with a woman he barely knew. She didn't know why a worldly and, she had to admit, lovely woman like Nina had pitched up in a rural backwater and agreed to marry someone who hadn't thought to mention that their future marital home once belonged to his ex-girlfriend. She didn't know whether spending time one on one with Scotty was a good idea or a calamity waiting to happen. And if it was destined to be calamitous, she didn't know who would suffer the most – him or her.

But Claire did know one thing: she was going to find out.

CHAPTER SEVEN

'Are you sure this is a good idea?' Vanessa asked the next morning. 'Actually, let me rephrase that: this is *not* a good idea.'

Claire froze midway through rifling behind the sofa cushions in a frantic search for her car keys. 'Why would you say that?'

Vanessa perched on the coffee table and set down her mug of tea beside her. She gave her niece a look that said, *Do I really need to spell it out?*

Claire sighed. 'Aunty Vee, for the hundredth time, Scotty is my friend. *Just* my friend. Why shouldn't Nina become my friend, too?' Her fingers closed around the wayward keys and she pulled them out with a triumphant flourish.

'Friends or not, Scotty was the love of your life. I just worry that forcing yourself to spend time with his fiancée to prove a point is not going to end well.' She took a sip of her tea.

Vanessa's tone was gentle, but her words struck Claire like a sledgehammer. 'The love of my *life*?' she spat. 'So if I can't be with Scotty I'm destined to be alone forever? Well, forget the shopping, I guess I might as well go and adopt fifteen cats right now.'

'There's no need for sarcasm,' her aunt said. 'You know that's not what I meant.'

'And what point am I trying to prove? That I can be a mature adult? That I'm not going to despise a woman just because a man I once loved chose her instead of me?' As soon as the words left her mouth, Claire realised how they sounded. 'I don't mean . . . I didn't want . . .' She let out an exasperated breath. 'He was never going to choose me. That's not what this is about.'

Claire sank onto the sofa and Vanessa moved to sit next to her. 'Then what is it about, sweetheart?' she said.

'It's about . . .' Claire looked around Vanessa's cosy living room, as if the words she was looking for could be hiding in a corner. Her gaze came to rest on her aunt's enormous white Christmas tree. It was the same one she'd had since Claire was a little girl, back when her parents were still together. She had always loved their family Christmases, filled with laughter and presents and way too much food. She remembered creeping into her parents' bedroom before sunrise on Christmas Day. Their windows would be wide open, the day already warm, and she would feel the soft, fragrant breeze caressing her bare arms as she tiptoed excitedly across the floorboards to rouse her father. Jim hadn't minded being woken early. He had been a typical farmer in that sense. The morning was the best part of the day, he had said – and Christmas morning was the best morning of them all.

But that had all been so long ago. Christmas would never be like that again. This town had a way of trapping people in the past.

'It's about moving forward,' she told Vanessa. 'Honestly, I have doubts about the speed of this wedding, but it's not because I still have *those* kinds of feelings for Scotty. This is about the future. His *and* Nina's.'

And mine.

Vanessa pursed her lips. She looked entirely unconvinced, but she didn't say anything further.

'Trust me, Aunty Vee. I know what I'm doing,' Claire said. She stood and picked up her handbag. 'I'd better get going or I'll be late to pick up Nina.'

Scotty was standing at the reception desk finalising a patient's discharge paperwork when his fiancée and his ex-girlfriend strolled past the clinic window, talking animatedly. Nina peered inside and waved when she saw him. Claire didn't even glance in his direction.

He felt sick. His guts churned with the bilious ferocity of a post-rugby grand final hangover.

'You all right, doc?' said his client Toby Watts. He clutched the leash of a glum golden retriever sporting a comically large Elizabethan collar. 'You look a bit rough.'

'Thanks, mate. You're too kind,' Scotty deadpanned. He knew he looked awful. He'd hardly slept a wink after dinner at Vanessa Thorne's place last night. The second his head hit the pillow his mind was racing, filled with thoughts of Claire.

Not Nina. Not his fiancée. *Claire.* His ex, the first woman he'd wanted to marry. Who was now taking the woman he *was* marrying to shop for a wedding dress.

How messed up was that?

'Sorry, buddy,' Toby chuckled. 'Listen, while I'm here, let's talk about food for the wedding. If you want a whole pig I'll have to order it right away . . .'

Scotty nodded and pretended to listen while Bindallarah's award-winning butcher droned on about suckling pigs and lambs and charcoal-spit rental. He knew he should be paying attention – people were pulling out all the stops to help Scotty arrange an eleventh-hour wedding at the least convenient time of year – but he wasn't.

He was still thinking about her.

He kept replaying the moment Claire had opened Vanessa's front door last night. The way her curls hung loose around her shoulders. The way she smiled when she saw him. Her short skirt and her long legs. That David Bowie T-shirt. *His* David Bowie T-shirt.

He wondered if she remembered that he'd given it to her. She'd swiped it from him that first week at university, when they'd fallen back into each other's lives and just as quickly into bed. After three years without her, three years of waiting to get over her and never quite succeeding, Scotty would have given her anything if it meant she'd stay.

But she didn't stay. Two years later she left him, shattered his heart almost beyond repair. Then she left the country. If he'd had any lingering hope of a future with her, Claire moving to America had been pretty unequivocal.

And now he was with Nina. Gorgeous, intelligent, charming Nina, who was as focused and decisive as Claire was scattered and hesitant. Kind, patient Nina, who came into his life just as he'd convinced himself he'd be alone forever. Nina, who had agreed to marry him, even though it was fast and probably crazy. Nina, who saw what a good team they made. Scotty was the envy of every straight man in town and he knew it.

But he had Claire, too, he reminded himself. She'd come back, in a way. They were friends and Claire seemed determined to be Nina's friend as well. He'd seen the brief flash of dismay that had hijacked Claire's face the moment she'd seen Nina. Women often looked at his fiancée that way. He knew he should feel grateful that he was going to be able to have both Nina and Claire in his life. He could have his cake and eat it. The woman he'd always wanted and the life he'd always planned. Just not the way he'd imagined either scenario.

Scotty realised Toby had stopped talking and was staring quizzically at him. He stared blankly back.

'So, what do you reckon?' Toby said.

'Sorry, mate, I missed that. Don't think I've quite woken up yet,' Scotty said with a forced laugh, shaking his head to try to shift the brain fog. 'What were you saying?'

'Do you want to come in tomorrow morning and place the order?'

'Um . . .' His mind drifted to Claire once again, taking Nina shopping for a wedding dress, offering to help him with the wedding preparations. He should just talk to her, explain the whole thing. She would understand. Hopefully. 'I will come in. Yes. And I'll bring Claire Thorne with me.'

Toby's mouth hung open. 'Claire Thorne?'

'She's back in town for the wedding. Helping me and Nina out with some of the arrangements.'

'You don't say.' Toby's tone was loaded. Scotty smiled and handed Toby the receipt for his dog's treatment. Half of

Bindallarah would find a reason to be in the butcher's shop the next day, he'd wager.

Scotty called for his next patient and resolved to put Claire out of his mind until he saw her in the morning. He was on a path he hadn't planned to travel, and it was entirely of his own making. He'd dug himself into a deep, deep hole and he had to try to haul himself out of it before it was too late.

CHAPTER EIGHT

Satin + Heels was their last hope. Claire and Nina had been to every boutique in Alison Bay. Claire had watched patiently as Nina had tried on any dress that looked even the slightest bit bridal. As Claire had predicted, she looked jaw-droppingly beautiful in every single one. She might have felt resentful if she hadn't found herself genuinely enjoying Nina's company.

Claire didn't have many girlfriends in Sydney – Jackie was as close to a BFF as it got. She'd lost touch with her Bindallarah schoolfriends when she went to boarding school, and the less said about the girls actually at boarding school the better. At university she and Scotty had been so wrapped up in each other that no one else really got a look in. She'd lived in an all-female dorm at college in America, and there were always plenty of girls to hang out with, but none of those friend-ships stuck once she moved back to Australia. It felt strangely exciting to be getting along so well with Nina – and just plain strange that she was Scotty's fiancée.

Maybe that was why she had vetoed every dress Nina had tried on. Nina wasn't fussy – she would have happily bought the first gown she'd seen. She was almost blasé about the decision. But nothing was quite right, at least not in Claire's opinion. She told herself she had a responsibility to make sure Nina didn't make a purchase as important as her wedding dress without properly exploring all her options.

But if she was honest with herself, Claire knew she was really just trying to buy more time – time to get to know Nina, to figure out whether she was right for Scotty.

'I swear I'm buying the first dress in this store that fits,' Nina said as she pushed open the door to Satin + Heels. 'I don't care if it's black or backless or made of wetsuit fabric.'

Claire giggled. 'You are seriously the most low-maintenance bride ever. I hope you don't mind me saying so, but when I first met you yesterday I kind of assumed you'd be one of those prissy girls who spend hours in front of the mirror every day.' She couldn't imagine Scotty falling in love with a vain woman, but surely Nina didn't look the way she did without a little bit of elbow grease.

'No way, I hate that stuff,' Nina said, wrinkling her nose. 'Honestly, I'd be happy to get married in jeans and a T-shirt. Except it's too darn hot in this country for jeans in December. And Scotty says I have to make *some* effort for this wedding.' She rolled her eyes as if to imply it was an unreasonable request.

Claire blinked in surprise as Nina glided to the store's formal section – a single rack of dresses in a corner by the fitting rooms. *Scotty says I have to make* some *effort.* It was a curious thing to say. Why would Scotty need to persuade his bride-to-be to glam herself up? Didn't Nina want to feel beautiful on her big day?

Claire had learned a lot about Nina in the three hours they had spent together trawling the shops of Alison Bay. She was older than Scotty: thirty-one to his twenty-nine. She grew up in Texas – Claire had been right about her faint southern twang – and came from a big family, though her parents had died when Nina was in college and none of her siblings was able to make it to Bindallarah in time for the wedding. She came to Australia a year ago with her boyfriend, some financial bigwig, but they split up not long after arriving. Nina had bounced around different places, often working casually as a vet nurse since she wasn't legally able to practise as a veterinarian. She met Bindy's mayor, Alex Jessop, at a yoga retreat in Queensland in October – she was a qualified instructor and teaching yoga had helped her pay for her vet studies. Alex persuaded her to move to Bindallarah and become the 'face' of his new yoga studio.

It wasn't meant to be a long-term thing, Nina told Claire. Her plan was to save ten thousand dollars to sit the National Veterinary Examination, which would mean she could register as a vet in New South Wales. Claire knew all about the notoriously tough exam – she'd purposely chosen an American university affiliated with her Australian alma mater for her postgrad studies so that her overseas qualifications would be recognised at home and she wouldn't have to take the test herself.

But then Nina met Scotty and all her plans went right out the window. They were engaged a month later.

'Hey, Nina,' Claire said, joining her in flicking through the dress selection. 'You haven't told me yet how you and Scotty actually met.'

'This one?' Nina said, holding up a dusky-pink strapless dress with a full skirt.

Claire shook her head. 'Too Molly Ringwald in *Pretty in Pink*.'

Nina returned it to the rack. 'It was his dog, as a matter of fact,' she said. 'You know Tank?'

Claire nodded. She chose a floor-sweeping pale-green Grecian-style gown and held it out to Nina.

'Well, I hit him with my car.'

The dress hit the floor. 'You did *what*?'

'I know,' Nina wailed. 'It's awful. I got horribly lost trying to find this cottage up in the hinterland that I was thinking about renting. I was stressed out and I guess I wasn't paying attention, because Tank ran right out in front of me and I just did not see him. It was right by Scotty's place.' She stopped herself and smiled. 'Your old place. Thorne Hill. Scotty picked up Tank and jumped in the car with me and we rushed him straight into town to the clinic.'

'So that's why Tank only has three legs?'

Nina nodded, cringing. 'We both worked on him – which technically speaking I should not have done – but we just couldn't save the leg. Can you believe Scotty wanted anything to do with me after that? I keep waiting for him to wake up one day and tell me he's come to his senses.' She held the green dress at arm's length, considering it coolly, as if revealing that she expected the man she was eleven days from marrying to change his mind was no big deal.

Was that why Nina was so laidback about buying a dress and planning the wedding? Did she not believe there would really *be* a wedding?

'Nina, it was an accident,' Claire said. She grasped Nina's forearm. 'Scotty knows that. Tank is fine, and it's actually a pretty great "how we met" story. Definitely one to tell your grandkids some day.'

For the briefest of instants, Claire was sure she saw a flash of fear in Nina's coffee-coloured eyes. It vanished before she could ponder what it meant. 'You don't really think Scotty would back out of the wedding, do you?' Claire asked.

Nina tossed her hair and laughed. 'Oh, I'm just being silly. Must be pre-wedding jitters or something,' she said. She waggled the dress hanger. 'I really like this one.'

'Great,' Claire said brightly. 'Go try it on.'

'No,' Nina replied.

'No?'

'I want *you* to try it on.'

Claire frowned. 'Me? Why? You're the one who has to wear it.'

Nina thrust the dress into Claire's hands. 'I'm sure it will fit. I want to see what it will look like from Scotty's point of view.' She planted her hands on Claire's shoulders and turned her to face the fitting rooms. 'I'm going to sit in that chair by the door. Imagine I'm Scotty and you're me, sashaying down the aisle to say "I do" and live happily ever after.'

Claire's head swam a little at the thought. 'You're planning to sashay?'

Nina smiled and crossed her arms. 'Go.'

Claire's feet were as heavy as lead as she plodded to the fitting room. She felt deeply uncomfortable. She closed the curtain and hung the dress on a wooden peg. Stepping out of her denim cut-offs and plain black tank top, she scrutinised her reflection in the full-length mirror.

This is a crazy idea.

Claire strutting around in the dress wouldn't tell Nina anything. They may have worn the same-sized clothing, but their bodies were completely different. Nina was a head taller, for a start. On her, the sleeveless gown's empire waist would show off her willowy arms and impressive cleavage. It would skim her shapely hips and hang just so over her pert bottom. Her figure was undulating, exotic, all mesmerising peaks and suggestive valleys.

If Scotty were to watch Claire walk down the aisle in this dress, all he would see was an ordinary woman with precious few curves swamped by the flowing fabric. It was a pointless exercise.

But she slipped the dress over her head, anyway, if only so that she could steal a couple of minutes to think about everything Nina had told her.

For a woman whose wedding was just days away, Nina didn't seem very excited. In fact, Claire mused, she seemed decidedly lukewarm about the whole thing. How many brides would be willing to stand idly by while their fiancé made all the arrangements – and with the help of his ex-girlfriend? Scotty and Nina's meeting and romance had been a whirlwind, their engagement lightning fast, but now that she had a metaphorical ring on her finger – because she still wasn't wearing an actual engagement ring – Nina seemed to have lost momentum.

Could it be that Nina shared Claire's doubts about the speed of it all? Maybe she wanted to pump the brakes, slow things down a little and think things through before making a lifetime commitment to a man she'd basically just met.

Perhaps it wasn't Scotty's good sense she should be appealing to, Claire thought. Nina might be the one who would respond to a rational argument for postponing the wedding.

Claire zipped up the dress and swept aside the curtain, stepping back into the shop with a flourish. She felt ridiculous, but if Nina wanted a show, Claire would give her a show. She clutched an invisible posy and weaved slowly between racks of garments towards the other woman.

Nina leapt up from her chair. She stood with her arms stiffly by her sides and pretended to blink back tears, imitating a nervous groom. But something told Claire that, come Christmas Eve, Scotty wouldn't be the one who'd be apprehensive about tying the knot.

'What do you think?' Claire asked.

'It looks really beautiful on you, Claire,' Nina said with what sounded like sincerity.

'Well, thanks, but we're supposed to be thinking about how it will look on *you*,' Claire reminded her.

Nina slapped her palm to her forehead. 'Right! Me. Okay,' she said. 'Well, I guess it will do fine.'

Fine? A growing sense of disquiet pricked at the edges of Claire's thoughts. She had to say something. 'Nina, are you okay? You seem a little . . . unenthused,' she began. 'If you're having doubts about the wedding, it's all right to say so. It's totally normal. This is a big step you and Scotty are taking. A *huge* step.'

Especially when you're taking that step at the speed of light, she managed to stop herself from adding.

Nina levelled a questioning gaze at Claire. 'I don't have any doubts about getting married,' she said in a clipped voice. 'Why would I?'

Her tone stung. 'Not about getting married. Just about everything happening so fast,' Claire said. She rushed to smooth things over. 'I just mean . . . not many women could be convinced to get hitched with only two weeks to plan.'

'Scotty didn't have to convince me of anything. Getting married on Christmas Eve was my idea.' Nina picked up her handbag. 'I'll go pay for the dress.'

Claire watched, disconcerted, as Nina took out her wallet and strode towards the counter. She scurried back to the fitting room and stepped out of the wedding gown. The mood had changed and she wasn't sure why. One moment Nina was talking about marriage to Scotty as disinterestedly as if it was a root canal, the next she was saying *she* had pushed for their truncated engagement. If she was in such a fever to become Mrs Scotty Shannon, why did Nina seem so dispassionate? Scotty deserved someone who would be counting down the seconds until she became his wife. If Nina didn't feel that way, then Claire *had* to make sure the wedding didn't go ahead – for both Scotty's and Nina's sakes.

Claire carefully placed the dress on its hanger. Wrapping herself in the fitting-room curtain, she leaned out and handed the gown to the smiling sales assistant, who carried it to the counter and zipped it into a garment bag.

By the time Claire had put her shorts and tank top back on and re-emerged into the shop, Nina was waiting outside, the garment bag slung casually over her shoulder. Through the window, Claire could see that Nina was talking to someone, a man with neatly trimmed dark hair who was wearing an unexpectedly hip royal-blue suit. He had his back to Claire, though she knew she would be unlikely to know him, even if she could see his face. If Bindallarah was as unfamiliar to her now as a foreign country, Alison Bay was another planet.

As a child, she had visited Ally Bay just once a year, making the thirty-minute drive from Bindallarah with her mother every December to shop for Christmas presents and supplies for the coming school year. Claire felt a little foolish as she remembered how she would barely sleep the night before the annual pilgrimage, as thrilled as if she were about to visit Paris or Rome instead of a torpid beachside hamlet in the northernmost reaches of New South Wales.

She left the store and was relieved when Nina flashed a bright smile in her direction, the strangeness that had passed between them just a few minutes ago apparently forgotten.

'Hey, Claire,' she said. 'Sorry, I was going to wait inside for you, but then I saw this guy passing by. This is my friend, Alex.'

The man in the blue suit turned around and, for what felt like the hundredth time since she'd returned to the district, Claire's jaw dropped.

'Claire Thorne,' Alex Jessop said slowly. The high school Neanderthal-turned-mayor gave her an appraising look. 'I heard you were back. Good to see you. You're looking great.'

Before she could reply, Alex planted a kiss on Claire's cheek and wrapped his arms around her.

'Of course, I forget you already know everybody in town, Claire,' Nina said, smiling.

'I don't know *everybody*,' Claire mumbled. 'Not any more.'

'But everybody knows you,' Alex said jovially, releasing Claire from his embrace. 'The Thornes have sure made their mark in this neck of the woods over the years.'

Claire felt her face flush. 'So, Alex, you're the mayor now.' She changed the subject. 'I did *not* see that one coming.' If Alex was going to make barbs about Claire's past, she would happily return the favour.

Alex chuckled. 'You're not the only one,' he said. His gaze roamed unabashedly over Claire's body and she felt exposed in more ways than one. 'It really is nice to see you, Claire. Can I buy you dinner while you're in town? I'd love to catch up properly.'

Claire was sure she heard Nina gasp. She felt a little breathless herself. Was she hallucinating or had Alex Jessop – the erstwhile muscled football jock who had scarcely given her timid, bookish teenage self the time of day – just *asked her out*?

She arranged her face into what she hoped was an apologetic expression. 'I don't think I'll have time, I'm afraid,' she said, her tone entirely unrepentant. 'Nina and Scotty's wedding is only a few days away and I've promised to help out with the arrangements as much as I can.'

'Huh,' he said, arching an eyebrow. 'Isn't that generous of you? Well, if you find yourself with a free evening, give me a call.' He extracted a business card from his back pocket and handed it to Claire.

She smiled and slid it into her handbag, making a mental note to deposit it in the first bin she saw.

'Nina, I'll call you later to go over the Christmas roster for the studio,' Alex said. He pecked Nina on the cheek and went on his way.

Nina waited until her boss was out of earshot, then turned to Claire. 'Well,' she said. 'That was weird. What's the deal with you and Alex?'

Claire shook her head. The encounter had left her feeling rattled and she didn't quite know why. 'There is literally no deal,' she said. 'We were at high school together and he was one hundred per cent awful. Boorish, mean, thought he was king of the castle. Seems like he's made quite the transformation.'

Nina looked sceptical. 'So you two never . . .?'

Claire frowned. 'Never what?'

'I don't know, dated? Made out? Secretly longed for each other?'

'Ew, no way!' She protested with all the vehemence of the dramatic teenager she had once been. 'Alex Jessop was *so* not my type. That was probably the most words Alex has ever spoken to me. The only guy I ever dated in high school was . . . was . . .'

Claire faltered. *Scotty.* She wouldn't really call those afternoons in the dunes and evenings on the stable roof at Cape Ashe Stud 'dating', but there was no doubt he had been the only member of the opposite sex on her radar back then – and for years afterwards.

'Scotty?' Nina supplied. 'It's okay, Claire. I know all about you and Scotty. You don't have to pretend you don't have a history.'

She wondered if Nina knew that Scotty had once wanted Claire to be his wife. He hadn't actually answered her yesterday when she'd made her awkward joke about Nina being his second choice.

'I just don't want you to worry that whatever Scotty and I once had has anything to do with me being here,' Claire said. 'I came back to Bindallarah because we're friends. *Just* friends. I only want what's best for him.'

'I'm not worried,' Nina said. 'I'm really glad you're here. I only want what's best for Scotty, too.'

She put her arm around Claire's shoulders and squeezed. Claire felt herself tense, and not just because even as a student in California she'd never managed to get used to that American touchy-feelyness. Her tension was guilt-induced. Nina thought they were on the same page, working towards a shared goal of helping Scotty plan an incredible wedding.

But somehow Claire doubted Nina would agree that what was best for Scotty was that they shouldn't get married at all.

CHAPTER NINE

Claire stood on the footpath and looked up at the blue-and-white-striped shop awning. Unpretentious block lettering declared it to be the commercial home of Tobias Watts: Artisan Butcher. 'Watt's the best meat? Watts's meat!' read a wooden signboard hanging underneath.

Claire shook her head. The only artisans in Bindallarah when she was growing up were the Country Women's Association quilters, who met in the community hall on the second Sunday of the month.

'Wow, Scotty, you sure know how to show a girl a good time,' Claire said with as much sarcasm as she could muster. 'Is this how you won Nina's heart? Taking her to all Bindallarah's hot spots?'

Scotty laughed loudly, his deep voice conveying genuine mirth, and Claire felt her stomach flip. She had loved trying to make him laugh when they were together. She'd almost forgotten that.

'It might not be glamorous, but it's probably the most

important part of the wedding,' Scotty said, nudging her good-naturedly with his elbow. 'And, besides, you offered.'

'I think the part where you and Nina promise to love each other forever is slightly more important than a pig on a spit,' Claire replied archly. From the corner of her eye, she studied Scotty for a reaction.

His gaze fell to his shoes. 'Well, yeah. That goes without saying,' he said softly, all traces of amusement gone.

Just say it.

Claire opened her mouth to speak, but couldn't find the words. What was the right way to say, 'Look, I know Nina is gorgeous, but I don't think her heart is truly in this and, besides, it's all happening way too fast and you're a fool if you marry her next week'?

There wasn't one.

It was Scotty who broke the silence. 'The thing about me and Nina is —'

But he was cut off by the jingle of the shop bell as Toby Watts yanked the door open and poked out his head.

'You two gonna stand there gabbing all morning or are you coming in?' he barked.

'Sorry, mate,' Scotty said with a forced laugh. He placed his hand on the small of Claire's back and guided her into the shop.

What? Claire's mind raced. What was the thing about Scotty and Nina?

She was surprised to find the shop empty. Scotty had confided that he thought Toby may have been less than discreet about Claire's involvement in the wedding. She had half expected to walk in and find it packed with curious

Bindallarahns – the way people always went to stickybeak at their neighbours' houses when they went up for sale.

'Welcome back to Bindy, Claire,' Toby said, giving her a cordial nod. 'Been a while.'

Claire steeled herself for the recrimination she was sure was coming. Toby was aged in his late fifties and had once been a good friend of her father's. He was also one of the people who had invested – and lost – the most money in Big Jim's get-rich-quick scheme. Toby had nearly lost his business and only just managed to hold on to it by the skin of his teeth. He'd never said so, not even when Jim had died, but Claire was sure Toby held her personally responsible – just like everyone else in town who'd been caught in her father's web of lies. If she had done the right thing and come back to Bindallarah to help Jim after her mother left, the farm wouldn't have hit the skids and he wouldn't have deceived his friends in his desperate attempts to save it.

But to her astonishment, Toby smiled and said, 'Good of you to help Scotty out with his shindig. You always were a good egg. Young fella needs all the help he can get, I reckon.' Claire's heart swelled, buoyed by Toby's generosity. Maybe she wasn't persona non grata in Bindallarah any more. The town had changed so much – maybe its residents' opinion of her had changed too.

Scotty rolled his eyes. 'I'm not totally incompetent, you know,' he said, but his tone was lighthearted. 'But yeah, it's great to have Claire here. I've missed her.'

She waited for him to clarify, to clear his throat and hurriedly add, 'We've all missed her.' But he didn't. He just looked into her eyes and smiled.

She felt small under his gaze, humbled by his affection for her even after she'd caused him so much pain over the years. 'I missed you too,' she said. *If only you knew.*

'Right, then. How many people you got coming to your do?' Toby asked. He pushed a sheaf of papers across the counter to Scotty. 'These are the catering packages and order forms.'

'Catering packages? Wow, Toby. You've come a long way from sausages and chops,' Claire said as she peered over Scotty's shoulder at the lists of street-food-style canapés and main-meal options.

Toby shrugged. 'Gotta give the folks what they want,' he said. 'And it pays to diversify. Learned that the hard way.'

The words hung in the air like a noxious gas. The confidence Claire had felt just moments ago withered and died. This town would not forgive her for what her father had done. She was an idiot to have hoped she could ever be redeemed.

As if he sensed her dismay, Scotty put his hand on her back again as he leaned in closer to show her the paperwork. It was such a small gesture, but it was an intense reminder of how well Scotty still knew her, even after all these years. He understood what wounded her, which cuts were the deepest.

'We've got two hundred on the guest list,' Scotty began, 'so I was thinking —'

'Two *hundred* people?' Claire interjected. 'That's practically the entire town.'

'Not quite,' Scotty replied, clearly amused by her outburst. 'Bindy's grown a lot, Claire. But, yeah, it's a reasonable-sized wedding. My family's been here a long time, remember. We know a lot of people.'

She knew he was right. Mike and Janine Shannon, Scotty's parents, had established Cape Ashe Stud nearly forty years ago. There were few people in the horse world in Australia, much less in Bindallarah, who didn't know the family. And with Scotty now one of the few vets in the district, he had friends far and wide.

And yet somehow Claire had imagined that Scotty and Nina's wedding would be a small affair. They'd been together such a short time, and Nina was so new to the town that Claire had pictured an intimate ceremony witnessed by just their families and a few good friends.

But then she wouldn't have made the cut, she had to admit. Claire could hardly expect to have qualified as a close friend when she'd been back in Scotty's life for mere months after an absence of eight years. So he was inviting lesser friends and acquaintances, too. She was on his B-list.

In her mind, she realised, a wedding arranged in such haste wasn't serious – at least, not serious enough for the whole town to turn out. It wasn't something people would change their Christmas Eve plans for. They wouldn't book expensive last-minute flights and rush their formal wear to the dry cleaner. It wasn't worthy of much of a fuss, because it surely wouldn't last. It *couldn't* last. What was that old saying? Marry in haste, repent at leisure.

That was what Claire believed – it was the reason she had come to Bindallarah – but clearly two hundred of Scotty and Nina's nearest and dearest didn't agree. Scotty and Nina may be marrying in haste, but their friends didn't seem to be worried that it was a mistake. They were going to converge on Cape Ashe Stud on Christmas Eve to watch Scotty and Nina tie the knot, because they believed the couple was the real deal. They believed their union would last.

Claire was the only one who thought otherwise. She'd assumed everybody could see the same impending disaster she could, but perhaps she was blind. The only one with doubts. And she *did* have doubts. Every time she saw Scotty, she had less faith in the fate of his marriage. Every moment she spent with him made her more convinced that his marrying Nina was the wrong move.

Every minute Scotty was by her side, Claire felt a growing sense of panic at the thought of letting him go.

'Okay,' Scotty was saying to Toby, 'let's make it two pigs on spits, your Tex Mex food truck and the salad buffet for the vegetarians. And what about just a barbeque for stragglers? Bacon-and-egg rolls at midnight, that sort of thing. Could you do that?'

'No worries, mate.' Toby took a stubby pencil from behind his ear and scribbled down Scotty's instructions. 'How are you for grog? It's not really my area, but I could probably sort something out. Package deal.'

'Thanks, Toby, but I've got it covered. Noel is doing a few kegs and a cocktail bar for us.' Scotty gestured beyond the shop window in the rough direction of the Bindallarah Hotel, where Noel Thomas had been the publican for donkey's years. 'The wedding's at five. Do you think you could be set up by three o'clock?'

Toby nodded and went to the register at the back of the shop to calculate the cost of Scotty's order.

'Well, that was easy,' Claire said. 'You don't need me here at all, Scotty. You know exactly what you want.' That was becoming increasingly obvious.

'I do need you here, Claire,' he said. 'You're the voice of reason. I probably would have only ordered a dozen snags and a loaf of bread if you weren't here to remind me of the ridiculous number of people coming to the wedding.'

She laughed, but Scotty let out a troubled sigh. 'This is a lot to handle in a short space of time. Honestly, I was feeling pretty stressed out until you offered to help.'

'Really?' Claire was taken aback. 'You haven't seemed stressed out at all. To the casual observer it looks like you're taking everything in your stride.'

Scotty gave a wry smile. 'I guess I'm a good actor.'

Before Claire could respond, Toby returned and handed Scotty an invoice. 'There you go, mate,' the butcher said. 'It's ten per cent up front, with the balance due the day before the bash.'

Scotty handed over his credit card and Toby retreated to the register once more. Claire seized the opportunity.

'Scotty, why get married so quickly? If you're feeling overwhelmed, just wait a while. There's really no need to rush,' she implored. 'Spend some time getting to know Nina better. Enjoy being engaged. Give yourselves a chance to figure out if this is truly what you want.'

She saw the muscles of his jaw clench as he gritted his teeth. Claire knew what that meant: he was annoyed. He was rarely angry, but she knew when his fuse was burning. The jaw clench was a classic Scotty Shannon tell. But whether he was irritated by what she'd said or simply the fact that she'd said anything at all, Claire couldn't distinguish.

'You're right. There's no need to rush,' Scotty said eventually, and for a beautiful instant her heart soared. 'But there's no need to delay either. We know what we're doing. What's the point in waiting?' His deep-green eyes bored into hers. 'Can you give me one reason why I shouldn't marry Nina on Christmas Eve, Claire?'

I can give you a thousand reasons, she thought. Her legs felt shaky under the weight of Scotty's intense gaze. *You just met. You barely know her. Nina seems weirdly detached from the whole thing.*

And I don't want to lose you.

The thought struck her with the devastating force of a freight train.

She didn't want to stop mattering to him. Maybe they would still be friends after Scotty married Nina, but it wouldn't be the same. Claire would return to Sydney and Scotty would get on with the business of being a husband and, inevitably, a father. She wouldn't have the same access to him – neither tangibly nor emotionally.

Claire didn't want the lifetime they had shared – give or take a few absences – to be less important to Scotty. And they would. A friendship would never compare to a marriage, no matter how longstanding or profound. It couldn't. It *shouldn't*.

But she wasn't about to tell Scotty any of this. It wasn't his job to allay her fears for their friendship when she'd shown him more than once over the years that she could take it or leave it. She wouldn't put that burden on him when he was already under so much pressure. Especially not in the middle of a butcher shop in Bindallarah.

Instead, she smiled and said, 'You always were so decisive, Scotty. What's your secret?'

She thought she saw a flicker of resignation in his smile. 'Some might call it stubbornness,' he said.

'Can you give me some tips? I feel utterly incapable of making decisions.' It was the most honest thing she'd said to him all morning.

'You're more decisive than you think,' Scotty said, echoing Jackie's sentiments of a few days earlier. This time his smile was warm, genuine. 'You just take your time with it. There's nothing wrong with that.'

Isn't there? she wanted to shout. Perhaps if she'd been a little less deliberate in her decision-making process over the years, she wouldn't be back in Bindallarah helping her first love choose the menu for his wedding.

CHAPTER TEN

It was nearing dusk by the time Claire staggered, exhausted, into Vanessa's cottage and collapsed next to Gus on the sofa.

'Tough day?' her cousin asked, looking up from her *Cosmopolitan* magazine.

'You have no idea,' Claire groaned, kicking off her rubber thongs. Her feet ached as intensely as if she'd run a marathon in stilettos.

She must have traipsed ten kilometres up and down Bindy's main street. After leaving the butcher shop, she and Scotty had gone to the bakery to choose a wedding cake. For once, he had lacked his usual resolve. He wanted an enormous traditional fruitcake, but with only ten days to go it simply wasn't possible. Claire had sold him on the benefits of a 'cake' made of tiers of individual cupcakes instead – one for each of his guests and easily able to be made within the ever-narrowing timeframe.

When Scotty had to get back to work at the clinic, Claire had continued on alone. She felt conspicuous as she shopped for streamers and balloons in the discount store. It seemed somehow wrong to be making decisions about the wedding with neither the groom *nor* the bride present. She tried calling Nina to ask her to come along, but the call went straight to voicemail and Claire figured she must be teaching a yoga class. She worried the decorations she chose were a little bit twee, but with nobody on hand to approve or reject her decisions, she wasn't sure what else she was supposed to do. Anyway, she reasoned, nobody was really going to expect sophisticated styling at a country wedding thrown together in mere weeks.

Next, armed with a list of Scotty and Nina's favourite songs, Claire met with the DJ – yet another old schoolfriend, Jared Miller, who was a surfing instructor by day and moonlighted as a one-man mobile disco – and vetoed all the gangster rap that inexplicably peppered his playlist.

Then she went to Bindallarah's lone florist. The wedding was cocktail style, meaning there wouldn't be a formal meal, so she didn't have to bother with table centrepieces. Claire chose two towering arrangements of natives to stand either side of the altar, and hoped Nina liked Australian flora as much as she did.

When the florist asked about the bride's flowers, Claire had balked. Surely, even with Nina's laidback approach to wedding planning so far, her bouquet was something she would want to choose for herself. Claire sent her a text message and Nina's reply was swift and direct:

Happy 4 U 2 decide. Whateva goes w green! N ☺

Hesitantly, Claire selected a soft-pink protea surrounded by cream roses, Esperance pearl and sprigs of eucalyptus. She was tempted to throw in some bright-red poppies for a truly Christmassy touch against Nina's mint-green dress, but something told Claire that this particular bride would prefer something understated.

'How was everyone?' Gus asked as Claire kneaded the burning arches of her feet with her thumbs.

'What do you mean?' she replied. 'Everyone who?'

Gus rolled her eyes, as if her older cousin was particularly dense. 'Everyone in *town*,' she said. 'Mum told me you've been worried they'd, like, chase you with pitchforks or something. So were they cool? Do I need to beat up anyone for you?'

Claire snickered. She didn't doubt that Gus would go in to bat for her if she asked her to. She may be just eighteen, but she was as assertive and unapologetic as any woman Claire had ever met.

'You know, it was okay,' Claire said. 'Kind of nice to catch up with people, actually.'

Vanessa was right. Claire hadn't realised it, but she *had* been skulking around town with her head bowed for the past five days. She was so sure the people of Bindallarah still detested her – still blamed her for deserting her father, for driving him to deceive them all – that she unconsciously expected abuse at every turn. Toby Watts's comments that morning had only confirmed that she wasn't welcome by anyone aside from Vanessa, Gus and Scotty.

And yet everyone else she'd spoken to throughout the day had been friendly. Some even seemed pleased to see her after such a long time. Karen Steiner, the bakery manager, once a close friend of Claire's mother, had wrapped her in a tight hug and made her promise to come over for coffee before she went back to Sydney.

At the discount store she'd bumped into Eloise Marshall, one of her best friends from primary school, who now worked on the checkout. Eloise had ignored the grumbling customers behind Claire in the checkout queue to show her photos of her kids and the house she was building just out of town.

Jared Miller had asked her all about her work as a vet – and then asked for her phone number. She gave it to him with the proviso it was to be used for wedding business only, but she felt surprisingly flattered that he'd asked.

'That's awesome,' Gus said. 'What were you so stressed about anyway? Why would anyone in Bindy have a problem with you? You haven't lived here in forever.'

'I think that's part of the problem. There were – are – people in town who thought that I should have come back here when my parents split up to help Dad with the farm. And that I *definitely* should have come back after he died and left a lot of people missing a lot of money.'

'And after Scotty asked you to marry him,' Gus said matter-of-factly.

Claire's jaw dropped. 'You *know* about that?' Except for Vanessa, she hadn't told a soul about Scotty's mad idea that getting married at twenty and twenty-one respectively would somehow fix everything.

'Everyone knows about that,' her cousin replied. 'This is Bindallarah.' The look she gave Claire told her Gus couldn't believe she was so clueless.

Claire groaned. 'Well, that's just marvellous,' she muttered. Just one more reason for the community to believe she was totally heartless.

Gus was unfazed by Claire's angst. 'So was Uncle Jim a crook or something?' she pressed.

Claire paused mid-lament, perplexed. Big Jim Thorne's many misdeeds were common knowledge in Bindallarah. Hell, he'd ripped people off all over the district. How was it possible that Gus didn't know all the sordid details of his transgressions?

'Gus, has your mum never talked to you about what happened?' Claire asked.

She shrugged. 'I was only ten when he died. All I know is that he was killed in a car accident. I suppose Mum thought I was too young for the full story,' she said.

Claire's heart gave a painful throb as she pictured Gus as a tiny and bewildered ten-year-old, frightened by the magnitude of her mother's grief over the loss of her brother, confused by the drama surrounding his death – and with absolutely nobody to talk to about it.

I should have been here, she thought. She was ten years older than Gus; she could have been a surrogate big sister to her. Another entry for her shame ledger.

'You went to boarding school when I was five,' Gus continued. 'I've heard people say stuff about you in town over the years, but nothing really bad. I think they felt sorry for you more than anything. Mum's always telling people how great you are. Scotty too.'

Claire's breath caught in her throat. 'Scotty? Really?' She tried to keep her tone neutral. 'You mean like in the last few months?'

'No, always. Ever since he moved back to Bindy after university.'

She didn't know what to make of that. The end of her relationship with Scotty had been crushing for both of them. It had never occurred to Claire that Scotty would have anything kind to say about her afterwards – especially not to people who would have been one hundred per cent on his side if he despised her.

'So will you tell me?' Gus asked. 'What really happened with Uncle Jim?'

Claire took a deep breath. Gus deserved to know the truth – if only to better understand why Vanessa had kept it from her for so long – but raking over the coals of her father's miserable last years was agony.

'Of course,' she began. 'You probably don't remember my mother, Emily, very well. She left my dad when I was sixteen, a few months after I went away to school, but they'd been very unhappy for a long time.'

'They split up after you went to boarding school? I thought their divorce was *why* you had to go away,' Gus said.

'Their marriage problems were part of it, but it was also about Scotty.'

Her cousin's eyes widened. 'They had a problem with Scotty? But everyone loves Scotty!'

Claire couldn't help but laugh. Scotty certainly was Mr Popularity in Bindallarah.

'They didn't have a problem with *him*. They had a problem with us being together. They thought we were too serious about each other, my mum especially.' She smiled sadly. 'Mum wasn't ever that keen on rural life. I think she worried I'd marry Scotty and stay here in Bindy forever. She wanted more for me.'

'What's wrong with Bindy?' Gus said with all the indignation of a teenager who had never lived anywhere else.

'Absolutely nothing,' Claire replied, and she realised she meant it. 'I didn't want to go. I begged them to let me stay. Leaving here was heartbreaking.'

'And then Aunty Emily left anyway.'

Claire nodded. 'She did. She moved to Perth, remarried. I've got three stepbrothers, you know?'

Gus wrinkled her nose. 'Poor you.'

'After Mum left, Dad really struggled to cope. He'd always liked a drink, but he really started hitting the bottle. The farm went downhill. He wasn't taking proper care of the cattle. The milking equipment was old and needed replacing, but the processing companies were paying less and less for raw milk and Dad just couldn't afford to upgrade. So . . .'

This was the part that always tore her up inside. The part where she'd tried to help, but didn't try hard enough.

'I offered to quit school and come home. Actually, I insisted. I told the principal I was leaving and everything,' Claire said. 'But Dad wouldn't let me. He told me it wasn't my job to solve his problems and that my education was more important. So I stayed.'

Claire lapsed into silence as she recalled the day she'd been summoned to Sister Hilaria's office to take a call from her father. The smug look on the nun's face as she watched Claire reduced to tears by Jim's rage at the other end of the telephone line. *It's not your decision to make, Claire,* he'd shouted.

'Then what?' Gus prompted softly.

'It's hard to say for sure, because Dad became quite secretive,' she said. 'He'd figured out that someone in town was telling me he was doing it tough. I think he suspected your mum, but it was —'

'Scotty,' Gus supplied.

Claire smiled. 'You guessed it. We were always in touch, though I didn't see him again for three years after I was sent to school in Sydney. He'd always planned to do his vet science degree at Sydney Uni, so I applied there, too.'

'You mean you didn't really want to be a vet?' Gus said, incredulous. 'But you're, like, the horse whisperer.'

'I didn't *not* want to be a vet. I've always loved animals and I absolutely adored spending time up at Cape Ashe Stud.' Claire shrugged. 'I just hadn't given it too much thought. I guess I wasn't used to making my own decisions. I had the grades, so vet science seemed like a natural choice.'

Liar. Scotty was the natural choice.

'So when Scotty was in Sydney with you, who was spying on your dad? Mum?'

She shook her head. 'Like I said, Dad made sure he always put on a good show, especially around Aunty Vee. He told everybody he'd decided to "diversify". He was going to grow acai berries.'

Gus nodded sagely. 'They're a superfood,' she said. Another *Cosmo* fact, no doubt.

'See, nobody in Bindallarah would have known that back when I lived here,' Claire said, rolling her eyes. 'But yes, they're one of those foods that hipsters like to post pictures of on social media. South American farmers couldn't keep up with the worldwide demand, apparently, so Australian growers were going to be rolling in cash. The climate up here is perfect, Dad said.'

'Sounds like a good idea,' said Gus.

'It was,' Claire replied. 'At least, it could have been.'

'Oh.'

'It was going to be an expensive operation to set up. Dad would have to import acai palm seeds from Brazil and build a processing facility. They're hard to process because the fruit is small but the stone is big, and they have to be harvested really quickly or they lose the health benefits people are so obsessed with.' Claire paused. 'You learn a lot about acai berries when your father uses them to defraud people of hundreds of thousands of dollars.'

'Why didn't it work out, then? It sounds like a great opportunity,' said Gus. 'Did the crop fail?'

Claire sighed. 'There was no crop. Dad convinced dozens of locals to invest in his scheme in exchange for profit share. Some of them put in their life savings and he promised them the world. But he didn't plant a single tree.'

'But weren't people suspicious? Didn't they ask where the trees were? The processing plant?'

She shook her head. 'Nope. He'd told them at the start that the trees were slow growing and it would be a couple of years before they saw any return on their investment,' Claire said. 'They were happy to wait. Everyone in Bindallarah trusted Big Jim Thorne.'

'Let me guess, he used the money to improve the dairy farm instead,' said Gus.

'Most of it. The rest of it he drank. His alcoholism got so bad he couldn't have made the farm profitable even with the most state-of-the-art equipment on the market.'

Claire's chest tightened and hot tears pricked at her eyes. She thought of her father hidden away in the hills above

Bindallarah, alone and desperate on his sprawling farm. An outcast by design, seeking solace in the bottom of a bottle.

'And somehow he hid it from all of us.'

Both Claire and Gus startled at the sound of Vanessa's voice. Claire turned to see her aunt leaning against the lounge-room doorframe, silhouetted by the fading twilight sun streaming through the glass front door.

Claire started to apologise for revealing the truth to Gus but stopped herself. Gus deserved to know why the ghost of Jim Thorne still haunted both her mother and her cousin.

'Why didn't you ever tell me any of this, Mum?' Gus said, a note of accusation in her tone.

'Because I thought there ought to be at least one member of the Thorne family who's not trying to carry a burden that isn't hers to bear,' Vanessa said simply. She focused her attention on Claire. 'Nobody in Bindallarah blames you for what your father did, sweetheart. You were just a child. How could you have been responsible?'

The tears that had been threatening spilled over in a torrent. 'He was my dad,' Claire sobbed. 'I should have known what was going on. I should have been here. He wouldn't have done it if I'd been around to help out. I abandoned him.'

Vanessa hurried to the sofa and wrapped her arms around her niece. 'Claire, *nobody* knew what was going on. Jim made sure of that,' she murmured into Claire's hair. 'You didn't abandon your dad. You were a teenage girl living her life, which is exactly what you should have been doing. Your being here couldn't have prevented the farm's downward spiral. Jim drove the property into the ground all by himself.'

'But at the funeral they said . . .'

'At the funeral people were angry. They were confused,' Vanessa said. 'Hurtful things were said in the heat of the moment. You know how small towns are. They took their frustrations out on us because they couldn't confront the man himself.'

'Wait,' Gus piped up. 'You're saying people didn't know Uncle Jim had fleeced them until after he died?'

'The full extent of the "fleecing", as you so eloquently put it, my darling, only became clear when I started digging around as the executor of Jim's estate,' Vanessa replied. 'If he hadn't drunk a bottle of Scotch and collided with a tree that night, he may have continued swindling his friends for years.'

Claire winced. It was a harsh assessment, but it was true. Who knew how many more thousands of dollars Jim would have stolen if he'd had the chance? His debts were so massive by the time he died that there was no way he ever could have repaid them without the extent of his scam becoming clear to everyone. He would have faced bankruptcy, prosecution, probably even jail time.

But having a convicted fraudster for a father would have been preferable to the reality, Claire thought. In her darkest moments, she wondered if he had driven his ute into that tree on purpose – if he thought it was the only way out of the mess he had created. It was just like Jim to try to spare Claire the fallout of his chaotic life. He was used to making big decisions on his daughter's behalf without ever asking what she thought.

'Wow, Claire,' Gus said. 'That's some heavy stuff you've been dealing with. I totally get why you haven't been back to Bindy for so long.' She paused, then added, 'You must really love Scotty Shannon.'

Claire let out a strangled sound that was a cross between a laugh and a choke. '*That's* what you got from all this?'

'Well, you've been so afraid of what the community thinks of you for so long, and the only person here – apart from me and Mum – who's always supported you is Scotty,' Gus said, ignoring Claire's umbrage. 'It makes sense that you'd put your fears aside to come back for him.'

'I do not *love* Scotty Shannon. He's my friend,' Claire protested. 'Why is that so difficult for everyone to understand?'

But Gus had touched on yet another truth that Claire didn't have the courage to admit. Her fears about being loathed by the people of Bindallarah weren't only about what her dad had done. They were also about what *she* had done to Scotty.

Gus was right: Scotty was the only person outside of her family who was always on her side. Everyone in Bindallarah loved Scotty Shannon. And now it turned out they all knew he'd proposed marriage after Jim's death – and that she'd shot him down in flames. Claire worried that people saw her not just as the selfish daughter of a con artist, but also as the callous wench who'd broken the heart of Bindy's golden boy.

'But you did come back for him,' Gus persisted.

'For his wedding. To a woman who is not me. Would I do that if I was in love with him?' *No, but you'd do it to try to fool people into believing you're a good person.*

'Well . . . yeah,' her cousin replied as if it were the most obvious thing in the world. She looked at Claire like she thought she was crazy. Or deluded. Or both.

'Well, I'm not,' she huffed. She crossed her arms and sank back into the sofa.

Gus wasn't deterred. 'You know, it would have made total sense if you and Scotty had ended up together. People are most likely to marry someone who lives nearby. It's called the residential propinquity effect.'

'Where on earth did you hear that?' said Vanessa.

'*Cosmo.*'

'In that case, it's clearly an incontrovertible fact,' her aunt replied dryly.

'It is! Look it up!'

'Even if it is a real thing,' Claire interrupted, 'Scotty lives here and I live in Sydney. We're not exactly next-door neighbours.'

'Not now, no. But you grew up in each other's pockets,' Vanessa said, looking thoughtfully at her. 'And you were a couple at university.'

'Don't encourage her, Aunty Vee. It's nonsense. Scotty is marrying Nina and I am not in love with him. End of story. Who wants a glass of wine?'

Claire stomped into the kitchen and opened the fridge. What did she have to do to convince people that her feelings for Scotty were purely platonic? And why was it so important to her?

Claire took out a bottle of chardonnay and extracted three clean wineglasses from the dishwasher. As she poured the wine, her phone buzzed in her back pocket.

She peered at the screen in disbelief. It was a text from Jared Miller.

Hey, Claire, great to see you today. Not strictly wedding business but . . . fancy meeting me for a drink tomorrow night? Jared.

Claire's finger hovered over the trash-can icon, but she hesitated. Gus's *Cosmo* pseudo-science had rattled her. Maybe there was something to it. She had to admit that most of the girls she'd grown up with had indeed married or were in long-term relationships with local lads. She probably would have too. She had to admit she hadn't had any great ambitions beyond Bindallarah before her parents sent her to boarding school and her world opened up. Maybe she was fooling herself. It wasn't like she was dazzled by the dating prospects in Sydney. Perhaps she'd always been destined to end up with a Bindy boy.

But that boy wasn't Scotty. She didn't want it to be Scotty, despite what her family seemed to think. He was off limits anyway.

Jared was nice enough. They'd got on well in high school and she'd enjoyed his company this morning. What could be the harm in meeting him for a casual drink? And if she were seen in public in the company of a man who wasn't Scotty Shannon, perhaps it would quieten those irritating whispers.

Claire hit 'reply'.

CHAPTER ELEVEN

Walking into the Bindallarah Hotel felt strangely illicit. The last time she'd set foot inside the Art Deco pub on the esplanade, Claire had been a child in the company of her parents. Counter meals at 'the Bindy' were a rare treat – as close to fine dining as it got back then. That cafés and restaurants – well, one restaurant – would one day fill the main street had seemed as unlikely to a young Claire as flying cars or holographic telephones.

But there was no question that Bindallarah had moved with the times – and so had the pub. Patrons entering the dingy front bar had once been greeted by sticky carpet and the inveterate tang of old beer. Now Claire entered a spacious and light-filled room decked out with Hamptons-style decor. To her left was a small stage with guitars and a drum kit set up, awaiting musicians. A blackboard on the wall displayed the Friday- and Saturday-night live-music schedule. To her right, a long bar made of white wood was lined with beer taps bearing the logos of local craft breweries she'd never heard of.

The rear section of the bar was a dining area; Claire could see an open kitchen that looked to be doing a roaring trade. Beyond it, a leafy courtyard beckoned.

The Bindallarah Hotel had been, as Jackie liked to say, 'glass-and-chromed'. Claire wondered what the town's long-time bar flies thought of the makeover. There didn't seem to be anyone aged over forty among the Friday-night crowd. The joint was jumping.

Somehow, over the hubbub of happy drinkers, Claire heard someone call her name. She peered through the cluster of bodies and spotted Jared sprawled across a cane sofa, a beer in his hand.

Nervously, she threaded through the crush until she was standing in front of him. 'Hey, Jared,' she said, hoping he wouldn't detect the slight tremor in her voice. It was crazy to feel so wobbly – she'd known Jared for years and this was just a friendly catch-up. But she'd never socialised in Bindallarah and she felt like she was on display. She pointed at his pint glass. 'Can I get you a refill?'

Jared jumped to his feet. 'Let me,' he said, pecking her on the cheek. 'What are you drinking? You look fantastic, by the way.'

Claire looked down at her outfit, an all-in-one shorts-and-top situation she'd borrowed from Gus. Her cousin had called it a 'playsuit', which probably explained why Claire felt like an oversized baby in it. But Gus had insisted that it showed off her legs and created the illusion of a waist, so Claire had dutifully left the house in it and tried not to dwell on the fact that she was the same size and shape as a teenager ten years her junior. It was probably time to stop hoping she would ever acquire actual curves.

But she pushed her insecurities down deep and instead smiled at Jared and said, 'Thanks. I'll have a glass of rosé, please.'

She took his place on the sofa and watched him make his way to the bar. This was going to be fun, she decided. She was going to have a good time. She *deserved* to have a good time.

Though she had only friendly feelings for Jared, there was no doubt that he was a good-looking man. It had been a long time since she'd enjoyed a night out with anyone – her shock-filled Sydney catch-up with Scotty didn't count – let alone someone so easy on the eye. Blue-eyed and tanned, with messy, sun-bleached blond hair, Jared had the broad-shouldered bearing typical of a daily surfer. Gus would have taken one look at his biceps and asked for 'two tickets to the gun show'. But his impressive physique looked natural rather than chiselled – Jared's muscles were obviously honed in the ocean, not the gym. Claire made up her mind to appreciate the pleasant scenery.

Had he always been this attractive? She couldn't remember if she would have thought him 'cute' when they were at school. Looking back through the lens of adulthood, she could only picture a teenage Jared as tall, thin and spotty. And, besides, she'd only had eyes for one gangly teenage boy back then.

And he had just walked into the pub.

Scotty saw Claire immediately, and as he made a beeline for her she felt her heart start to beat double time. She glanced at the bar. The queue was three-deep; Jared would be a while.

'Claire!' Scotty said, sounding genuinely happy to see her. 'I didn't expect to see you out tonight. I just finished work and thought I'd stop in for a quick one. Are you here with Vanessa and Gus?'

'Uh, no. Actually, I'm —'

'Wait. You don't have a drink,' Scotty cut in, pointing at Claire's empty hands. 'What can I get you?'

'That's okay,' she said. 'I've got a glass of wine on the way.'

'Oh?' Scotty turned and scanned the punters at the bar. When he didn't see anybody he could identify as an obvious drinking buddy, he turned back to Claire, his face creased with confusion. 'Who are you here with?'

Claire felt a twinge of guilt, but silently rebuked herself. *Just relax.* She had nothing to feel guilty about.

'Um, Jared. Jared Miller?' As if Scotty wouldn't know who she was talking about.

'Ah! Wedding business. But come on, Claire, you don't need to spend your Friday night vetting the DJ's playlist.' There was a beat of silence, then Scotty frowned. 'But didn't you talk to Jared about the wedding music yesterday?'

He was still standing while she sat and Claire felt cowed by his towering presence. 'I did, yeah. This isn't about the wedding.'

She watched as comprehension dawned. 'Are you on a *date* with Jared Miller?' Scotty's tone was disbelieving, and Claire had to admit that it stung. Was the possibility that she was on a date really so preposterous?

The guilty feeling in her stomach was abruptly replaced by a spark of irritation. She stared at him with all the defiance she could muster. 'I don't think that's really any of your business, Scotty,' she said crisply. 'Do I need your permission to come to the pub on a Friday night?'

His astonishment was still writ large on his face. Scotty slowly shook his head, as though he was struggling to process what she'd said. 'I just . . .' he began. 'I didn't realise you were looking to meet somebody.'

As if Scotty had poured petrol on a campfire, the annoyance flickering inside Claire suddenly flared into a full-scale blaze. She stood up and leaned as close to him as she dared.

'Why wouldn't I be looking to meet someone, Scotty?' she hissed. 'I'm twenty-eight years old. Everyone I know is either married or getting married or having babies or whatever. Am I supposed to help you plan your wedding and then just disappear back to Sydney, alone? Don't I get to think about my future, too?'

Scotty took a step back, aghast. Claire understood his surprise – she was pretty shocked herself at the words that had just tumbled out of her mouth. She hadn't meant to say those things. She wasn't aware she even *thought* those things.

Scotty's expression grew stony. 'Of course you do, Claire,' he said coldly. 'I've only ever wanted you to think about your future, remember? For a long time I thought I might be part of it.'

She glared at him, completely lost for words. He was throwing her rejection of his marriage proposal in her face. Now. After eight years. Little more than a week before his wedding to someone else.

'How dare you,' Claire said eventually, her voice a whisper. 'That is so unfair.'

Jared suddenly appeared at Claire's side and handed her a condensation-covered glass of wine. He didn't seem to notice that the tension between her and Scotty was thicker than the sea air on a humid summer's night.

'Hey, man,' Jared said, clapping Scotty on the back. 'Changed your mind about letting me put N.W.A on the wedding playlist?'

Scotty didn't acknowledge Jared's quip. 'Have a good night,' he said gruffly, and stalked away.

Claire sagged into her chair, her legs shaky. She took a fortifying gulp of her wine.

'Are you okay? That looked heavy,' Jared said, sitting beside her. His face was the picture of concern and Claire felt a wave of affection for him. Jared was sweet and uncomplicated – and more perceptive than she'd given him credit for. Why couldn't she have fallen for someone like him all those years ago, instead of someone who constantly pushed and challenged her, and arrogantly assumed he knew what was best for her?

She plastered on the brightest smile she could muster. 'I'm great,' she said. 'I think maybe Scotty and I are a little stressed out, what with the wedding so close.'

Jared chuckled and sipped his beer. 'And you're just the helper,' he said. 'Imagine how you'd feel if you were the bride.'

Claire knew it wasn't a criticism, but Jared's words felt like a slap. She was just the helper. If only she could figure out how to help herself.

Scotty sat at the bar and glowered. He should have just left, should have gone home and drank alone like the sad case he was. Did it count as drinking alone if you had a three-legged dog for company?

But he stayed at the pub. It was better to be around people, he figured. Around friends. Mates he'd known forever, who wouldn't remind him how gutless he was. Maybe he would text Nina and ask her to meet him for dinner after she finished teaching her sunset yoga class on the beach. He'd barely seen her all week and he felt the need to check in, to make sure they were still on the same page with all this wedding stuff.

It was loud in the pub, but every now and then Claire's mellifluous laugh would drift above the racket. He'd chosen a seat at the far end of the bar, with his back to Claire and Jared so he didn't have to watch them on their date. But he could still feel her there. He always sensed her, wherever she was, even when there were hundreds of kilometres and years of silence between them. She was like a thought he couldn't articulate or a moment he couldn't forget.

More like a nightmare I can't forget.

But that was unfair. Scotty didn't want to forget Claire, though his life would certainly be easier right now if he had. She had hurt him once, sure. But he figured he had deserved it, trying to run her life the way he had. He'd tried to play Mr Fixit when what he should have done was just hold her hand while she figured it out for herself.

He never should have asked her to marry him back then – and he definitely shouldn't have alluded to it tonight. What was he thinking? Claire lugged around enough shame about her past with her. Scotty felt sick that he'd added to it. What he'd said to Claire had been straight-up cruel.

He heard her laugh again and his head throbbed. Seriously, Jared Miller? He was a nice enough bloke, but he was no match for Claire. Jared was fun – easygoing and straightforward, what you saw was what you got. Claire had hidden depths, layers that Scotty had barely begun to peel back. She was fiercely intelligent, complex, fragile.

No, not fragile. Scotty caught himself. He'd made that mistake before. Claire was no weakling. She was as tough as a Mallee bull. She just didn't know it.

If anyone was weak in this scenario, it was him.

What could Claire possibly see in Jared? Scotty knew many girls liked that salt-crusted surfer-dude vibe he had going on, but Claire wasn't the type to fall for looks alone – that she'd ever been with Scotty was proof of that. Still, even Jared was punching above his weight with Claire. She was classically beautiful, like a painting, with her pale skin, smattering of freckles and dark curls. When he'd walked into the pub and seen her sitting on that sofa in those tiny shorts, Scotty couldn't take his eyes off her. He'd felt heat pooling deep within him. Something stirred in a place that had no business being stirred by a woman who was not his fiancée.

But it was all a moot point. Claire was with Jared, and he had to admit she was probably a better match with him – at least aesthetically speaking – than she had ever been with Scotty. He was no stranger to punching above his weight himself. He knew he was no oil painting. It was yet another reason he couldn't quite believe Nina had agreed to marry him.

He drained his beer and signalled to the barman for another, his fourth. He had to stop thinking – about Claire and Jared, Nina, the wedding. Maybe getting off his face would help him switch off his brain.

But before he could take another sip, Scotty's phone rang. His brother's name flashed up on the screen. He smiled. He could always count on Chris for a solid night out.

'Little brother,' he said. 'Whatever you're doing, stop it

now and get your arse to the pub. I've decided you're throw-ing me a buck's show.'

But Chris's voice was panicked. 'Mate, we've got a problem at Cape Ashe,' he said. 'It's Autumn.'

Scotty's head cleared, the effects of the three beers he'd downed dissipating in an instant. 'The foal?' She wasn't due for another month, but horses were always getting themselves into trouble – especially pregnant ones.

'I dunno,' Chris replied. 'She's been off her food all day. Now she's really struggling to breathe. She's making a bloody terrible noise.'

'Have you taken her temperature? Does she feel hot?' It wasn't a particularly warm day, but with Autumn's recent malignant hyperthermia diagnosis, heat stroke was an ever-present threat.

'Her temp's up, but I don't think it's heat stroke. She doesn't have any of the other symptoms of it. Can you get up here, bro?'

Scotty opened his mouth to say 'of course' but stopped. The best-case scenario was that Autumn would need to be transported to the clinic for treatment. Chris's call had sobered him up, but he knew he'd drunk too much to drive the narrow country roads to Cape Ashe Stud in the gathering darkness, much less tow a horse float back into town.

And worst case? Autumn could need emergency surgery in situ. Scotty couldn't operate on his brother's pregnant mare with three beers in his system – not legally and definitely not ethically.

'Mate, I can't do it,' he said. 'I'm three beers in.'

A stream of expletives issued from Chris's end of the line. 'What can we do, Scotty? She's in a really bad way. Can you call one of the other vets?'

Scotty groaned. He employed two other vets at the clinic, both part-time. Charlie had already flown to Tasmania to spend Christmas with his family and it was Eleanor's day off. On any other evening, he knew he could call her and she'd drop everything to help, but her husband was away on a golfing trip and she was flying solo with their four kids.

The nearest vet hospital besides his was at Alison Bay. Even if he could get hold of them after hours, they were at least a half-hour's drive away. If Autumn was in respiratory distress, she may not have that much time.

Claire's giggle floated above the dull roar in the pub once more. *Of course.* He hadn't seen Claire or Jared come back to the bar for more drinks, so she couldn't have finished her first glass of wine. It wasn't ideal – stone-cold sober was ideal – but it was his only option.

'Try to keep her calm and cool. We don't want the MH flaring up on top of whatever else is going on,' Scotty instructed his brother. 'I'll be there in fifteen minutes.'

Scotty left his untouched beer and hurried across the bar to the sofa where Claire and Jared still sat talking, their heads close together. Jared's hand rested across the back of the sofa, nearly touching Claire's shoulders, and Scotty had to fight the urge to slap it away.

Claire looked up in surprise when Scotty loomed before her. 'How many drinks have you had?' he said.

A look of undisguised disgust crossed her face. '*Excuse me?*'

'Steady on, Scotty,' Jared said, a note of warning in his voice.

'Just tell me,' he said. 'Please.'

Claire sighed and held up her wineglass. It was still half full. 'Just this one. Okay, Dad?'

Scotty nodded. 'Great. Come with me.' He held out his hand.

Neither Claire nor Jared moved. They just stared at him, dumbfounded. Finally, Jared said, 'I think it's time for you to go, mate.'

'Please, Claire,' Scotty said. 'It's my brother's horse – you remember Autumn?'

'Malignant hyperthermia,' she said. Jared looked at her like she was speaking Swahili.

'Yeah, but this is something else. Airway, from what Chris said. She needs to be seen right now, but . . .'

Claire frowned. 'But what?'

'I've had too much to drink. I shouldn't drive, and even if I did I definitely can't operate on her, if it comes to that. You're the horse guru. Will you help?'

Claire got immediately to her feet and turned to Jared. 'I'm so sorry, Jared. I treated Autumn in Sydney last week. I can't not help her.'

'Of course,' he replied, rising to stand beside her. 'I completely understand. Go do your thing.'

She gave him a quick hug. 'I've had a really good time catching up. I'll call you, okay?'

Jared smiled. 'Make sure you do.'

Claire turned to Scotty and held out her hand. 'Keys.'

Scotty fished them out of his pocket and handed them over. 'We'll need to stop at the clinic to get my instruments,' he said.

'No, we'll need to stop at Vanessa's house to get *my* instruments.'

'You brought your instruments on holiday?' He stared at her, amazed.

Claire shrugged. 'A girl never knows when she might need a scalpel. Now let's go.'

CHAPTER TWELVE

Claire knew the way to Cape Ashe Stud like the back of her hand. She'd made the journey from town or from Thorne Hill more times than she could count, first on her bike and later, when Scotty got his learner driver's licence, in the turquoise Mazda 121 his parents had bought him. He'd been so embarrassed by that car, but Claire had loved it. To her it had represented freedom – from her parents' increasingly volatile marriage, from their objections to her deepening relationship with Scotty and from the looming threat of boarding school. She had often persuaded him to take to the open road, just the two of them, even though he was supposed to have a fully licensed driver in the car whenever he was behind the wheel. She'd been a bad influence on him from the start.

Now, she was in Scotty's car again, but this time it was the hulking black four-wheel drive she'd seen the day he brought Autumn to the clinic in Sydney. Claire had protested when he'd insisted she drive the beast – she was much more comfortable in her little hatchback – but Scotty was over the limit and if the mare needed treatment at his clinic, Claire's car wasn't up to towing the float.

And so she bounced down the slim dirt lanes in the dwindling light and took the precariously tight bends as fast as she dared behind the wheel of an unwieldy vehicle that made her feel small and out of control.

Or maybe it was Scotty who made her feel that way. He sat in grim silence, but Claire could see he was doing the jaw-clenching thing again. His brooding presence made her stomach knot. The idea that he could possibly be angry with her was galling. He had ruined her evening with Jared and was dragging her to the middle of nowhere to treat a pregnant horse that might not even survive until she got there. And now he wasn't even going to speak to her? Where did this guy get off?

'Don't even worry about this, Scotty,' she said when the tension in the car finally got too much. Her voice dripped with sarcasm. 'You can thank me later.'

He looked at her, surprised, almost as if he'd forgotten she was there. 'Huh?'

Claire let out an exasperated breath. 'I'm doing you a favour here,' she said. 'I was having a really nice time with Jared, but I dropped everything to come and help you. And you're sitting there scowling and grinding your teeth like I've done something wrong.'

Was it her imagination, or did Scotty bristle when she mentioned Jared?

He turned to stare out of the window. Finally he sighed and said, 'You're right. I'm sorry. You haven't done anything wrong.'

'I know I haven't,' she snapped. 'I don't need you to absolve me, thanks very much.'

Scotty fell silent again as the car's headlights illuminated a carved timber sign hanging on a post-and-rail fence. Cape Ashe Stud. In spite of her annoyance, Claire smiled. That sign had been there for at least twenty years, changing only with the addition of a threadbare Christmas wreath every December. Such a humble advertisement for one of the most renowned horse studs in the country. It was typical of the Shannon family's approach to their business. They were in it for the love of horses, not the money or the kudos, though they'd earned plenty of both over the years.

Claire swung the four-wheel drive onto the gravel driveway and sped past the main house, where Chris now lived with his family, to the stables beyond. The huge pine tree in the front garden was hung with twinkling Christmas lights, just as it had been every year when she was a teenager.

In fact, every light on the property seemed to be blazing. Chris had even switched on the floodlights in the exercise arena adjacent to the stables. She could see Scotty's little brother – now a strapping man himself – rushing in and out of a stall as she approached.

She shuddered. With no streetlights or road noise, nights in the hinterland were almost eerily dark and silent. There was something about seeing a building brightly illuminated against an onyx sky, sensing frenetic activity when there should have been stillness, that Claire found deeply unsettling. Growing up, she had loved the quiet of the country, that feeling of splendid isolation. But tonight, Cape Ashe Stud looked to her like a foreboding island in the middle of a churning, black sea.

Chris approached the car as Claire pulled up next to the stables. She rolled down the tinted window and his jaw dropped.

'Claire!' he said. 'Of course. I should have known Scotty would rope you in. Thank you so much. You made it in record time. Haven't forgotten the way here after all these years, eh?'

'Hey, Chris,' she said. 'I'm happy to help. Where's Autumn?' She opened the car door and stepped out. As she turned to close it, she shot Scotty a pointed look. *At least one of the Shannon brothers remembered his manners*, she said with her eyes.

'This way,' Chris said and hurried towards the stall she'd seen him emerge from moments ago.

Claire opened the back door and grabbed her instrument box. Scotty still hadn't moved from the passenger seat. 'Are you coming?' she said.

Her voice seemed to jolt him out of his reverie. He pushed open the door and jumped out. 'I am,' he said. 'Just let me know what you need from me. You take the lead.'

Another wave of irritation crashed over her. 'Well, obviously, Scotty,' she said. 'That's the whole reason I'm here.' She shook her head. He'd seemed sober enough in the pub – at least he'd had the self-awareness to know he wasn't up to treating Autumn – but maybe those three beers had gone to his head more than Claire had realised. Why else would he be trying to micromanage a situation his own actions had excluded him from? It wasn't like her to be so snippy, but she was in no mood to be told how to do her job.

Without giving Scotty the chance to further annoy her, Claire followed Chris to the stable block and Autumn's stall. She heard the mare well before she saw her. Autumn was coughing. It was a strange sound – like a cross between a sneeze and a bark – and, to Claire's dismay, each cough was followed by a deep, rattling wheeze as Autumn tried to drag air into her lungs.

Claire stopped to wash her hands in the stable sink, then thrust the stall door open with her hip and went inside. Scotty was close behind her. Immediately, she could see that Autumn was in agony. The heavily pregnant horse's neck was extended and she was holding her head down, a clear sign that she was trying to alleviate pain or pressure, most likely in her throat. There was swelling below her jaw and Claire could see that the lymph nodes around her throat were inflamed. She pressed her fingers to one of the lumps – it was rock hard.

But the most worrying thing was Autumn's nose. It was crusted with a thick, yellow discharge.

Scotty saw it at the same time Claire did. They exchanged a loaded look.

It didn't escape Chris. 'What is it?' he demanded. 'What's wrong with her?'

'Stethoscope,' Claire said to Scotty. Turning to Chris, she added, 'Just give me a sec.'

Wordlessly, Scotty opened her instrument box and retrieved the stethoscope. He handed it to Claire and watched as she pressed it to the flat plane between Autumn's eyes. Gently, she tapped her index finger all over the horse's head.

'What's she doing?' she heard Chris whisper.

'It's called percussion of the sinuses. She's listening for a hollow sound,' Scotty said quietly. 'If it doesn't sound like that, it means there's fluid in Autumn's skull.'

'Fluid? Like water?'

Scotty shook his head. 'No, mate. Not like water.'

Claire moved to Autumn's chest and listened there. Then she removed her earpieces and faced Chris.

'It's pus. Her lymph nodes are full of it and her throat and larynx are severely inflamed, which is why she's struggling for breath,' she said, her tone grave. 'Autumn has Strangles. It's a very serious and highly contagious bacterial disease.'

Chris groaned. 'I know what it is,' he said, burying his face in his hands. 'I've seen it before, but not for years. I thought they couldn't get it in summer. And Autumn's had the vaccine – all my horses have.'

'It's unusual to see it outside of winter, but not unheard of. And you'd know that the vaccine isn't one-hundred-per-cent effective,' Claire replied. 'In Autumn's case, the fact that she's pregnant and also has an underlying genetic condition may mean her immune system is weaker than it usually would be.'

'She must have been infected when she was down south,' Scotty said to his brother. Claire heard the urgency in his voice. 'You need to get on the phone to them now.'

'You'll also need to get all your other horses into isolation well away from here,' she said. 'And call your grooms. Everything needs washing and disinfecting as soon as possible. Saddles, blankets, food boxes – the lot.'

Chris nodded, his face ashen. 'Okay. I'll call everyone in now,' he said. He ran his hand down the mare's flank. 'But what about Autumn? Will she be all right? Please, Claire, just do whatever you can for her.' He sounded close to tears.

'The first thing I need to do is help her to breathe properly. We can't transport her – it will stress her too much and time is just not on her side,' Claire said. She spoke slowly and deliberately, in spite of the urgency she felt, so that her words could penetrate Chris's distress. 'I need to bypass the inflammation that's obstructing her airway and I'm going to do that by performing an emergency tracheotomy.'

He looked at her, horrified. 'Cut into her throat? Won't that hurt?'

There was no way to sugarcoat it. 'Yes. We can't sedate her because there's a chance it would make her breathing issues even worse,' she said. 'But she's already in terrible pain, Chris. And it's preferable to the alternative.'

'Mate, it's the only way to save Autumn,' Scotty said, gripping his brother's shoulder. 'You've got to trust Claire. She's already saved Autumn's life once. When it comes to horses, I'm telling you there's nobody better.'

Claire felt her cheeks flush with pride at Scotty's endorsement. She knew that what he thought of her veterinary skill shouldn't matter to her – *she* knew she was a good vet – but it did. What Scotty thought of her in general mattered. It mattered a whole lot.

Chris took a deep breath. 'Okay. Whatever it takes,' he said. 'The tracheotomy – will it fix her?'

Again, Claire looked to Scotty. She had an obligation to tell Chris that Autumn's prognosis was bleak. Strangles could lead to anaemia, inflammation of the heart, even lung abscesses. Plus, there was the added risk that the stress of the illness would trigger another heat-stroke episode. As Chris was a life-long horse owner and the owner of an equine business, Claire knew that he appreciated how serious the mare's condition was. But she didn't want him to lose hope – she could see how much he loved this horse. She needed Scotty to guide her, to help her decide how 'real' to get with his little brother.

Scotty gave an almost imperceptible shake of his head. Claire got the message loud and clear. *Go easy.*

'It will fix her breathing problems straightaway,' she said. 'And I'll give her some pain relief, so she'll be a lot more comfortable. After that it's a matter of treating with antibiotics.'

She didn't tell him that sometimes the antibiotics didn't work – that they could even make the condition worse. There was no point. The drugs were her only option.

Instead she added, 'Autumn is one tough horse, Chris. We've seen that already in the way she came through the heat stroke last week.'

Had it really been only a week ago that Scotty had arrived at the clinic with Autumn? It felt like a lifetime. Claire couldn't believe how much had changed in her life in seven days.

Chris seemed heartened by Claire's words. He even managed a wobbly little smile. He pressed his cheek to Autumn's belly. 'Hang in there, girl,' he said quietly. Her ragged breathing seemed to calm slightly at his touch. Then Chris turned to Claire. 'I'll leave you to it. I'll be down at the house making calls. Just yell if you need anything.'

Chris left and it was just her and Scotty. The stall that had comfortably accommodated three adults and a pregnant horse just seconds ago now felt too small. Claire could almost feel the nervous energy vibrating within him.

She needed some fresh air – a moment to collect her thoughts before she operated, away from the dizzying closeness of him. *Propinquity.* Isn't that what Gus had called it? The word rolled around in her head like a marble.

She stepped around him and grabbed a box of surgical gloves and a container of antibacterial soap from her kit. 'Help me scrub in?' she said over her shoulder as she left the stall.

Scotty followed Claire to the sink. He washed up first and donned a pair of gloves, then watched as she took an elastic band from her pocket. Holding it between her teeth, she twisted her curls into a messy bun and secured it with the elastic.

Scotty chuckled. 'Look out,' he said. 'Claire's not here to mess around.'

She planted her hands on her hips and raised her eyebrows, daring him to elaborate.

'You've always done that. Put your hair up when you really mean business. It's one of your little rituals.' He leaned forward and tucked an errant curl behind her ear. 'I love it.'

The air felt charged, fizzing with something other than the summer humidity. But there was no time to contemplate whatever this current was that ran between them. Scotty was right: Claire *did* mean business. She turned on the tap and pumped a dollop of soap into her cupped hands. She scrubbed her hands three times, then shook them dry and held them up to Scotty.

Slowly, deliberately, he eased the gloves on, one finger at a time. She'd had surgical assistants help her scrub in before a procedure a million times. It was a necessary chore that she could complete with her eyes closed. But this was different. It felt incredibly intimate.

She felt his warm breath caressing her skin as he bent his head low. She saw the focus in his eyes as he concentrated on the task. She noticed for the first time a sprinkling of silver strands in Scotty's dark hair and smiled. He would hate that he had grey hair at twenty-nine, she knew, but it made perfect sense. Scotty had always been more advanced than his years. He was an old soul.

Soul mate.

The thought came from nowhere, unbidden and unwelcome. Claire snatched away her hands. 'Thanks,' she said. 'Let's get on with it.'

She felt foolish, wasting precious seconds imagining that something as banal as Scotty putting on her gloves held deeper meaning. There was no meaning. She was at Cape Ashe Stud as a professional, helping out an old friend – an *engaged* old friend – who was in a bind.

They returned to Autumn's stall. The mare seemed more distressed now that Chris wasn't there to soothe her. Every breath rattled and groaned like a steam train.

Claire positioned herself and her sterile instruments by Autumn's head and gestured for Scotty to stand beside her. 'You've done a trach before, right?' she said.

He nodded. 'Yeah, plenty of times, but, um . . .'

'But what?'

'Always as the lead surgeon. Not as an assistant. Well, not since uni.'

She fought the urge to roll her eyes. Of course Scotty wasn't used to assisting in surgery. Playing second fiddle wasn't his thing. He preferred to call the shots.

'Okay, I need you to hold her head up and straight. Like this.' Claire gently guided Autumn's head into position and held it firmly. The mare tried to shake free, jerking her head backwards and letting out a short, sharp squeal. 'She doesn't like it, because it hurts and she wants her head down. You have to hold on tight.'

'Got it,' Scotty said. He placed his gloved hands over Claire's. The warmth of him was electricity. She felt herself shudder as if she'd been shocked. 'Are you okay?'

She extracted her hands from beneath his. 'Fine,' she said quickly. She reached for her scalpel. 'Ready? She's going to lurch and pull, so be prepared.'

Scotty nodded and braced his legs against the stall wall. 'It's all right, girl,' he murmured to Autumn under his breath. 'You're going to be okay, mama.'

Claire scrubbed the surgical site near the top of Autumn's neck with antiseptic liquid, then made the incision. The horse tensed and squealed, but Scotty held fast and she hardly moved.

'I can see the trachea,' Claire said. She made a small cut in the windpipe and there was a rush of air through the incision as Autumn was at last able to take a deep breath without pain. Claire felt the mare relax as she put the tracheotomy tube in place, the panic Autumn had felt as she'd struggled to breathe immediately easing.

Claire's own breath came out in a rush as she slumped back against the wall. The procedure had taken less than five minutes, but she felt like she'd climbed a mountain. She wasn't sure whether it was the pressure of racing against the clock or the added distraction of Scotty standing so close to her while she worked. Either way, she was exhausted.

Scotty released Autumn and, without warning, wrapped his arms around Claire. 'Great job, Thorne. This horse is bloody lucky she knows you,' he said. 'We all are.'

Claire felt herself relax, just as Autumn had. She rested her head against Scotty's chest and let her eyes drift closed. Being held by him was so comforting. It always had been. He was so solid, so steadfast. Being in Scotty's arms was her safe place. It felt natural, she realised – dangerously so.

Eventually, though he gave no indication of wanting the moment to end, Claire extracted herself from his embrace. 'I still need to drain the abscesses, get some fluids into her and start the antibiotics,' she said, all business once more. 'She's not out of the woods yet. Let's give her a few moments of peace. I want to get her heart rate down before I continue.'

She put her instruments back in their box and peeled off her gloves. She would have to scrub in again in a few minutes' time, but that was okay – it was more important to allow Autumn to calm down and reduce the risk of triggering another heat-stroke episode.

Claire stepped out of the stall into the still night and leaned against the stable wall, breathing deeply. She shook out her hair and rubbed her temples. The spicy-sweet scent of the light-bedecked pine tree filled the balmy air. How she had missed that smell. It just didn't feel like Christmas without it.

Scotty smiled as he emerged from Autumn's stall and came to stand next to her. 'Do you hear yourself, Claire?'

She blinked, confused. Had she said something wrong? 'What do you mean by that?'

'You say you're not decisive, that you don't know what you want, but listen to yourself. And look at what you've just done,' he said. 'From the moment I asked for your help tonight, you just took charge. You knew exactly what to do and you did it. You saved Autumn's life. Even though I ruined your date.'

She looked away. Down the driveway, inside the main house, Claire could see Chris pacing agitatedly in the kitchen,

his phone pressed to his ear. She needed to tell him the procedure had been a success. And she would, just as soon as she
mustered the energy.

'It's not the same thing,' she said at length.

'It's not?'

'No,' she said, shaking her head. 'It's different at work.
I have fewer options to choose from and in most cases I can
predict the outcome of whatever decision I make. I can trust
myself more. And *other people* trust me to make the right call.'

Scotty frowned. 'And it's not like that in life? You don't
think people trust you?'

'Nobody ever has,' she said, and she heard the bitterness
in her voice. 'My whole life, people have made my decisions
for me. Mum and Dad decided I'd never amount to anything
in Bindallarah, so they sent me away. Dad decided I couldn't
come back to help him on the farm after they split up, then
he decided I couldn't handle his problems, so he lied to me
instead. Vanessa decided I couldn't manage his estate after he
died and just made all the decisions about the farm herself.'

As the words passed her lips, Claire realised for the first
time that they were true. She hadn't capriciously left her
father's estate for Vanessa to unravel. She hadn't thrown his
problems at her aunt's feet and skipped off to the United States
without a backward glance. Vanessa had simply taken it upon
herself to do those things. She had never asked Claire what she
wanted. Not once.

She felt her stomach starting to churn with anger. What
she'd said to Scotty was the absolute truth. Nobody had
trusted her to play any part in the decisions that affected her.
And she had grown so used to it, become so accustomed to

having decisions made for her, that she had lost the ability to do it for herself.

'And you,' Claire said, her voice barely audible. 'You did it too.' She looked up at Scotty. His green eyes reflected the pain in hers.

She expected him to protest, to tell her she was crazy. Instead, he held her gaze and said, 'I know. I'm sorry.'

His words knocked her for six. 'You *know*?'

He nodded sadly. 'When I asked you to marry me it was because I'd decided it was the most sensible thing. If we were married we could run Thorne Hill together, make it work somehow, even though we were both so young.' He wearily ran a hand over his face and through his hair. 'I didn't ask you what you thought, if you actually wanted to keep the farm. I never even *asked* you.'

The look of self-focused disgust on his face wounded her. Claire attempted a smile. 'And here I thought you proposed to me because you loved me and you wanted to be my husband.' It was a lame attempt at a joke, but she had to do something to try to assuage the ache in her chest.

The disgusted expression gave way to horror. 'I did! I always – I wanted . . .' Scotty sighed, his frustration obvious. He was silent for what felt like hours. When at last he spoke again, his voice was gruff. 'I loved you more than anything, Claire. When you left and went to America, it ripped my heart out. But I know now why you had to do it. You had to take control of your life. And . . . and I deserved it. I deserved to lose you.'

She wanted to shake him, to wrap her arms around him and tell him he was wrong. He didn't deserve what she had done to him. Scotty had made mistakes, missteps driven by the hubris and unfettered optimism of youth, but the truth was that she was unworthy of him – both the idealistic boy he had been then and the thoughtful man he had become. She had always known it and she had spent eight years wishing she could undo it, wishing she could travel back in time, say yes to his proposal and then do whatever it took to become a better version of herself.

But she couldn't go back. She could only go forward. Scotty was moving on – with Nina. Whatever her misgivings about his coming marriage, Claire knew she had to free Scotty from this guilt he carried. They couldn't both spend their lives wallowing in the miseries of their shared past.

'You didn't lose me, Scotty. You escaped me,' she said. 'I wouldn't have made you happy in the long run.'

'I disagree,' he replied.

And then he was in front of her, his hands on her waist, pulling her to him. She knew what was coming next; she saw him make the decision. His frown relaxed as his lips claimed hers.

CHAPTER THIRTEEN

Claire had kissed Scotty thousands of times. She had covered his body in kisses from the top of his head to the tips of his toes, and he hers. They had lost entire evenings kissing in movie theatres and dimly lit bars. But this kiss was different.

This time felt like the first time.

Scotty was tentative at first, softly grazing her mouth with his. But when Claire responded by pressing her body against him, she felt his hunger overtake him. He expertly parted her teeth with his tongue and deepened the kiss. He was all urgency, all need. He wound his hands through her curls as hers drifted to his waist and up under his shirt. She felt his soft skin, the taut plane of his stomach, the way the muscles in his back moved beneath her fingertips.

Scotty gently pulled her hair, easing her head back, and started kissing her neck. Claire shuddered as she gazed up at the starlit sky. Her breath came in short, sharp rasps. The ache in her chest migrated to an altogether sweeter, more pleasurable location. He knew exactly what he was doing. It was his signature move when they were together, the one that always made her want to . . .

'No!' She pushed him with more force than she had intended and he staggered back several steps.

Scotty touched his fingers to his lips as if still looking for hers. 'What's wrong?' he panted, trying to catch his breath.

'We can't do this,' Claire said. 'You're engaged to be married, Scotty.'

He put his hands on his hips and stared intently at his boots. He nodded. Slowly, his breathing calmed. When he looked at her again, there was something animal in his gaze.

'Then why do I want you so much?'

He stepped towards her, seeking to claim her again, but she moved away. She wanted him too. The throbbing between her thighs told her how much. But he wasn't hers any more. He was Nina's.

And Claire was convinced beyond a shadow of a doubt that their marriage would be a cataclysm of epic proportions. If kissing an ex-girlfriend didn't prove it, she wasn't sure what would.

She couldn't skirt the issue for another second. It was time to lay her cards on the table.

'Don't marry Nina,' she said.

His eyes grew wide. '*What?*'

'I didn't come back to Bindallarah to help you plan your wedding. I came here to stop it. It's a mistake, Scotty. It will be disastrous for both of you,' Claire said. 'I like Nina. I do. But she's a stranger. I know she has doubts. And you obviously do too, or you wouldn't be here, kissing me. Call it off. Please. For both your sakes.'

She scanned his face for a sign that her words had hit the mark, but Scotty's expression was inscrutable. Claire felt desperate. He had to see that she was right. He simply had to.

'Say something,' she pleaded.

Scotty straightened his shoulders and appeared to steel himself. 'Claire, I'm going to ask you a question and I'm only going to ask it once,' he said. 'I need you to answer honestly. Will you do that?'

She nodded.

'Do you still have feelings for me?'

Not that. Anything but that. Jackie was right – she'd suspected Scotty had been cagey about his relationship with Nina because he was trying to spare Claire's feelings. His question made it perfectly clear that he suspected those feelings went well beyond the bounds of friendship.

'It doesn't matter how I feel, Scotty. What matters is how *you* feel about Nina. Do you love her enough to spend the rest of your life with her?'

And did he believe Nina loved *him* that deeply? Claire definitely had her doubts.

'Just answer the question,' he said. 'You promised.'

She searched for the right words to explain how she felt about him. In one sense she had deep feelings for him. He made her laugh, both online and in person. He made her feel safe. He made her feel *seen*. She cherished her memories of the love they had once shared and felt ashamed that she'd been so cavalier with his heart. She was happy, beyond happy, that he was back in her life. She was just so glad, so grateful, to be able to call Scotty Shannon her friend.

Maybe, if things had been different, she might have considered herself worthy of a second chance with Scotty. If they had found each other again under different circumstances, the fact that they were both a little older and a little wiser might have meant they'd be great together.

But if returning to Bindallarah had revealed anything, it was that everything had changed. What Claire really wanted, she understood now, was their past. She wanted a chance to make it right. But the past was gone and she had to accept that.

'I don't have *those* kinds of feelings for you, Scotty, I swear. This isn't about me trying to win you back or take you away from somebody that you love. It's really not,' she said haltingly. She felt the sting of tears. 'Maybe you and Nina are meant to be together, but you can't know that after a month. You just can't. If you marry her now, you'll get your heart broken. I care about you too much to stand by and watch that happen.'

It was like a light was extinguished behind Scotty's eyes as she watched. All the passion, the fire she had felt in him just moments ago, seemed to drain away. His face fell and his shoulders sagged as though he was collapsing in on himself. The transformation frightened her and again she fought the urge to go to him, to pull him close and never let him go.

When Scotty spoke again, his voice was flinty. 'Thanks for your help with the plans, but I think it's probably a good idea if I handle things myself from here.'

'Scotty, don't,' she pleaded. 'If you'd just let me —'

'I'm marrying Nina on Christmas Eve, Claire. It's happening,' he said. 'Perhaps it's for the best if you don't come to the wedding.'

Claire was stunned. She had misjudged him – misjudged *them*. She had believed their friendship was strong enough that they could say anything to each other, share even the most uncomfortable truths, the way they used to. But Scotty couldn't handle her honesty. He thought she was lying – that she was motivated by lingering feelings for him instead of a genuine desire to spare him from the agony of a bad marriage. It hadn't occurred to her that he could not only dismiss what she said but reject her entirely.

'I want to come to your wedding, Scotty. If you truly feel that marrying Nina will make you happy, then I respect that. I want to be there to share that moment in your life.'

I can't lose you again, she screamed inside her head.

He drew himself up to his full imposing height and squared his shoulders. 'I'd better check in with Chris. I'll let you finish up with Autumn,' he said. 'You drive my car home. I'll crash here tonight.'

He turned and walked away. Claire watched him stride towards the house and wondered if she was witnessing Scotty Shannon vanishing from her life once again.

Scotty didn't go into the main house. He knocked on the door, told his brother that Autumn was breathing well, and then, when he was sure Claire would be back in the stall tending to the horse, he doubled back to the stables.

He went to the far end of the building and, as quietly as possible, used a low-hanging eucalyptus branch to haul himself onto the sloping tin roof. During the day, the view from up here was spectacular, a vista that spanned the hills and the valley beyond, right down to Bindallarah and out across the Pacific to the horizon. When Scotty and Chris were kids, their parents had tried to forbid them from climbing onto the roof. It was steep and precarious in places, and in the searing summer sun the tin got lava hot – hot enough to burn their skinny bare legs.

But they'd sneaked up there anyway, especially Scotty and especially at night. In the dark he couldn't see anything but the lights of the main house and the stars. He wrapped himself in the blackness like it was a warm quilt. He'd always loved his roof perch. He loved that it caught the mellow sea breezes, that it was silent but for the horses' gentle music below. It was his thinking place.

And often, in the heady first incarnation of his relationship with Claire, they had done a lot more up there than think. He shivered as his brain uploaded a highlights reel. Memory was a funny thing. Sometimes he imagined his fingertips still tingled with the touch of her creamy skin.

Scotty could hear Claire now, speaking quietly to Autumn as she worked. 'I'm so sorry, my love,' she was saying. Apologising for the pain she was causing the mare. In his experience, it was unusual for a vet to talk to her patients, to seek to calm and reassure them. Most vets were all business, especially out here in the bush, focusing on the injury or illness rather than the patient as a sentient being. But then, there wasn't much about Claire that could be described as 'usual'.

He'd heard it said that the best veterinarians weren't those who loved animals – they were often too emotional and got too attached. The best vets were those who loved science, loved puzzles, wouldn't rest until they solved the mystery and fixed the problem, but could keep the animal itself at arm's length. That was Scotty to a tee. Even when Nina had hit Tank with her car, the part of him that was racked with panic at the prospect of losing his beloved dog had shut down as the vet in him had taken over.

Scotty was all about getting to the bottom of things. And yet Claire was the better vet. She was emotional and unapologetic about her care for her patients. He remembered how broken up she'd been about losing a horse to laminitis on the night she first contacted him on social media. She loved animals and science in equal measure – and he could never get to the bottom of her. She was a puzzle he simply couldn't solve, just as he couldn't figure out how to shake her from his heart. Trying to do either only seemed to make things worse.

He couldn't believe he'd kissed her. He hadn't meant to. But *she* wasn't meant to stand in front of him and tell him how lucky he was to be free of her. She wasn't supposed to rush to reassure him that she had only platonic feelings for him. Scotty didn't have the words to tell her that, despite everything, he didn't think he wanted that freedom. He couldn't articulate his confusion, so he had showed her instead.

He had felt Claire respond. She had kissed him back with every bit as much desire as he'd felt thundering through his veins. *She wanted me too.*

But then it had all gone to hell. Scotty groaned as he recalled how she'd pushed him away.

You're engaged to be married, Scotty.

He'd let it go way too far. What must she think of him now? *It's just a kiss*, he'd told himself as he pulled Claire to him. But of course it was so much more than that. It was an announcement. He might as well have shouted it through a megaphone: *Scotty Shannon has no integrity.*

How could he ever expect Claire to have faith in him when he'd just been unfaithful to his own fiancée – with her? Scotty had allowed his lingering attraction to Claire to overwhelm him, let himself give in to his still-simmering desire for her, and in the process had made her an unwilling participant in deceiving Nina. And why? Because Scotty was sure that Claire must feel the same magnetic pull towards him that he felt for her. He thought it was fear that had made Claire say she wanted nothing more from him than friendship. That kiss was carnal, wanton, unbelievably sexy – anything but platonic.

But that was his thing, wasn't it? Deciding how Claire felt and what Claire wanted without ever asking Claire. He had manipulated her because he wanted *her* to decide this time. He wanted Claire to choose him, even though he'd already chosen somebody else. Did he really need his ego stroked that badly? He wasn't just a liar – he was arrogant and cruel. He was a fool.

Scotty had told Claire not to come to his wedding because he couldn't bear to have her watch him marry Nina knowing he had already been disloyal. Claire would never forgive him, because it was unforgivable.

And if she left his life again – left for good this time – he would never forgive himself.

CHAPTER FOURTEEN

Saturday morning dawned overcast, hot and humid. The air was heavy and stifling, and there was the occasional ominous rumble of thunder in the distance. Claire was glad. The black clouds were the perfect complement to her dark mood; the tumultuous atmosphere matched the turmoil in her head. And at least she could blame the uncomfortable conditions for the violet circles around her eyes, instead of admitting the real reason she hadn't slept a wink last night.

She curled up in the worn armchair on Vanessa's back patio, cradling a mug of tea and listening to the intensifying wind tossing the branches of the fig trees. Just as she'd done all night long, Claire replayed the events of the previous evening in her mind. The race to save Autumn. Begging Scotty to call off the wedding. Assuring him she wasn't acting out of some twisted desire to win him back. The way he walked away from her without a backward glance.

The way he kissed me.

She shook her head to dislodge the memory. She hadn't been kissed like that in a very long time. Claire couldn't recall the last time she had felt her body respond to a man the way she had answered Scotty last night. There had been others in the eight years since she'd last been with him – it wasn't like she'd lived the life of a nun – but none of them came close to matching the physical connection she and Scotty had always shared. It was as though Scotty had staked a claim the first time he kissed her, and her body wouldn't let him relinquish it no matter how forcefully her brain insisted she move on.

Claire was shocked by how intensely, how viscerally, she had craved him as they kissed. If she hadn't come to her senses and pushed him away, she didn't know how far she would have taken it. She knew, though, that she wanted to take it all the way.

But none of it mattered now. It had been a moment of madness, lust clouding her better judgement. It meant nothing and thinking about it was pointless. Claire had asked him to reconsider marrying Nina. She had appealed to his logic – to the scientist in him. But Scotty had made it perfectly, painfully clear that the wedding was happening. That was that. End of story.

Unless . . . Claire wondered if Scotty would tell Nina about the kiss. Surely he wouldn't want to start their married life carrying a secret like that. Scotty was nothing if not honest. And if he did tell her, what then? Claire didn't know Nina well enough to discern whether she was the forgiving type. Discovering that your fiancé had kissed another woman a week before your wedding *seemed* like it would be a deal-breaker – but Claire had learned the hard way that apparently nothing was what it seemed when it came to Scotty and Nina.

I have to tell her.

An image flashed before Claire's eyes. Storming into the ceremony on Christmas Eve, just as the officiant asked if anyone knew of any reason why Scotty and Nina couldn't be married. Pointing at Scotty and declaring, 'He kissed me!' Watching as it all imploded.

Claire chuckled in spite of her disquietude. It was too melodramatic for words. Sure, it would probably do the trick, but she wouldn't do it. She came to Bindallarah to try to reason with Scotty, to make him see sense, not to destroy his wedding like some cartoon villain. Simply sabotaging the event would be easy – she would only need to cancel the celebrant or hide Nina's car keys on the day. It wasn't just about ensuring Scotty didn't tie the knot on Christmas Eve. It was about understanding *why* he wanted to get married so quickly – and convincing him to ask himself that question, too.

So, no. Nina didn't need to hear that particular news update from her. Scotty may have betrayed Nina's trust, but Claire couldn't betray his.

Could she?

There was a ruckus from within the house and Gus suddenly appeared on the patio, looking as gleeful as if Christmas had come a week early.

'Are you serious?' she said in a loud stage whisper, her eyes shining.

Claire frowned. 'Good morning to you too?'

'Scotty Shannon's car is out the front,' her cousin said. 'Is he here? Did you guys *do it*?'

'Sshhh,' Claire hissed. Gus's 'whisper' was louder than most people yelled. Claire didn't need any sharp-eared neighbours getting hold of that particular rumour. 'Scotty isn't here. And no, we didn't "do it".'

Well, not quite.

Gus crossed her arms and glared expectantly.

'There was an emergency up at Cape Ashe last night. I treated one of the horses and then I drove Scotty's car back to town. That's it.'

'I don't believe you. Why are you sitting out here looking all broody and lovelorn? What aren't you telling me?' Gus demanded, narrowing her eyes.

'I didn't sleep well. It was a stressful night. Because of the *horse*,' Claire clarified in response to her cousin's knowing smile. 'That's all.'

'Hmm,' Gus said, clearly unconvinced. 'What about your date, then? Did you do it with Jared?'

'Gus! Jared is just a friend. It wasn't a date. I didn't do it with anyone, okay?'

Claire had almost forgotten about Jared. He'd been understanding when she had raced out of the pub with Scotty, but she knew she owed him an explanation. Being abandoned halfway through the evening had to sting a little, even though they weren't technically on a date. It was only a casual drink, but he was fun and she had enjoyed his company. She resolved to call him later in the day.

Claire drained the last of her tea and stood up. 'I'm going into town,' she said. 'I need to take Scotty's car back to the clinic and do some Christmas shopping. Want anything?'

Gus pouted and shook her head. 'Only the truth,' she said dramatically.

Ha. Claire hardly knew what the truth was any more.

*

Claire swung Scotty's four-wheel drive into the car park behind the clinic and killed the engine. There were no signs of life inside the squat brick building. She knew she should have called Scotty and asked what he wanted her to do with the car, but she couldn't bring herself to dial his number. If he no longer wanted her at his wedding, he probably wasn't interested in speaking to her either.

She pulled the key from the ignition, climbed out of the car and locked it. Then she wrapped the key in a sheet of Bindallarah Veterinary Hospital letterhead she'd found in the glove box and slid it under the clinic's back door, watching it skid across the shiny linoleum floor.

Claire pulled her phone from her bag and began composing a text message.

Your car is parked at work. Posted the key thru the clinic door. Please tell Chris I'll come up this afternoon to check on Autumn.

Her thumb hovered over the 'send' button, but she hesitated. She couldn't just leave it at that. Scotty thought Claire had lied to him. He thought she'd only been pretending to be his friend all this time – that she really wanted him to call off the wedding because she was jealous. And that made her feel sick.

I'm sorry about last night. I wish I hadn't said anything. I don't want anything more from you than what you can give, I promise xx

She sent the message. Her heart leapt when three undulating dots appeared inside a bubble on the screen, indicating Scotty was typing. It felt like years passed before he replied.

Thx. Will tell Chris. Autumn doing well.

Claire stared hopelessly at the screen for another minute, waiting for a second message. There had to be more. But the dots disappeared. Scotty had said all he was going to say.

She felt the first fat drops of rain as she walked down a short side road from the clinic's back entrance to Bindy's main street. Or were they tears? It hardly made a difference either way. Claire couldn't remember ever feeling so bleak.

The main street was thronged with people. Though some would work right up until the next Friday, many had finished for the year the day before and had travelled from all over the district to shop for Christmas gifts and entertaining supplies. But the main reason most people had converged on Bindallarah today was to meet friends and gossip.

Claire had forgotten what a big social occasion the weekend before Christmas was in the community. Twenty-first-century Bindy felt less remote than it ever had, but for the older farming families, who lived on outlying properties and rarely visited town for anything more interesting than stock feed or tractor parts, the annual Christmas catch-up was an event. Cars drove by with tinsel wound around their radio antennae and joke reindeer antlers attached to the windows. She watched families promenade up and down the esplanade – the men and boys in freshly laundered shirts and jeans with sharp creases ironed in, the women and girls in pretty summer dresses – and felt warm inside. She wished she'd made more effort with her own attire that morning. She knew she looked glum and washed-out in her floor-sweeping black maxi dress. She had dressed to match her mood, and it was far from merry.

It meant something, this festive ritual. Bindallarah meant something to all these people. For perhaps the first time since she'd arrived a week ago, Claire felt truly glad to be home.

She had to move on. All these people were living their lives, going about their business in a town that was unrecognisable from the one she'd left as a scared fifteen-year-old. They may have stayed in Bindallarah, but they'd grown in a way Claire hadn't. They'd had families, joined sports teams, bought houses, started businesses, formed book clubs, and forged deep, lasting friendships.

They had built lives, and what had she done? Gone to America, qualified as a horse specialist, returned to Sydney and started working. It looked impressive on paper – she'd built a career she loved and was good at. But she'd forgotten to build a life she loved, because she couldn't let go of the one that had been snatched away from her.

Scotty had – he'd let go of Claire and embraced Nina, invested his whole heart and soul in their future with the sort of carefree courage Claire envied. Maybe it was time she threw a little caution to the wind, too. She owed it to herself.

'Who are you spying on?' came a voice from behind.

Claire let out a startled squeak and jumped what felt like a metre in the air. She whirled around to see Alex Jessop, holding up his hands in a gesture of apology.

'Whoa! Sorry, Claire. I didn't mean to scare you,' he said, looking sheepish.

'Alex,' she said breathlessly, clutching at her chest as if it would calm her racing heart. She wondered if a swift kick to his shin would make her feel better. 'Don't sneak up on people like that.'

'You looked like you were pretty deep in thought there. Something on your mind?'

She opened her mouth to tell him to mind his own business, but was stunned instead to hear herself say, 'I was just thinking about how lovely Bindy is. I've spent the past thirteen years telling myself this town is a backwater, but it's not. At all. I think it was just easier to believe that than to think about how much I missed the place.'

Alex's face lit up. The wide smile suited him, made his hazel eyes twinkle. 'Well, as the mayor, I'm very happy to hear you say that,' he said. He looked different today in board shorts and a T-shirt instead of his smart business attire – he was friendlier somehow, less intimidating. 'And as not-the-mayor I'm pretty stoked too.'

'You are?'

'Definitely. I'm glad I bumped into you, actually. I was starting to worry you weren't going to call me.' When Claire stared blankly at him he added, 'Dinner, remember?'

Dinner? She did remember – she remembered bumping into Alex in Alison Bay on Wednesday, when she'd been wedding-dress shopping with Nina and he'd been wearing a sharp suit and a leer. He had given her his business card and asked her to call him. It hadn't occurred to her that he was serious.

'Wow,' Claire said. 'Alex, I'm sorry. I didn't think you meant it.'

Now Alex looked bewildered. 'Why would you think that?'

'Oh, I don't know. Maybe because I haven't seen you since my father's funeral eight years ago, and before that I hadn't seen you since high school when, let's face it, you weren't exactly my biggest fan. You weren't particularly welcoming the other day either.'

'Oh man,' Alex groaned. He rubbed his fingers along his stubbled jawline. 'I'm an idiot. I was trying to be the cool guy the other day. I'd heard you were back in town, but seeing you there with Nina was so unexpected, I think I freaked out a bit.'

Claire frowned. None of this made sense. Was Alex Jessop really telling her she made him nervous?

'I was a jerk to you at school, Claire,' he went on. 'I know that. At the risk of sounding like a sexist moron, it was because I liked you. I didn't know how to talk to girls. I had no social skills. All I knew back then was footy and partying.'

A sudden gust of wind buffeted her and Claire felt like it might actually knock her off her feet. What Alex was saying to her was as astonishing as if she'd just discovered that the sand on Bindy Beach was really sugar. And it *was* sexist – 'boys only tease girls they like' was basically page one of the *Sexism Handbook* – but it was also an attitude typical of most of the fifteen-year-old country boys Claire had grown up with. Typical of most of their fathers, too, she suspected.

But just like the town he now presided over as mayor, Alex seemed to have moved with the times. Although it seemed he could still use some help on the talking-to-girls front.

'Are you telling me you had a crush on me, Alex?' she said. She couldn't conceal her amazement.

He shrugged in a way Claire found oddly endearing. 'Big time. But you were Scotty's girl. Everybody knew that,' he said.

Claire flinched. *Scotty's girl*. Back then, knowing people thought of her as someone's possession would have made

Claire furious. She would have seen it as an affront to her bur-geoning teenage autonomy. Now it just made her sad. Nearly fifteen years later, she wasn't sure she was even Scotty's friend.

I have to move on.

It was her only option. The past was of no use to her. She had to decide how she was going to go forward.

'What are you doing right now?' she asked.

Alex's eyebrows shot up so quickly Claire thought they might disappear right off his face. 'I was going to grab a coffee and do some Christmas shopping,' he said. 'Why?'

'Same here. It's not dinner, but would you like to spend the morning together, Alex?'

It was the first time in her life Claire had asked a man on a date. It was terrifying.

'Yes, Claire,' Alex replied, flashing a relieved smile. 'I would like that very much. Where to?'

'Bindy Brew?' She knew it would be packed with locals, but for once that thought didn't scare her. Since her talk with Gus, Claire no longer expected harsh words from everyone she encountered. In time, perhaps she would truly believe she wasn't to blame for what her father did – and in the mean-time she felt less inclined to bow and scrape to anyone in town who still thought she should. Her father had tried to take his guilt to his grave. Maybe Claire's final gift to him would be to let him.

And, besides, being seen with Alex would help to hose down those persistent rumours about why 'Scotty's girl' had finally come home.

Alex nodded and they walked side by side in the direction of the café.

'Look, can I tell you something?' he asked, not looking at her. 'I just want to be honest so there're no misunderstandings.'

Claire felt a surge of anxiety. 'Okay,' she said slowly.

'My parents lost money in your dad's acai berries scheme. Not a lot, and they got it all back when the farm was sold. There are no hard feelings at all, not from anyone in my family. We all know you had nothing to do with it.'

She let out the breath she didn't realise she was holding. 'Thanks. I appreciate that.' She appreciated Alex being upfront with her even more. She was so tired of second-guessing what everyone thought of her. Trying to figure out people's motives and agendas was exhausting.

'In a way, I have Big Jim to thank for helping me become mayor,' Alex continued.

That stopped Claire in her tracks. 'That seems unlikely,' she said dubiously.

They arrived at Bindy Brew. Though the queue at the takeaway window was predictably long, there were plenty of free tables inside. Claire led the way to a table for two by the window.

'I'm serious. I really love this town,' Alex said. 'When I saw what your dad had done to try to save his farm, it really got to me. Nobody should have to feel that deception is the only way to keep a roof over their head. I knew that Bindy needed to change. The local economy had shrunk almost to the point it didn't exist. The town was dying and taking the whole district with it. And then . . .'

He faltered and looked down at the table, pretending to study the menu.

'And then what?' Claire prompted.

Alex looked at her for a moment and she could see he was trying to figure out how to frame what he wanted to say.

'I've got a picture of you in my head at Jim's funeral. I'd never in my life seen a human being look as broken as you did that day, Claire,' he said softly. 'I made a promise to myself right there that I'd do whatever I could to bring this town back to life. To make sure other families would survive.'

Claire felt her throat tighten. *Damn it.* She wasn't going to cry in front of Alex Jessop, especially now that she was on a date with him. But his kindness and concern touched her deeply.

She was grateful when the waiter appeared at their table to take their order. Claire suddenly realised she was famished. She'd left Vanessa's house without eating breakfast and she'd missed dinner the night before when she left the pub to treat Autumn. She ordered poached eggs on toast with a side of bacon, a hash brown and an extra-strong coffee. Alex was impressed and said so.

'So, you went to New York?' she said when the waiter had left, determined to shift the focus of the conversation away from her and her splintered family.

'Yeah. I did a bunch of business and economics courses over there, and did a masters in Australian local government management online while I was at it.'

'We must have been in America at the same time,' Claire said.

'We were. I always kind of hoped we'd bump into each other,' Alex said, chuckling. 'Hey, in a country of three hundred million people, it didn't seem entirely impossible.'

'Amazing,' Claire said, shaking her head.

'What is?'

'Just that there was somebody thinking about me all that time and I never had any idea.' She'd been too busy thinking about Scotty all those years, but Alex was interesting, urbane and charming. Who knew how different things might have been if she had known he was interested? Maybe there was something to Gus's residential propinquity theory. Claire had just been too blinkered to realise there were other romantic possibilities in Bindallarah.

Alex ducked his head, but not before Claire saw his cheeks flush a telltale pink. 'What can I say? You made an impression on me, Thorne.'

Her coffee arrived, along with Alex's green juice, and she gazed out of the wide window as she sipped it, contentedly listening to him talk about his adventures in the Big Apple. The wind had picked up and the rain was coming down steadily now, but it only seemed to make the people outside more jubilant. Little kids jumped in puddles as their parents attempted to shield them with umbrellas. The sound of laughter and happy chatter mercifully drowned out the competing Christmas carols emanating from every storefront on the street.

Claire felt . . . if not quite happy, then something close to it. The events of last night lingered in the back of her mind. She was still confused, still bereft at the thought of not having Scotty in her life. She remained convinced that his marrying Nina was completely crazy.

But she felt hopeful. That was it. It took her so long to identify the feeling because it was so unfamiliar to her. Hope. *How about that*, Claire thought.

And then she saw them. Scotty and Nina.

Nina charged along the street, threading her way between shoppers, while Scotty hurried after her. He caught up with his fiancée right in front of Bindy Brew. Just a few inches of glass separated them from where Claire sat eating breakfast with Alex. He didn't appear to notice them and neither Scotty nor Nina cast a glance inside the café.

Nina was upset. Scotty looked as exhausted as Claire felt. He grabbed Nina's elbow and she spun to face him, her rain-soaked hair swinging out behind her. Anger flashing in her pretty eyes as she spoke to him, stabbing her index finger into his chest. Passers-by cast surreptitious glances in the couple's direction; clearly their spat was attracting attention. Claire was no lip-reader – she couldn't make out what Nina was saying – but she didn't need to be to see that she was giving Scotty a no-holds-barred serve. His response was more sub-dued. He seemed to be trying to placate her, holding out his hands in front of him as if to say, 'I surrender.'

Claire froze. *He must have told her about the kiss.* What else would drive chic, collected Nina into a public argument with her fiancé a week before their wedding? Why else would Scotty be pursuing her through the streets, all but prostrating himself at her feet? Nina must know.

As Claire watched, Nina wrenched her arm from Scotty's grip. She dropped her arms to her sides and stared at the foot-path. Her anguish was clear. Scotty ceased his appeals and just stared helplessly at her. At last, she looked up at him. She said two words and this time they were as clear to Claire as if Nina had shouted them into her ear.

Tell Claire.

When she turned again and walked away, Scotty didn't move to follow. He stood rooted to the spot and raked his fingers through his hair. Then he looked absently through the window of Bindy Brew.

Their eyes met. A faint smile played across Scotty's lips as he recognised her. His gaze shifted to the next chair at Claire's table. The smile vanished.

Scotty looked from Alex to Claire and back again. He clenched his jaw and shook his head.

'Scotty,' Claire said, startling Alex. He followed her gaze to the window, but Scotty wasn't there.

He'd already disappeared into the rain.

CHAPTER FIFTEEN

The more Claire thought about it, the more indignant she felt.

Scotty had looked angry when he saw her sitting with Alex. He had shaken his head like a disapproving schoolteacher. What right did he have? Not twelve hours before, Scotty had kissed her despite being engaged to someone else – a fact it seemed Nina was painfully aware of. Then he had uninvited her to the wedding that he had practically begged her to attend only the week before. And now he was going to get his stethoscope in a twist because Claire dared to have breakfast with an old friend?

The *nerve* of the guy. Who did Scotty Shannon think he was?

Alex had known immediately that something was up.

'Are you okay, Claire?' he'd asked after she'd blurted Scotty's name for no apparent reason. 'You look like you've seen a ghost.'

She had responded with a bitter laugh. Wasn't that the truth? Scotty was like the ghost of Christmas past: he just kept turning up to remind her of everything she'd done wrong in her life.

Alex, on the other hand, was all about the future. His family could have been ruined by what Big Jim had done, but Alex had chosen instead to see it as a blessing in disguise. He had used it to make life better not just for himself, but for the whole town. Claire had to admit that was kind of a turn-on.

'I'm fine, Alex,' she'd told him. 'I'm going to be fine. Hey, you're going to Scotty and Nina's wedding, right?'

'I sure am.'

'Would you like to go with me? Like, as my date?' Claire didn't know if people took dates to weddings. At this point, she didn't much care. She was going to Scotty's wedding whether he liked it or not and she'd be damned if she was going to turn up alone.

'Um, yeah,' Alex had said, grinning. 'That'd be great. Definitely.'

They'd finished their breakfast and spent some time pottering in the shops. Claire bought a beautiful hand-painted silk scarf as a Christmas gift for Vanessa and a wedding planner notebook as a tongue-in-cheek present for Gus – it would go nicely with the subscription to *Cosmo Bride* she planned to buy for her online. She didn't necessarily understand her young cousin's wedding fixation, but she had a new-found respect for people who knew what they wanted from life and pursued it with gusto.

Well, *most* people. People whose goals weren't as reckless as marrying someone they hardly knew.

When the Christmas crowds filling Bindy's main street got too much, Claire bade Alex farewell and they went their separate ways. Now she headed for the beach, her favourite route back to

Vanessa's cottage. Somehow it was even more beautiful on this tempestuous morning than on a sunny day, the moody sea foaming and tossing beneath a portentous sky. The rain had stopped, but the wind howled like a gale in a Gothic novel. Claire's bare skin stung where the sand whipped against it.

She thought about Alex as she walked. Claire had enjoyed their spontaneous morning date – in fact, she was surprised by how content she felt in Alex's company. Did he make her weak at the knees? No – but she still had a lot of years-old baggage to discard before she was truly comfortable with this 'new' Alex Jessop. Maybe, if she were willing to give him a chance, that chemistry would develop.

Alex wasn't like the men Claire usually dated. The long hours and erratic shifts she worked in Sydney meant her options were pretty much limited to other vets. No, she realised, *she* had limited her options to other vets. Men who, like her, were deliberate, methodical and rarely saw the sun.

Alex was the polar opposite. He was ebullient and enthusiastic, a bit of a wheeler-dealer, but in an honest and undeniably charming way. He reminded her of a labrador: positive, intelligent, and always looking for the next adventure.

Was that bad, she wondered? Comparing a potential boyfriend to a family pet? This was all new to her. She'd enjoyed the company of two very different but equally nice men in Bindallarah – it was more exposure to the opposite sex than she'd had in two months in Sydney.

And one incredible kiss.

Claire tutted, mad at herself as her thoughts drifted back to Scotty yet again. He was under her skin like a splinter she just couldn't extract. And she knew why. It was because, in spite of everything, in spite of her anger and confusion, she couldn't stop worrying about him. She was even more concerned now that she'd witnessed his argument with Nina.

Did Nina know about the kiss? What Claire had witnessed on the street seemed to suggest she must, but she knew better than to assume anything when it came to Scotty. If Nina *had* called off the wedding, surely Scotty would be feeling devastated. But what if she hadn't called it off? What if they were still going to get hitched on Christmas Eve? Claire didn't know which scenario was worse.

And what did Nina mean when she said, 'Tell Claire'?

She wondered if she should find Nina, talk to her, figure out for sure what she knew. If Scotty had told her about the kiss, then Claire owed her an apology. And if he hadn't, what then? Though she had resolved earlier to keep her mouth shut, Claire just couldn't shake the feeling that Nina deserved the truth. But would it help her? It might only wound her. Claire just couldn't decide what was the right thing to do.

She reached the northern end of the beach and climbed up through the dunes to Vanessa's front gate. Her aunt was in the front garden, wearing an oversized straw hat and deadheading her rosebushes.

'Hello, sweetheart,' Vanessa said. 'Gus told me you were up and about early this morning. Christmas shopping?'

Claire nodded, glad she'd thought to hide the bag that held the silk scarf inside the one containing Gus's notebook. 'Let me guess,' she said. 'Gus also told you her wild conspiracy theory about why Scotty's car was here earlier?'

Vanessa's mouth twitched. 'She may have mentioned something to that effect.'

Claire rolled her eyes. 'You know there's not a word of truth to it, right? Scotty did not stay here last night. I had his car because I did a tracheotomy on a horse at Cape Ashe. I've just dropped it back to the clinic.'

'You don't owe me any kind of explanation, darling,' Vanessa said with what Claire knew was deliberate neutrality. 'What you do in Scotty's car is your business.'

Immediately, Claire felt irked. The contentedness she'd felt just moments before disappeared as quickly as the morning's rain had blown through. There it was again: that old assumption that there had to be more to the Claire-and-Scotty story. Her aunt's feigned disinterest only reminded Claire that some people were still trying to make decisions for her – still deciding how she felt and what she wanted. Nothing Claire said made a lick of difference. It was exhausting.

And she'd had enough.

'Aunty Vee, why didn't you let me take care of Dad's estate?'

Vanessa dropped her secateurs and stared at Claire, aghast. 'Goodness, what a question. Where did that come from?'

'I've been doing some thinking lately. About my life,' Claire said quietly. 'About the decisions I've made and those that were made for me. It seems to me there were a lot of things I should have had a say in, but I wasn't given that opportunity.'

Her aunt pressed her lips together in a thin line and wiped her palms on her trousers. 'Jim didn't name an executor in his will. We thought – your mother and I – that it would just be easiest if I took care of it.'

'But why? I was his next of kin. I was old enough. Didn't you think I deserved to be involved?'

'Honey, you were so young. You'd just lost your dad in the most tragic way and you had so much on your plate already with your studies and your relationship with Scotty. I didn't want to burden you.' Vanessa took a deep breath. 'And honestly, once I started to understand what a mess my brother had left behind, I did make a conscious decision to keep it from you as much as I could.'

Claire sat down heavily on the timber steps that led from the garden path to the verandah. She rested her forehead in her hands. 'It wasn't your decision to make, Vanessa. Don't you see? He was my father. Thorne Hill was my home and you sold it off like it meant nothing.'

'Thorne Hill had to be sold, Claire. Your father's debts were enormous. It was the only way to square the ledger,' she said. There was an edge to her voice now; she was growing defensive. 'There wouldn't have been any money for your American adventure without selling the farm.' She jutted her chin defiantly.

Claire knew she was being terribly unfair. Yes, Vanessa had presumed eight years ago to know what was best for her, but somebody had to. Her father was dead and her mother was no use to her – she didn't even travel from Perth for Jim's funeral. And Vanessa had lost her big brother. She was trying to do the right thing by her niece while wading through her own grief and trying to come to terms with Big Jim's many betrayals.

But in that moment, Claire didn't care. She was too tired to be charitable, too worn out to take a single step in another's shoes, much less walk a mile. She just didn't have it in her to try to see things from everyone else's perspective any more. Nobody, it seemed, had ever tried to see things from hers.

They just barged in and turned her life upside down, over and over again.

'You know something, Aunty Vee? I don't think I've ever made a good decision.'

Vanessa's stony expression softened. 'Oh, Claire. Of course you have,' she replied.

'No,' Claire said, shaking her head. 'I really haven't. Every decision I've ever made, I should have done the opposite.'

It was true. None of her choices had made her happy, not really. Well, except becoming a vet – but she could have done that without travelling halfway around the world and breaking her own heart in the process.

'I should have come home after Mum left, no matter what Dad said. I should have tried to save the farm,' she said. 'I shouldn't have run away to the US after Dad died. I should have finished my studies in Sydney and then come back to Bindy like Scotty wanted.'

I shouldn't have left Scotty. I should have said yes. I shouldn't have kissed him back last night.

I shouldn't have stopped *kissing him last night.*

'Like Scotty . . .? Sweetheart.' Vanessa came to sit next to her. 'All this soul-searching – is it about the wedding?'

Claire hesitated, then nodded. She felt pathetic. It was ridiculous to admit that an ex-boyfriend's wedding had thrown her into such a tailspin. But it had. The week she had been back in Bindallarah had been exquisite and painful and revelatory and terrible all at the same time.

And Scotty had been at the centre of it all. Just like he always had.

'Don't you like Nina?'

'Nina's great! She's perfect,' Claire wailed. 'I truly think she's a lovely person and I can see why Scotty's mad about her.'

'But?'

'But . . . how do they know? They met a month ago. *Four weeks*, Aunty Vee. How can they be sure?'

Vanessa shrugged in a way that said, *You're asking me?* 'I don't think anybody is ever sure. Some people are just more willing than others to take the chance.'

'It might be an awful, terrible, horrendously bad decision, though. It might make them both miserable,' Claire countered.

'Or it might be a wonderful, magical, joyous decision. It might make them both blissfully happy,' said Vanessa.

She supposed her aunt might be right, but Claire simply couldn't quash her doubts about the match. She thought back to her day of dress shopping with Nina, when the bride-to-be had seemed so unfussed about the wedding. She was sure she hadn't imagined it. And, obviously, Scotty kissing Claire last night wasn't normal behaviour for a loved-up groom, even one who insisted his wedding would go ahead no matter what. They both had reservations, she was certain of it.

Just because somebody could ignore their gut instinct, it didn't mean they should. Having the ability to drown out the little voice in their head whispering 'this isn't a good idea' wasn't necessarily a good thing. Charging ahead with a plan when all evidence pointed to going back to the drawing board wasn't always a sign of strength.

Claire knew all too well that it was often a bright-red flag that signalled weakness.

In an instant, Claire's thoughts swung a hundred and eighty degrees. She couldn't give up trying to save Scotty and Nina from themselves. If Scotty wouldn't listen to reason, she would take her case to the High Court of Nina. She had to tell her about the kiss. It was the right thing to do, Claire was almost certain of it.

And if it wasn't . . . well, what was one more bad decision?

Claire still couldn't quite believe Bindallarah had its own yoga studio. Growing up, the CWA had held a weekly class, run by an ancient hippy couple who lived in an actual treehouse outside Alison Bay.

But Yoga by Nina was the real deal – even if technically it was Alex's business and not Nina's. Claire emerged from the staircase that led up from the kids' clothing store and peeked through the studio door into a tranquil oasis of plush cream carpet, leafy green pot plants and a wall of floor-to-ceiling mirrors.

It still had the unique aroma of cloying incense and sweaty sneakers that all yoga studios seemed to share, however, so she was pleased to see that Bindy hadn't grown too big for its boots just yet.

A schedule tacked to the door advertised more class styles than Claire knew existed running six days a week. A quick glance at the Saturday column told her that the next class wasn't until later in the afternoon. She went inside and found Nina alone, sitting barefoot and cross-legged on the floor with her back to the mirror. Her eyes were closed and she appeared to be meditating.

The thick carpet absorbed Claire's footsteps and Nina didn't hear her come in. She waited awkwardly for a few moments, hoping Nina would sense her presence, but she seemed to be in a deep trance.

Claire didn't want to just start talking – Nina would likely have a heart attack. Eventually she settled for quietly clearing her throat.

Nina didn't startle. Instead she exhaled through her nose and calmly opened her eyes, as if she'd been expecting company and Claire was right on time.

'Claire! How lovely to see you,' Nina said warmly. She stretched out her legs and stood up.

Claire was taken aback. This wasn't the greeting she'd expected from the fiancée of a man she'd passionately kissed the night before. She wasn't sure whether to feel relieved or disappointed. She had come to confess, but there was a part of her that hoped Scotty had already done it.

Claire had meant it when she told Vanessa that she thought Nina was lovely. She didn't relish the prospect of hurting her, but she had to believe that a little pain now would spare both Scotty and Nina a lifetime of agony.

'Have you come for a class?' Nina went on. 'The next one isn't until four, but I'd be happy to book you in. Your first class here is free.' She crossed the studio to a small desk in the corner and picked up what looked like an enrolment form.

'Uh, no. Yoga isn't really my thing.' All that deep breathing, contemplation and being at one with the universe made Claire feel itchy. 'I came to see you.'

'Oh, you're so sweet,' Nina said, smiling brightly. 'I was going to call you today, actually. I just talked to Scotty.'

Uh-oh.

'You did?'

'Yeah. We decided that we can't possibly get married —'

'*What?*'

'— without having bachelor and bachelorette parties. Although apparently you call them bucks' and hens' nights here? Which is one more thing I don't get about Australia, but that's fine. So will you come?'

Claire's head was swimming. 'Um, Nina, I need to —'

'It's super casual. No strippers or anything awful like that,' she said, wrinkling her nose. 'We're breaking with tradition and having a joint party. You know, since the wedding is only a week away.'

'When is it?' Claire asked in a reedy voice.

'Thursday night, seven-thirty, on the beach. We were going to have it at Cape Ashe, but all the horses are in isolation so we can't do it.'

Autumn. Claire really needed to get back up to Cape Ashe Stud to see how the mare was coping and show Chris how to clean the trach tube. Under normal circumstances she would have headed back there first thing, but last night had been anything but normal. Claire's mind definitely hadn't been on the job all day.

'I know,' she said absently.

'Oh, that's right! Scotty told me you were up there last night,' Nina said. She swiped at the air as if amazed at her own forgetfulness.

'He did?' Claire studied Nina's face for any hint that she knew what had happened. 'Did he say anything else?'

'Only that you were amazing.'

Well, *that* was certainly open for interpretation.

'God,' Nina said, perching on the edge of the desk. 'I can't tell you how much I miss working as a vet. I was actually a bit jealous when Scotty told me what the two of you did last night. I love teaching yoga, but the sooner I can get my permanent residency and take the NVE, the better.'

It was almost painful listening to Nina talk about her plans for the future, knowing what she knew. Would she feel as positive about what was to come if she knew she was about to marry a man who had already been unfaithful to her?

There was only one way to find out.

'Nina, I really have to tell you something,' Claire said, the words tumbling out. 'Last night, after we operated on Autumn, Scotty —'

'Don't.'

It was a single word, but it shook Claire to her core. 'Sorry?' she whispered.

Nina left the desk and walked slowly towards Claire. When she reached her, she smiled and took her hand.

'You don't have to tell me anything, Claire,' she said.

'Nina, you don't understand. Scotty —'

'I know Scotty means a lot to you,' Nina cut in again. 'And I know you have questions about this wedding. I appreciate your concern, Claire. I truly do. But you don't need to worry about me.'

Claire didn't know what to think, particularly the way Nina emphasised the last word. She had never felt so mystified in her life. It seemed like Nina was telling Claire she knew about the kiss. But if she knew, why was she being so kind?

'Just tell me what's going on, Nina,' she implored. 'Please.'

Nina smiled, but she looked sad. 'I really wish I could, but it's not my place.'

Claire shook her head. 'I don't understand any of this.'

'That kind of makes two of us.' Nina's laugh eased the tension slightly. 'A week ago my life was normal, kinda boring even. I was just teaching yoga, going to the beach, and hanging out with the local vet. Then he calls me up and asks me to marry him and everything goes bananas.'

Claire frowned. 'Scotty proposed over the phone?'

'I know. So romantic, right?' Nina said, rolling her eyes. 'He'd been in Melbourne at that conference. He actually woke me up at, like, midnight. I was so annoyed because I teach a dawn class on Saturdays, so I always go to sleep early on Friday nights.'

It suddenly felt like all the air had been sucked from the room. 'This was Friday last week?' Claire said. She wanted to be sure she'd heard Nina correctly. 'Midnight last Friday?'

A curious look crossed Nina's face. 'Yeah,' she said slowly. 'Why?'

Claire began to tremble. Nina and the yoga studio seemed to fade away. She knew this feeling. The last time she'd felt it was eight years ago, the night Scotty had asked her to be his wife.

It was anger. Pure white-hot rage.

That Friday was the day Scotty had turned up at the clinic in Sydney with Autumn in the throes of heat stroke. Claire had met him for a drink that night and he'd told her about his quickfire engagement.

But she had been at home in bed by ten p.m., tangled in sweaty sheets and staring at the ceiling as she had tried to make sense of it all.

Now Nina was saying Scotty popped the question at midnight. That meant he proposed *after* he'd already told Claire he was getting married. He had lied to her.

He had lied all along.

CHAPTER SIXTEEN

Claire practically sprinted back to Vanessa's place, cursing herself all the way for choosing not to drive into town.

Yes, it was bad decisions all the way today – and every day.

Somewhere along the way, the fury she'd felt when she dashed out of the yoga studio had morphed into searing pain. Claire wasn't sure what hurt worse. Was it the fact that Scotty had lied to her a week ago when he'd said he was engaged to Nina before he actually was? Was it the fact that he'd *kept* lying the entire time she'd been back in Bindallarah?

Or was it the fact that something about seeing Claire in Sydney had made Scotty rush back to his hotel that Friday night, pick up the phone and propose marriage to a woman he'd known for a month?

Because that was clearly what had happened. Spending a couple of hours in Claire's company was apparently so unpleasant for Scotty that he had dashed off and asked Nina to marry him.

She couldn't believe she'd been so stupid. She had let Jackie's insistence that something still burned between Claire and Scotty start to sink in. Against her better judgement, Claire had let herself consider – even hope for – the possibility that there was a chance for them. And believing that possibility existed, even for a little while, had felt wonderful.

But Scotty, meanwhile, must have been watching the clock that night in the pub, counting the seconds until he could extricate himself from Claire and throw himself at the feet of the woman he *really* wanted.

He had asked Claire to come to his wedding out of some old sense of obligation. He had extended the invitation because he had good country manners, not because deep down he was uncertain and wanted Claire to talk some sense into him. Scotty didn't have doubts about marrying Nina. It was all in her head. He was right to suspect she had come to Bindy with an agenda. How could she have been so blind?

And – *oh God*. She had insisted on helping with the wedding arrangements, insinuating herself into proceedings like some oblivious party guest who won't leave at the end of the evening. And Scotty had agreed – he'd let her make a fool of herself because she meant nothing to him.

But he meant everything to her. She loved him. Not just as a friend, though he was the best friend she'd ever had. Not just as an old flame she still had a soft spot for. Not as someone who would drift in and out of her life over the years – a Christmas card here, a catch-up coffee when they happened to be in the same city.

That would never be enough, she understood now. Scotty had lied to her about the timing of his engagement, but Claire had been lying to herself about her feelings for him for years. She didn't reach out to him on social media six months ago hoping for some friendly chitchat. She wanted him back. Jackie, Vanessa, Gus – they were all right. Everyone saw it except Claire.

Nor did she come back to Bindallarah only because she was alarmed by Scotty's rush to the altar. He and Nina could have had a ten-year engagement and Claire still would have despaired at the match. She had appealed to him – to both of them – to cancel the wedding not because of some benevolent concern for their future happiness, but because of a selfish, craven fear for her own. She didn't want him to marry anyone. Ever. She only wanted him to want her.

Everything Claire had said and done over the past week was an attempt to hide the truth from herself. Every decision she'd made then unmade, every time she'd flip-flopped on whether or not it was her responsibility to try to prevent the wedding from going ahead, every time she had resolved to move on with her life only to find herself consumed once again by thoughts of Scotty – it was all a trick. Claire had thoroughly bamboozled herself. In trying to stop Scotty from tying the knot, she had instead tied *herself* up in knots. How would she ever begin to untangle the mess she'd made of her life?

Claire reached Vanessa's front door and raced inside. Ignoring Gus's startled greeting, she grabbed her car keys from the hall table and returned to the street. She got into her car, turned the key in the ignition and pressed the accelerator flat to the floor. She had to get away from this town – away from Scotty and Nina, away from the wedding that was thundering towards her like a freight train, away from all of it.

She had begun to think she might have been wrong about Bindallarah, even started to imagine a peaceful, happy life in the town she'd once loved so much she'd been heartbroken to leave. But that was crazy. There was nothing for Claire in Bindy. Trying to imagine a future here with Alex or anybody but Scotty Shannon was folly.

Claire was lost without Scotty. That was the agonising truth from which she'd been working so hard to distract herself. She had loved him since she was fifteen years old and she wanted him, *all* of him, all to herself. Forever.

But she was too late. That was never going to happen. And so she had to go.

'Mate, is Claire here?'

Chris looked up at Scotty and shook his head. He was on his knees, his arms submerged elbows-deep in a trough of sudsy water. It reeked of the antiseptic solution he was using to disinfect every item of horse tack at Cape Ashe Stud. With close to fifty horses on the property, it was going to take days, even with the help of the half-dozen stablehands he'd roped in. But there was no getting around it – it was the only way to prevent the Strangles that had nearly claimed Autumn from spreading to the rest of the stable.

'Nah,' Chris said. 'She was here last night to check on Autumn, but she didn't stay long. Have you tried her aunt's place?'

Damn it. Scotty had been to Vanessa's cottage last night, as soon as Nina had told him about her odd conversation with Claire at the yoga studio. It was Claire's cousin, Gus, who said she might have come up to Cape Ashe.

'How was she? Did she seem okay?' Scotty asked.

Chris stood up and shook the water from his hands. He regarded his brother with suspicion. 'She seemed a bit wound up, come to think of it. Not her usual chilled self,' he said. 'Why? You two have a blue or something?'

Scotty let out a long breath. 'I don't know, mate. Kind of. I saw her yesterday with Alex Jessop and . . . things are a bit weird.'

He wasn't about to tell Chris that he'd kissed Claire less than forty-eight hours ago almost exactly where he now stood. Or that late yesterday he'd had a phone call from Nina, who seemed to think she'd said something to Claire that she shouldn't have, though she couldn't work out what it was.

He needed to talk to Claire, straighten this mess out. He'd let things go way too far.

Chris crouched down and plunged his hands back into the trough again. 'So? Alex is a good bloke. You're not jealous, are you?' His tone was jovial, but when Scotty didn't respond his eyes widened in surprise. 'Wait, *are* you jealous?'

'I'm not jealous,' he said. 'What I am is a bloody idiot.'

'Whoa,' Chris replied. 'Do we need a beer for this?'

'It's ten a.m., bro.'

'I didn't ask what time it was.'

Scotty nodded and followed his brother down the driveway to the main house. Inside, Chris's wife, Amber, was helping their son, Matty, build a tower out of Lego blocks. She gave him a friendly wave from the living room as Chris took two bottles of beer from the fridge and gestured for Scotty to take a seat at the kitchen table.

Sometimes it struck Scotty as absurd that Chris was younger by two years. Scotty had always thought of himself as focused and decisive, always ready to step up or step in, but really it was Chris who was the more mature of the two of them. Chris just got on with things. While Scotty had worked twenty-four-seven to establish his clinic, Chris had taken over Cape Ashe Stud on their parents' retirement and quietly taken it to the next level. Shannon-bred horses were more highly coveted than ever before. His marriage to Amber was rock solid and drama free; along with Matty, they were a tight family unit working towards shared goals.

Scotty, meanwhile, had jumped from fling to fling while tearing himself up over a woman he'd loved and lost. Now he was a week away from marrying another woman – one he didn't love.

'How do you do it, Chris? This life business. I haven't got a clue what I'm doing,' Scotty said.

Chris twisted the tops from the beer bottles and slid one across the table to his brother. 'What's going on, mate?' he said, his eyes darkening with concern. 'You getting cold feet?'

'It's Claire. I can't get her out of my head.' He took a long pull on his beer.

'What are you talking about? You're about to *marry* Nina.'

'I am actually aware of that, Chris,' he said dryly. 'But I just . . . I can't let her go.'

'Mate, Claire let *you* go. Remember? Eight years ago, when you proposed and she left the country. Don't get me wrong, I like Claire, but you deserve better, Scotty. She's caused you enough pain over the years.' Chris drank from his own bottle.

'I *knew* she'd try to mess things up,' he added under his breath, almost to himself.

Part of Scotty knew Chris was right. Another part of him wanted to tell his little brother in no uncertain terms to watch his damn mouth.

'I'm the one who's messed everything up. I wasn't honest with Claire. I didn't tell her the real reason I'm marrying Nina,' he said.

Chris stared at him, open-mouthed. 'You're joking.'

Scotty shook his head. If *only* he were joking.

'So Claire thinks . . .?'

Scotty nodded.

'But *why*? Why would you do that?'

Scotty stared at the table in silence. He'd asked himself that question a million times.

'I think I was hoping,' he said eventually, 'that if Claire thought she was going to lose me for good, she might finally make up her mind.'

'Oh, mate,' Chris said quietly. 'Claire's not going to make a play for you if she thinks you're in love with Nina. She's not like that. You *are* a bloody idiot.'

Scotty laughed in spite of his misery. It was the first time he'd smiled in what felt like days. 'Have you been talking to Nina? She said pretty much the same thing yesterday. Yelled it at me in the middle of the main street, actually.'

Chris smiled. 'So what are you going to do?'

Scotty took a deep breath.

'I'm going to tell Claire the truth,' he said. 'But first I have to find her.'

CHAPTER SEVENTEEN

Claire thought she'd been rumbled on the first night. She'd chosen the furthest corner of Thorne Hill to pitch the tent she'd hastily bought at the discount store on Saturday afternoon – a copse of shady gums at the edge of Bindallarah Creek. There were a hundred acres between her and the farmhouse, and the undulating landscape ensured that neither she nor her car could be seen from the road. She figured Scotty wasn't likely to be kayaking on the creek or mending far-flung paddock fences when he had the clinic to run and Christmas Eve was just days away. Nobody would find her out here unless they knew exactly where to look – and the squire of Thorne Hill wouldn't be looking for her anyway.

But Claire hadn't counted on curious dogs.

She had just drifted into a fitful sleep on Saturday night when she was woken by an almighty splash. She lay in the stifling tent for what felt like an eternity, listening to something thrashing and snuffling in the creek just beyond the flimsy nylon. When at last she dared to switch on her torch and peek out, Claire had almost fainted with relief at the sight of Tank chasing moonbeams as they rippled across the still water.

The relief was swallowed by panic when it occurred to Claire that where Tank went, Scotty usually followed. But as the minutes ticked by with no sign of him, she realised the three-legged dog was simply doing his duty as Thorne Hill's resident canine, stopping to cool off as he patrolled the perimeter to make sure the property was free of unsavoury characters – characters like his master's heartsick ex-girlfriend, who was hiding in plain sight.

Tank didn't seem to have any suspicions about Claire, though. In fact, he actually seemed to like her. He had come back to visit every evening since, gratefully gulping whatever tidbits she had to share with him, then curling up next to her to listen to the rainbow lorikeets and cockatoos shrieking as the sun sank in the sky.

He watched her now as she dismantled the tent and rolled up her sleeping bag. She had hardly needed it – the mercury hadn't dipped below twenty degrees on any of the four nights Claire had been camping out. She wished she'd invested in a mosquito net or some insect repellent, though – she was covered in bites from top to toe. Her father would be appalled by her terrible outdoor skills.

Claire knew it was crazy to have come to Thorne Hill. How would she ever explain herself to Scotty if he found her there? But she couldn't stay in Bindallarah and risk running into him on the street, seeing the look of pity in his eyes as he was forced yet again to endure the presence of a woman who just wouldn't take the hint. The chances of finding herself face to face with him on his own property were much smaller, she decided.

Scotty had no inkling that Claire was there if his increasingly frantic 'Where are you?' text messages and missed calls were any indication. She wondered why he cared. Surely he was glad she'd left town. He must be grateful she wasn't still badgering him to cancel his wedding. Claire ignored all his attempts at contact until he texted to say he was on his way to Bindy police station to report her as a missing person. She replied then to say she was camping and had unreliable mobile reception. It was the same story she'd told Vanessa and Gus, though she'd made them promise not to say anything to Scotty about her whereabouts.

When she went to Cape Ashe Stud to check on Autumn on Saturday afternoon, Claire had briefly wondered if she could secrete herself there. But with Chris in the main house, his parents in their home up on the ridge and staff coming in and out of the property all day, it was much more likely that Claire would be sprung. Her heart gave a little lurch as she realised there would be even more activity at the property this week with wedding preparations in full swing. She should have told Chris that the equine quarantine meant the event couldn't go ahead, she thought. Shutting down the venue was a surefire way to derail a wedding. Any cartoon villain worth her salt should have known that.

Another missed opportunity.

Besides, Thorne Hill was the only place aside from Cape Ashe where Claire had ever felt truly happy. She had loved growing up there. Even when her parents' conversations had grown terse and her father had started drinking more, it had been her sanctuary, the one place she always felt at ease – until she was sent away to school and the life she had loved was ripped from her.

It now made more sense to her that Scotty had bought the place. It was an incredibly beautiful property and it deserved to be in the care of someone who saw that beauty, who understood its potential instead of bemoaning its limitations the way Jim always had. She hoped Scotty would be happy there, him and Nina and the children they would have one day.

She had retreated to Thorne Hill because she needed time to get her head together. She needed the space and tranquillity of her childhood home to try to find peace within herself. Claire had hoped that coming back to Thorne Hill would help her finally say goodbye to her past – all of it.

Had it worked? She didn't quite know yet. She was still in love with Scotty – that hadn't changed – but she'd accepted that it made no difference. She'd missed her chance with him. It hurt to admit it and it probably always would. But Claire hoped it would hurt less in time. Maybe the pain would become something she could live with.

'Off you go, Tank,' she said to the watchful dog. 'Go home. Where's Scotty? Find Scotty.'

Tank took off in the direction of the house as fast as his three stubby legs would carry him. Claire watched as he grew smaller and smaller in the distance, feeling a little guilty. She knew Scotty wouldn't be at the house. His and Nina's joint bucks' and hens' party was set to start in an hour. Scotty would be at the beach by now.

And soon, so would she.

*

Flaming bamboo torches lit the path through the dunes to the beach, but Claire would have found her way without them. The cacophony of music and merry voices mixed with the scent of barbequing meat and drifted into the night sky in a cloud of muggy sea air. The whole town seemed to have converged on Bindallarah Beach for Scotty and Nina's party. The sand was a writhing mass of people. The golden glow cast by the torches illuminated Santa hats and tinsel accessories on those who had clearly decided the event should do double duty as a Christmas party.

Claire paused at the bottom of the path, taking in the scene. She saw Nina right away, wearing a stunning beaded kaftan that sparkled as it caught the light. She was also wearing a tiara, a sash that proclaimed her the 'Bride-to-Be' in swirly pink lettering, and what looked suspiciously like penis-shaped earrings. Surrounded by a gaggle of women no doubt quizzing her for every detail of the wedding, Nina was smiling, but Claire thought she detected something guarded in her expression.

Nearby, she saw Chris Shannon with his wife, Amber, and Scotty's parents, Mike and Janine. Claire wondered who was looking after their little boy, Matty, when it seemed the entire district had turned out for the party. She saw Vanessa and Gus, who was swirling her wine around in her glass as ostentatiously as a sommelier.

But she didn't see Scotty anywhere.

Claire made her way hesitantly towards the party. Vanessa saw her approaching and waved. Claire headed in her direction, but she hadn't taken more than three steps when she felt a strong hand close around hers.

'There you are,' said a deep voice. 'I've been looking for you.'

Claire turned to see Alex, smiling warmly. Her heart sank a little as she realised she could add his name to the list of people she was fated to disappoint.

'You have?' she said.

'Yeah! You kind of vanished off the face of the earth after our date on Saturday.'

Claire winced. She had completely forgotten to let Alex know she was heading for the hills. Her head was all over the place, but that was no excuse for rudeness.

'I was hoping we could hang out again,' he went on. 'Was it something I said?'

Alex was joking, but Claire realised it kind of *was* something he had said. At breakfast on Saturday he had told her, *You were Scotty's girl – everybody knew that.* Nina's revelation about the timing of Scotty's proposal may have been the catalyst for her bush sabbatical, but Alex's offhand remark had stirred something in Claire – something long buried. She saw now that she had been thinking of herself as Scotty's girl for years, even though they weren't together, whether she deserved to or not. She'd expected Scotty to miraculously know that she might want him back some day – and to just wait patiently until that day arrived, no questions asked.

'Hey, Alex, on Saturday you said you wanted to be honest so that there were no misunderstandings,' Claire said. 'Can I do the same?'

Alex nodded. 'Yeah,' he said slowly.

'I think you're lovely, but I don't think there's a future for us. I'm really sorry.'

His face fell. 'Oh. Okay,' he said. 'Can I ask why? Is it because I was such a jerk in school? You can't forgive me?'

'No! Alex, no, it's not about that at all,' Claire said, squeezing the hand that still held hers.

She thought about giving him the easy answer. *I live in Sydney, you live here, our lives are too different, it would never work, et cetera, et cetera.* It would be a plausible excuse to hide behind. But Alex had been honest about his feelings for Claire. She knew he deserved the same from her.

She took a deep breath. 'It is about the past, though,' she said. 'Specifically, my total inability to let go of it. I thought I had, or I never would have gone out with you, but recent events have shown me that I've been kidding myself.'

Comprehension settled on Alex's face. 'Oh,' he said again. His gaze drifted across the crowd to Nina. 'This must be really tough for you then.'

Claire wanted to hug him. It was such a kind thing to say. Alex was a truly decent man. She wished she could make herself fall for him. For what felt like the hundredth time that day, she cursed her stubborn heart.

'It's been an experience,' she said with a hollow laugh. 'But I'm figuring some stuff out. I am really sorry if I led you on.'

His smile returned. 'Don't sweat it. I got to tick "go on a date with Claire Thorne" off my bucket list, so I'm all good. And I do appreciate you telling me where you're at.'

This time she did hug him.

'Hey,' Alex said when she released him. 'If it wouldn't be too weird, do you still want to go to the wedding together? I hate going stag to those things and, correct me if I'm wrong, but maybe you could use some moral support?'

Claire considered the offer. She was still determined to go to the wedding. It would be gut-wrenching to watch Scotty promise to love someone who wasn't her for the rest of his life, but she knew she needed to see it. Her brain knew Scotty was lost to her, but her heart still wouldn't believe it without incontrovertible proof. She needed that thing her American college friends always talked about: closure.

Would it be so bad if she had her emotional catharsis in the company of an attractive man who looked great in a suit?

'I would love that, Alex,' Claire said. 'Thank you.'

'Cool. I'll pick you up from your aunt's place at five. I'm going to grab a drink. Can I get you something?'

'Maybe later,' she said. 'I'm going to go say hi to a few people.'

Alex gave her shoulder a final reassuring squeeze and disappeared into the crowd. Claire did want a drink. She needed something to calm the jittery feeling in her stomach, but she also wanted to keep a clear head. She had to talk to Scotty. It was difficult enough keeping her wits about her when she was in his presence without alcohol clouding her thoughts.

Claire weaved through the sea of faces she knew so well, smiling and waving at people she'd known all her life, people who had welcomed her back to Bindallarah when she feared they would cast her off. The sense of familiarity was comforting, not oppressive as Claire had once felt. Tonight, this community felt like her safety net, a security blanket that had wrapped her up before and would again if things fell apart.

When things fell apart.

Finally, when Claire had walked what seemed like the length of the beach, she saw Scotty. He was walking away from his party, heading towards the path that led through the dunes with his head down and his hands in his pockets.

'Scotty!' she called, but he didn't seem to hear her over the pounding of the waves against the shore. Either that or he just didn't want to talk to her.

But she wanted to clear the air between them – to tell him she knew he hadn't been truthful about the timing of his engagement to Nina, and that she understood why. She broke into a jog and followed, catching up to him as he was halfway up the sandy path to the car park. It was quiet here, sheltered. The sound of the party receded behind the towering sandhills.

'Scotty, wait,' Claire called again.

This time he turned around and she was relieved to see he wasn't wearing high heels or comedy breasts or whatever else grooms were commonly forced to don at bucks' parties. In fact, Scotty was casually gorgeous in dark-blue jeans and a fitted button-down shirt.

But when Claire's gaze alighted on his face, she gasped. Maybe it was the long shadows cast by the full moon or the dim artificial light that extended from the car park, but Scotty looked awful. His eyes were dull and his face unshaven. He seemed to have aged ten years since Claire's last glimpse of him on Saturday morning.

When he realised it was her, Scotty closed his eyes and blew out a long breath. Claire heard him whisper something. She couldn't be certain, but it sounded like *Thank God*.

It seemed like hours passed before he opened his eyes again. 'I thought you'd gone,' Scotty said flatly.

Claire felt herself deflate. He didn't want anything to do with her. This was going to be harder than she'd imagined.

'Nope, still here,' she said. 'I'm sorry, Scotty. I know you don't want to see me, but I just need to —'

'No, I mean I thought you'd left. I was *worried* that you'd left,' he cut in. 'Nobody's heard from you in days.'

'Oh . . .' She wasn't sure how to respond. She thought Scotty wanted her out of his life – now it sounded like he was chastising her for not keeping him properly informed. 'I went camping. I sent you a message.'

'One message,' he spat, 'that didn't tell me where you were or who you were with. I thought something had happened to you. I've been going out of my mind, Claire.'

Claire gritted her teeth and fought to damp down the irritation that sparked inside her. *What do you care where I go?* she wanted to shout. *You're about to get married, and you've been lying to me all along.*

Instead she said, 'Where are you going? The party's this way.' She attempted a smile as she jerked her thumb over her shoulder.

'I'm going into town to get more drinks,' Scotty replied. Then his shoulders sagged and he sighed. 'Actually, that's not true. Chris offered to go, but I said I would because I needed an excuse to get out of there.'

At once, the prickly feeling in her stomach was washed away by concern. 'Why?' Instinctively, she took a step towards him. 'Scotty, are you okay? What's going on?'

He looked at her then. *Really* looked at her, his gaze asking a question she couldn't comprehend. 'I lied to you.'

'I know.'

She heard his sharp intake of breath. 'You know? How?'

Claire looked down at her feet, at the sand covering her toes. The fine white powder was cold despite the warmth of the evening and Claire wished she'd worn shoes. She felt chilled to the bone.

'Nina told me,' she said. When Scotty tipped his head back and looked to the sky she rushed to add, 'She didn't mean to. I put two and two together and figured out that you proposed to her after we went out that night – *after* you'd already told me you were engaged.'

His gaze returned to her. 'And?'

Claire squared her shoulders. This was it. 'And it's okay,' she said. 'I understand why you did it.'

Scotty studied her for a long moment. 'I don't think you do,' he said.

'I know you were trying to spare my feelings, Scotty. You were worried I'd read something deeper into our friendship – something that isn't there – and you knew that Nina's the one for you, so you jumped the gun in telling me the news.' She shrugged. 'It's quite sweet in a ham-fisted kind of way. I do appreciate you looking out for me and I'm sorry I've been such a nightmare.'

There. She had said her piece. Leaving out the inconvenient I'm-still-in-love-with-you part, obviously, but that was her own sorry mess to untangle. The most important things were apologising for her meddling and trying to salvage some semblance of a friendship with Scotty. She would figure out the rest later. What was it they said in those twelve-step programs – the first step is admitting you have a problem?

Scotty's mouth hung open. He looked at Claire like he didn't know whether to laugh or cry.

'You think I lied because I was trying to do the right thing by you?' he said. 'Trying to do you a *favour*?'

Claire arched an eyebrow. 'Weren't you?'

'No! I was trying to . . .' Scotty faltered and looked to the heavens once more. It was as if he was hoping the stars would spell out the words he was looking for. 'Did you?'

'Did I what?'

'Did you' – he made air quotes with his fingers – '"read something deeper into our friendship?" Did you think we were going to be more than friends?'

She bit her lip. 'I don't think I realised it at the time, but . . . yes. There was probably a part of me that hoped there might still be a chance for us.'

Scotty groaned. It was a raw, primal sound and it shook Claire to her core.

'But I don't feel that way now,' she said, reaching it out to him, pressing her palm to his chest. 'I promise.' It wasn't technically a lie. She loved him, but she had finally stopped kidding herself that there was any hope for them.

'Then what are you doing here, Claire?'

An uneasy feeling settled in the pit of Claire's stomach. 'What?'

'Why are you here? In Bindy? You told me on Saturday night that you came back to try to convince me to cancel my wedding, but I *am* going to marry Nina on Christmas Eve,' he said with heat in his voice.

'I know that,' she said meekly.

'Have you changed your mind then? Or do you still think it's a bad idea for me and Nina to get married?'

She hesitated, then nodded. Knowing that her feelings for Scotty were the real reason she didn't want him to tie the knot in four days' time didn't change the fact that marrying a woman he knew virtually nothing about was, empirically speaking, completely insane.

'So if you're not sticking around so that you can support me on my wedding day, then what is it?' he demanded.

Claire turned her head and peered into the darkness. She felt helpless. 'What do you want me to say, Scotty?'

'I just want you to be honest with me. With yourself,' he said, his voice rising with every word. 'You say you hoped there was a chance for us. Why didn't you do something about it? You tracked me down, remember? You had months before I met Nina to make a decision about us. But you didn't.'

He took a step back and Claire's hand, still pressed to his chest, fell away. 'You don't want me, Claire. You've made that clear, over and over again,' he said. 'And I can't keep waiting and hoping that you might change your mind. I'm not going to keep putting my heart on the line for you to stomp all over it.'

Claire reeled. Scotty's words were like a physical blow. She had no idea, not a clue that he felt that way.

You had months to make a decision about us.

All that time they'd spent reconnecting – time Claire had spent convincing herself she wasn't falling in love with him again – Scotty was just waiting for her to want him.

She had thought it impossible that Scotty could still have feelings for her after the way she had broken his heart eight years earlier. Everything that had happened since she'd come back to Bindallarah Claire had tried to see through his eyes – the eyes of a man who'd stopped loving her long ago. But now she saw that he hadn't stopped loving her back then. Incredibly, he had held her in his heart through all the years of silence, in the hope that she would find her way back to him.

Every time they'd swapped silly messages, she suddenly understood that, in his own way, Scotty was asking her the same question: *Will you love me again?* But Claire hadn't answered him. She'd been afraid to tell him what she wanted, afraid even to admit it to herself.

She had been paralysed by indecision, by the fear of making the wrong move – and so, in the end, doing nothing had become a decision in itself.

'Why didn't you tell me?' she whispered.

'Because, as you pointed out just the other night, I have a bad habit of confusing what I want with what you want. I didn't want to make that mistake again.' He laughed and it was a desolate sound. 'So I guess I just made a whole lot of different mistakes instead.'

Claire felt wretched. If only Scotty knew how desperately she *did* want him, how having lost him was eating her up inside. She had emerged from her hideaway at Thorne Hill determined to let him go, but now she opened her mouth to tell Scotty that she loved him, that she hadn't stopped in thirteen years and she never would.

But the words wouldn't come. Tears came instead, rolling down her face like plump summer raindrops.

Claire's own inaction had driven Scotty into Nina's arms. He wasn't asking her to confess her feelings now. He was telling her she was too late. He might have still loved her six months ago, but since then Claire had done everything in her power to obliterate those feelings. Her eleventh-hour declaration of undying love would make no difference.

Scotty watched her cry, his face stony. He made no move to comfort her.

'I didn't know,' she managed to choke out at length. 'I'm so sorry, Scotty. I just didn't know.'

As Claire turned and walked sadly back to the beach, she thought she heard Scotty call her name, but it was consumed by the sound of the waves and her own ragged sobs.

It was all too late.

CHAPTER EIGHTEEN

Nina found him pacing the car park a few minutes later.

'Hey,' she called out. 'Everything okay?'

Scotty looked up to see his fiancée gliding towards him, her brightly coloured dress billowing around her like a cloud. God, she was a stunning woman. He knew every bloke in town thought so. Why couldn't he fall in love with her? Why didn't the sight of Nina wearing a beautiful dress in the moonlight have the same effect on his body as the sight of Claire in hospital scrubs in a veterinary supply cupboard?

'I saw Claire head up this way,' she said as if she were reading his mind. She reached out and squeezed his arm. 'And then I saw her a few minutes ago, walking down the beach in tears.'

Shame sat like a heavy stone in Scotty's gut. He'd promised himself he would tell Claire the truth tonight. Instead he'd yelled at her and made her feel once again that everything was her fault. He was a coward.

'I didn't tell her,' he said.

Nina tried unsuccessfully to conceal her dismay. 'Oh, Scotty. Why not?'

He shook his head. *Why not?* He'd had plenty of opportunity, not just a few minutes ago, but for the past two weeks. He'd even started to come clean just now, but when he admitted he'd lied and Claire said she already knew, he'd been knocked off his axis.

Then she'd revealed that what she knew was only the tip of an iceberg of deception, and he just couldn't bring himself to disabuse her of the belief that he was still a good guy. Talk about clutching at straws.

It had been like a punch to the throat, Claire saying she understood why he'd told her he was engaged when he wasn't. All the air just went out of him. She thought he was trying to protect her, when the whole time he'd thought only of protecting himself, of getting what he wanted no matter what it took.

What he wanted was *her*. Claire Thorne. She was complicated and mercurial, she excited and infuriated him in equal measure, and she'd had his heart since he was sixteen years old.

Except she didn't know it – Scotty's clumsy manoeuvring had made sure of that.

'She knows we got engaged after I saw her in Sydney,' he told Nina.

'Aha,' she replied. 'So I *did* put my foot in my mouth when we spoke at the studio. I'm so sorry, sweetie.'

'It's not your fault, Nina. All of this is my doing.'

'So just tell her the rest of it. Before it's too late. Not telling Claire the whole story is only going to make things worse,' she said.

Scotty shook his head. 'I can't. Maybe if I'd been honest from the start, she might have understood. But not now. I know her – she'll never forgive me.'

It's already too late.

'Then . . .' Nina used her index finger to turn Scotty's head towards her. She looked him directly in the eye. 'We should call off the wedding.'

'What? No!' he said. 'Nina, I would never do that to you.'

She pressed her hand to his cheek. 'Scotty, you're a good man and an incredible friend,' she said softly. 'But you're getting nothing out of this and you stand to lose so much.'

'That's not true.'

Nina smiled. 'Which part?'

'Anyway, the wedding is in four days. Everything is arranged.' *Thanks to Claire.* 'We can't cancel now.'

'We can't cancel the *event*,' Nina said pointedly. 'But we still have two weeks after that to decide if we're going to get married.'

Scotty sighed. He seemed to be doing that a lot lately. 'I gave you my word. I won't let you down.'

'Mr Decisive,' she said. 'Solver of the world's problems. Don't forget, Scotty, that you don't have to cling to a mistake just because you spent a lot of time making it.'

'That sounds like something straight out of the yoga handbook.'

Nina arched an eyebrow. 'Maybe it is, but it doesn't make it any less true.' Her tone turned serious. 'I'm giving you an out. No strings attached. It's up to you.'

'Thank you,' Scotty said. 'I'll think about it.'

But he knew he wouldn't call off the wedding. He'd made a promise to Nina and she didn't deserve to have her life turned upside down because her fiancé had a schoolboy crush he couldn't get over. Scotty's word was his bond. He always did what he said he would.

There was no reason to cancel the wedding anyway. He knew where Claire stood. She didn't want him. She had been unequivocal about that – he'd just been too hard-headed to see it. In fact, Scotty understood now that Claire had been telling him for years that she could do without his love. It was time he started listening.

'Come on,' she said. 'Let's get back to our party. People will be wondering where we've got to.'

Nina turned and went back down the path to the beach. Somehow, Scotty managed to put one leaden foot in front of the other and trail after her.

He followed his wife-to-be back to a celebration for their sham wedding, while the woman he'd always dreamed he would marry was out there somewhere, alone, in the dark.

The shrill ring of her mobile phone roused Claire from sleep on Thursday morning. She sat up with a start, her head spinning. Her mouth felt as dry as the sand on Bindallarah Beach. But this wasn't a hangover. She hadn't had a single drink at Scotty and Nina's party.

This was *actual* sand. She had fallen asleep on the beach and she was covered in it. Claire felt parched and shaky. She figured the salty air had made her dehydrated – that or the hours of violent sobbing she'd enjoyed the night before.

Without warning, a deluge of gut-wrenching snapshots of the evening crashed into her brain with the force of a rogue wave catching a swimmer unawares. Realising she'd wasted months trying to delude herself that she wasn't still in love with Scotty, when all he needed to hear was that she was. Learning he'd been ready to give them a second – or was it a third? – chance if only Claire had managed to stop vacillating long enough to make a decision.

Finally understanding that Scotty would not be coming back to her. Ever.

Claire fought back a fresh batch of tears as the magnitude of her loss sank in. She had squandered her last chance to have the love of the only man who had ever made her happy – and she hadn't even known she was doing it.

Her phone trilled insistently and with trembling fingers Claire retrieved it from her bag. *Good old Bindy*, she thought as she saw that her wallet and keys were still in there. Searching for her belongings after waking up on a Sydney beach wouldn't be such a heartening experience, she knew.

Claire frowned as she saw Jackie's name flash up on the screen. She had been keeping her friend up to date on the disaster that was her life in Bindallarah via text message, but they hadn't spoken since Claire had left Sydney nearly two weeks earlier.

'Jackie?' she said by way of a greeting. 'What's up?'

She expected Jackie to launch into a detailed description of some horse emergency she needed help with. Instead she said, 'Thirty days.'

Claire's brain was still too foggy to say anything more intelligent than 'Huh?'

'I've been thinking about your one-and-only's shotgun wedding,' Jackie said.

'It's not a shotgun wedding, Jac. Nina's not pregnant. I've seen her sink half a bottle of rosé in one go.' It was a catty thing to say, but she couldn't muster any magnanimity at this hour. She recalled the horrified look that had crossed Nina's face when Claire had jokingly mentioned her future grandchildren the day they'd gone dress shopping. She was certain no bundles of joy were imminent.

'Maybe not, but something just didn't sit right with me about it,' Jackie went on.

'That makes two of us.'

'Right? So I finally got around to doing a little bit of googling.' Jackie suddenly fell silent.

'And?' Claire prompted. Her friend was acting like Hercule Poirot laboriously explaining how he'd solved a murder mystery.

'And it turns out you can't get hitched in New South Wales until you've lodged a Notice of Intended Marriage,' she said triumphantly.

'So? I'm sure Scotty and Nina are on top of the paperwork.' Claire frowned.

'No,' Jackie said, and Claire could practically hear her rolling her eyes. 'You can't legally get married until thirty days *after* you lodge that notice. They got engaged on the Friday night of the heat stroke, right?'

It was seeing Scotty in the flesh after eight long years that made that day significant in Claire's memory rather than Autumn's first brush with death, but she replied, 'Yeah.'

'And Scotty didn't get back to Brindywoopwoop until the Monday after you saw him here in Sydney?'

'*Bindallarah*.' Jackie was doing it on purpose now, surely. 'And yes, that's right.'

'So even if he and Little Miss Yoga were at the registry to file their form at nine o'clock on the Tuesday morning —'

Claire could suddenly hear her heartbeat pounding in her ears. 'They can't legally marry until . . .' She squeezed her eyes shut and pictured a calendar in her head. 'The middle of January.'

'January eighteenth, to be exact,' Jackie confirmed.

'So . . .' Claire shook her head, trying to make sense of it.

'So what the hell is this charade you're subjecting yourself to on Christmas Eve?' Jackie supplied.

The words on the tip of Claire's tongue were a little more colourful, but Jackie had summed up the gist of her feelings.

'Are you sure about this, Jackie?' she said. 'There must be some explanation. Are there exceptions to the thirty-day rule?'

'There are,' she replied, 'but none of them seem to fit. It's stuff like work or travel commitments, religious reasons, legal proceedings. I'll text you a link. Call me back when you've read it.'

Claire promised she would and ended the call. Seconds later, a text message arrived containing a link to the website for the NSW Registry of Births, Deaths and Marriages. Claire clicked on it and her internet browser opened automatically. She suddenly felt absurdly grateful for Bindallarah's decent mobile phone reception. Only a few years ago, she would have had to dash back to Vanessa's place and fire up her wheezy old desktop computer to try to figure out why the man she inconveniently still loved had lied to her about his wedding date.

None of it made sense. Why were Scotty and Nina racing to the altar on Christmas Eve if their union couldn't be legal for another fortnight? Was this what Nina was hinting at when she said it wasn't her place to tell Claire what was really going on?

Claire couldn't imagine any reason they would have been granted an exemption. It was unlikely either of them had to race off to deal with some urgent work-related thing. She couldn't think of any pressing commitment that would require a veterinarian's attention over the Christmas period, at least not outside of Bindallarah. And yoga was hardly a deadline-driven occupation.

Religious reasons were out, too. Scotty was an atheist and, while Nina obviously had a spiritual side, Claire was fairly confident she wasn't a regular churchgoer. Besides, marrying at Cape Ashe Stud meant they had to have a civil rather than religious ceremony – surely, if she were devout, Nina would have insisted on a church wedding.

Legal proceedings? Claire had done jury duty years earlier and knew the courts shut down over the Christmas period, so that was out. For a second she wondered whether Scotty or Nina was about to be sent to prison, but dismissed the idea as crazy just as quickly. *At least try to stick within the realms of reality, Thorne.*

Claire kept reading. There was one possibility listed on the website that Jackie hadn't mentioned: medical reasons. She broke out in a cold sweat.

She knew who that exemption was for. It was for people who were sick. Really sick. People who weren't going to make it.

She dialled Jackie's number.

'What do you think?' was her friend's opening gambit.

'One of them must be terribly ill,' Claire said, her voice barely a whisper.

There was a pause. 'That's what you've come up with?' Jackie said eventually.

Claire couldn't respond. If she tried to speak she knew she would scream.

As if sensing her turmoil, Jackie huffed out a breath. 'Claire, get a grip. Nobody's dying,' she said.

'How do you know?'

'Because if they'd been granted an exemption on that basis they'd be married by now. Those are for people who have hours to live, not weeks.' Her words were blunt, but there was kindness in her voice. She must have felt Claire's panic. 'Trust me. Scotty is a *very* healthy-looking man. He certainly didn't look sick to me the other week, and didn't you say Nina's some glowing Italian-American supermodel?'

Jackie was right. Neither Scotty nor Nina appeared to be unwell, and Claire was certain the bush telegraph would have told her otherwise. Illness was almost impossible to hide in a town the size of Bindallarah. The CWA would organise a meal-delivery roster at the first sign of a sniffle.

Claire stared out to sea as she tried to fit the pieces of the puzzle together in her mind. The overcast conditions of the past few days had blown through and the sky was a deep, cloudless blue. It was shaping up to be a spectacular Bindy Christmas – at least in terms of the weather.

She felt herself start to relax a little. She needed to take Jackie's advice and try to maintain some semblance of perspective. It was just so hard to do when she was beginning to doubt whether anything Scotty had told her was the truth.

'What else could it be? None of these exemptions applies,' she said. 'So how can they be getting married on Christmas Eve if they only lodged their Notice of Intent nine days ago?'

'That's exactly my point. They can't be,' Jackie replied.

'But that means . . .'

'Yep. The most obvious option is usually the answer. This wedding – or at least this wedding ceremony – is as fake as a three-dollar note.'

CHAPTER NINETEEN

Alex gave a low whistle as Claire opened the front door on Sunday evening.

'Wow, Thorne,' he said. 'You scrub up all right.'

'Is it okay?' she said, casting a critical eye over her outfit for what must have been the fiftieth time.

She was wearing another one of Gus's cast-offs. Gus had taken one look at the random assortment of dresses Claire had thrown into her suitcase two weeks earlier and declared them all hideous. She had to admit her cousin had a point. Claire hadn't packed anything that was really suitable for a wedding, because she had left Sydney determined there wouldn't *be* a wedding. In her head, she had been certain she could convince Scotty that marrying Nina was lunacy.

How wrong she had been. About everything.

So now she was wearing the dress Gus had worn to her school formal: a dove-grey gown with cap sleeves, a lace bodice and a flowing chiffon skirt. With the help of a

YouTube tutorial, Claire had wrangled her long curls into a fishtail braid, which hung over one shoulder.

'Okay? It's breathtaking,' Alex said and Claire felt her cheeks flush. 'Are you really sure about this "just friends" business? Because I've got to be honest, I'm having some distinctly unfriendly thoughts about you right now.'

She laughed, grateful for Alex's bawdy humour. Maybe a bit of levity would help alleviate the feeling that she was going to a funeral rather than a wedding.

'You're looking pretty sharp yourself, Jessop,' she shot back, mimicking his jovial tone. If he noticed that she'd sidestepped his question, he didn't say so. He *did* look great, this time wearing a tailored eggplant-coloured suit. Once again, Claire silently scolded her obstinate heart for refusing to be moved by anyone other than Scotty. 'Not many men can pull off a purple suit, but you're working it.'

'Well, you know, it's Christmas Eve. I figured I could get away with something a little more festive. Shall we?' Alex cocked his elbow and Claire took it, letting him lead her to the gleaming sports car parked at the kerb.

'Nice wheels,' she said as she eased herself into the low-slung passenger seat and gathered her flouncy skirts around her. 'Not much good on dirt roads, though. I'm guessing you won't be taking over your parents' farm one of these days?'

He laughed and started the engine. 'Nah, that's more Callum's scene,' he said, naming his older brother. 'I may be a country boy, Claire, but this baby has only ever seen tarmac.'

They sat in companionable silence for a few minutes as Alex drove out of town and up into the hinterland. The sky above the hills was beginning to turn a dusky-pink colour. It was a beautiful evening for a sunset wedding – even a pretend one.

'So you must know Nina pretty well, being her boss,' Claire said, affecting what she hoped was a neutral tone.

She saw Alex cast a sidelong glance in her direction. 'Yeah, she's a pretty fantastic woman,' he replied. 'I like her a lot.'

'So do I,' Claire said. She meant it. She thought Nina was great – just not for Scotty. 'Were you surprised when she and Scotty got engaged so quickly?'

Alex considered the question. 'Yes and no,' he said eventually. 'I didn't realise they were that serious, to be honest. I mean, I knew she and Scotty had been out a few times, but I talk to Nina literally every day and she never mentioned marriage.'

Ha, Claire thought sourly. She knew what it was like to think you knew someone and yet still be totally blindsided by their life choices.

'But then,' Alex went on, 'you know what Scotty's like. Once he makes up his mind about something, that's it. He's the most bull-headed bloke I reckon I've ever met. All the Shannons are the same. They should raise cows, not horses.'

Was that true? Claire had never considered Scotty's intractable nature in the broader context of his family. But thinking about it, she realised Alex had a point. Chris was every bit as determined as his older brother. He'd been a new broom at Cape Ashe Stud – Claire had been blown away by the changes she'd noticed there, all of which Chris had proudly told her he'd made since taking the reins.

Even the boys' parents, Mike and Janine, shared the stubborn streak. Scotty loved to recount the tale of how everyone in the district told them they were crazy when they announced they were establishing a horse stud. *This is cattle country* was the consensus in Bindallarah at the time. *You want to breed horses, head six hundred clicks south to the Hunter Valley.*

But the young Shannons wouldn't be dissuaded and their sons had obviously inherited their tenacity.

'What do you think this wedding is about, Alex?' Claire said. 'Is it the real deal?'

'That's an interesting question,' he replied, his tone guarded. 'Don't you think it is?'

Claire gazed out of the window at the trees whizzing past. 'I don't know what to think any more.'

Alex didn't respond. He turned off the road and eased his fancy car into the driveway of Cape Ashe Stud. The flaming bamboo torches that had lit the path to Scotty and Nina's beach bash on Wednesday night had been recycled – now wrapped in silver tinsel, they led the way past the main house and stables to the large paddock that had been set aside for guest parking.

Alex found a spot and killed the engine, then hurried to Claire's side of the car to open her door. She giggled as he extended a hand like he was her butler.

'Such a gentleman,' she said, not bothering to try to hide her surprise. 'How come you were never like this at school?' Claire grasped his fingers and tried to appear elegant as she hoisted herself out of the car.

'My motives are purely selfish. Those shoes you're wearing are totally impractical for walking on grass. I just don't want you taking me down with you when you fall over, which you definitely will.'

She elbowed him good-naturedly, not wanting to admit he was on the money. The vertiginous heels Gus had convinced Claire to wear not only mercilessly pinched her feet, they also sank into the grass with every step. She was glad she'd thought to bring a pair of thongs in the car with her at the last minute – there was no way she'd make it through the night in her borrowed shoes.

It was going to be a long walk to the fairy-lit clearing she could see at the top of a small rise behind the paddock. Claire could see dozens of guests already mingling in the velvet dusk. Just as at the beach party, some wore Christmas hats with their wedding finery. She gasped as she spied Nina among them.

She knew this was a low-key wedding, but she hadn't expected to see the bride casually chatting with well-wishers before the ceremony. Wasn't she supposed to arrive fashionably late and make a grand entrance?

Though one glance at Nina told Claire she would make a show-stopping entrance no matter when she arrived. She looked incredible in the pale-green gown Claire had helped her pick out. Her hair tumbled down her back in loose waves and a single diamond pendant glittered at her throat.

Nina looked up and saw Claire and Alex approaching. She waved and even from a distance Claire could see the anxiety in her eyes.

She looks scared.

Not nervous. Not like she felt the excited last-minute jitters expected of a woman about to marry the love of her life. This was doubt. This was fear.

Or was Claire just projecting her own feelings about the wedding onto Nina? It was probably a figment of her imagination – just like so many other things had been lately.

She felt panic start to claw at her as she scanned the growing crowd for Scotty. If Nina was on meet-and-greet duty, he surely would be too. She wasn't prepared to see him, to watch him smile and laugh and shake the hands of the people who had come to watch him get married. *She* had come to watch him get married, because she knew it was the only way to rid herself of the dream of him – to exorcise his ghost once and for all. But she wasn't ready. Not yet.

She needed a few more minutes to get used to the idea that she was about to say goodbye to the only man she'd ever loved.

'Are you okay, Claire?' Alex asked suddenly.

'Yes,' she said a little too quickly. 'Why wouldn't I be?'

He looked down at her white-knuckled grip on his hand. 'No reason. It just kind of seems like you're trying to break my fingers.'

'God, sorry, Alex,' she said, releasing his hand. He shook it and flexed his fingers several times. 'Actually, you know what? You were right about these ridiculous shoes. They're killing me already. I'm going to go put my thongs on.'

He flashed a cheeky grin. 'I'm not one to say I told you so . . .'

'Yes, yes, you're very astute,' she said, returning his smile. 'See you up there?'

He nodded and continued along the path. Claire took off her shoes and breathed a sigh of relief as the pain in her feet abated. She hurried back to the unlocked car and threw the offending heels in the back seat, then slid her feet into her rubber thongs.

And then she kept right on walking – away from the wedding.

She went to the stables and paused, listening. Usually she would hear the soft chorus of a dozen or so mares chuntering in their stalls. But tonight all was quiet, the horses having been dispersed for their own safety to isolated paddock shelters dotted around the Shannons' vast property.

Only one horse remained in the stable block. Claire slipped into Autumn's stall and found the mare standing motionless but for the occasional swish of her tail. Her stillness alarmed Claire and she hurried to her, checking that her trach tube and incision site were clean and running her hands over her satiny hair to ensure she wasn't too warm. Everything seemed normal, aside from the distended belly that told Claire the arrival of Autumn's foal was imminent.

She realised that Autumn's inactivity wasn't caused by illness. She was still simply because she was tired. She was heavily pregnant and had fought her way back from the brink of death twice in as many weeks. The mare was just trying to rest, to replenish and ready herself for her next great challenge.

'I think I could learn a thing or two from you, girl,' Claire said softly as she stroked Autumn's muzzle. 'Less do, more be. Maybe I wouldn't be quite so crazy then, huh?'

'You're not *that* crazy,' came a voice from behind.

She turned to see Scotty leaning against the doorframe, his hands thrust in his pockets. Her heart sank as her eyes devoured him. He wore a charcoal-grey suit with a skinny black tie and had used a copious amount of gel to tame his hair. He looked like a schoolboy going to his first job interview. Or a country vet on his way to go through the motions of pretending to marry a stranger.

He was beautiful.

She heard Scotty's breath catch in his throat as he looked at her. 'God, Claire. You look . . .' His gaze travelled the length of her body, then back again. He cleared his throat. 'That's a lovely dress.'

'What are you doing here, Scotty? Shouldn't you be getting ready to say "I do"?' Had he come to remind her that she'd missed out? To warn her not to make a scene and ruin his big day?

To tell her she wasn't welcome there at all?

He came into the stall, stepped close enough to her that she could feel the heat of him radiating against her bare skin. When he looked down at her, Claire felt small and exposed. He towered over her in her flat shoes. Scotty had no idea how easy it would be for him to break her open in that moment.

'I've hardly seen you this week,' he said. 'Not since . . .'

A bitter laugh escaped her lips. He made it sound like they were old girlfriends who were overdue a catch-up. 'Not since Wednesday night,' she supplied. 'I didn't think you wanted to see me, Scotty. You seemed pretty adamant that I've done my dash with you.'

He looked away from her, absently reaching out to pat Autumn's nose. Seconds passed, but it felt like days.

They hadn't spoken at all since the party. Unlike the volley of calls and messages he'd sent after he kissed her and she fled to Thorne Hill, this time Scotty hadn't even tried to contact her. Claire was glad. She wasn't sure she would have been able to summon the courage to confront him with what she knew about the wedding. She didn't know if she was strong enough to hear him lie to her again.

'The things I said to you at the beach that night . . . I shouldn't have unburdened myself like that, dumped all that stuff on you. It wasn't fair to you,' Scotty said. 'I'm sorry, Claire.'

Sorry he said it the way he did, she thought, but not sorry about what he'd said. He meant every word. He was done with her.

'Look, Scotty, if my being here tonight makes you uncomfortable, you can say so,' she said. 'I'll understand if you want me to leave. I'm sure Alex or Vanessa won't mind running me back into town.'

Scotty took a step back. 'Alex? You came with him?'

Claire nodded.

'And, what, are you two together now?' He clenched his jaw.

She frowned. 'No, we're just friends,' she said deliberately. 'What does it matter to you anyway? You're about to marry Nina.'

Claire bit her lip. It was the closest she'd come yet to admitting to Scotty that she was jealous of his intended; that she wished she were in Nina's glamorous shoes instead of her own cheap thongs. She could never compare. She should have seen that from the start.

It was Scotty's turn to laugh; his was every bit as bitter as hers had been. 'You're right. It shouldn't matter. But it does,' he said. He closed the gap between them and let his hands rest on her hips. He leaned in close. 'You've never done your dash with me, Thorne,' he whispered.

Her thoughts were a maelstrom as his lips brushed her ear. *This is wrong! He's five minutes away from getting married!*

And yet Claire felt her body respond to his touch the way it always had. She rose up on her tiptoes and tilted her face towards him, aching for another kiss that would feel like the first – the one they'd shared on the roof of the stables thirteen Christmas Eves ago.

This would be their last first kiss.

She closed her eyes as she felt his warm breath on her cheek. And then . . .

'Scotty! Where are you, bro?' Chris's voice shouted from somewhere close by. 'Let's get this show on the road.'

'Time to rock'n'roll, mate,' yelled another voice, followed by a burst of male laughter.

Scotty pulled away from her as sharply as if she had burned him. His emerald eyes widened in horror. He backed out of the stall.

'I'm so sorry,' Scotty said. 'For everything.'

And then he was gone.

Scotty stood at the altar, sweating into his wool suit as the guests took their seats. The temperature had to be close to thirty degrees, despite the lengthening shadows. Why had he picked Christmas Eve? What kind of idiot got married outdoors in the middle of summer?

Nina stood opposite, looking gorgeous in her green dress. But she wouldn't meet his gaze and Scotty felt her hand trembling when he took it in his.

They'd decided not to bother with the whole walking-down-the-aisle thing. None of Nina's family was in attendance, so there would be no traditional 'giving away' moment. There wasn't much about this wedding that was traditional – least of all the fact that it wasn't really a wedding at all.

It looked the part, though. The branches of the surrounding trees were festooned with fairy lights and the streamers and balloons Claire had bought. Scotty was sure he hadn't hung them the way she would have, but decorating wasn't exactly his strong suit.

He saw Claire slip into the chair next to Alex Jessop and wondered if she'd noticed the decorations, if she thought he'd created a fitting setting for a hasty betrothal. Alex turned and said something to Claire. She nodded and gave him a shaky smile, but her eyes glistened. Scotty knew she'd been crying.

Scotty's heart rate kicked up a gear as he watched Valda Chadwick advancing down the aisle towards him, clutching an official-looking leather compendium. Nina had balked when he'd booked a real marriage celebrant, but Scotty had insisted. It wasn't going to look legit if he asked Ken Broome from the footy club to officiate, was it? And Valda was okay with performing the fancy ceremony now and then doing it again, officially, in January.

A hush descended on the crowd as Valda took her place in front of them. Nina suddenly turned to Scotty, panic in her eyes.

'Are you sure, Scotty?' she whispered. 'Are you *really* sure you want to do this? It's still not too late to change your mind.'

'Shall we get started?' Valda said pleasantly.

He gazed out at the congregation – if that was the right word for a group of people witnessing a civil ceremony that wasn't legally binding between two people who didn't love each other. The faces of two hundred friends, acquaintances and family members beamed back at him. They all thought they were watching a fairytale love story play out: the joining of two people who were so mad about each other they decided to throw caution to the wind and get married after just six weeks.

Well, all but one of the wedding guests felt that way. As Scotty's gaze alighted on Claire, something broke inside him. She was the only person in his life who had expressed doubts about the speed of his relationship with Nina. The only one who seemed to care about his wellbeing – or his sanity. Her concern for him wasn't driven by the feelings he'd so fervently hoped she still had for him, but by genuine care nonetheless. Care that he'd repaid with lies and manipulation and more lies.

Claire's face was the picture of misery. Hardly surprising, since he'd nearly kissed her just minutes ago and then left her alone in a horse stall while he went off to marry another woman.

Scotty turned to Valda. 'Absolutely.' He tried for resolute, although his voice sounded flat. Best to just get on with it now. He had no choice but to lie in the bed he'd made and let Claire find someone who actually deserved her.

Valda opened her compendium. 'Friends and family, on behalf of Nina and Scott, I would like to welcome you all to the beautiful Cape Ashe Stud this evening. My name is Valda Chadwick and I am a marriage celebrant duly author-ised to solemnise this marriage in accordance with the laws of Australia,' she read.

Nina hid a smile. 'Scott?' she mouthed.

Scotty nodded. He'd almost forgotten the name every-one called him wasn't the name his parents had given him at birth. 'Scott' sounded so formal, so adult. It was a name for a man who knew what the hell he was doing.

'We are here today to celebrate with Nina and Scott a very important moment in their lives,' Valda continued. 'While they may have known each other for only a short time, that was all the time they needed to know they wish to spend the rest of their lives together as husband and wife.'

A chorus of *awww* came from the crowd.

'All of life's most important relationships can be found within a marriage. A husband and wife are each other's best friend, staunchest ally, biggest critic' – Valda paused for knowing laughter – 'patient teacher, loving listener and passionate lover.'

Scotty's gaze met Nina's and he saw his own shock reflected back at him. *Where did that come from?* He cursed himself for failing to read through Valda's speech before he had signed off on it. His grandmother had heard that. He didn't want people picturing him and Nina in the throes of passion.

One person in particular.

'But marriage is also a decision,' she went on. 'It demands that two people commit to walking through life together, weathering whatever storms and challenges may come their way. It is not a decision to be made lightly. Nina and Scott have made that decision and that is why we are all here this evening.'

There was that word again. *Decision*. Claire couldn't make one, so Scotty tried to make it for her. But every decision he made, it turned out, was the wrong one.

'A little bit of housekeeping now and then we'll get to the bit you're all waiting for,' Valda said conspiratorially. 'Before you are joined in marriage, Nina and Scott, I am required by law to remind you of the solemn and binding nature of the relationship into which you are about to enter. With that in mind, I ask you and the witnesses present whether you know of any impediment that should prevent this marriage today. Speak now, et cetera . . .'

More laughter. Scotty stared down at his shoes. He couldn't bring himself to look at Nina or their guests. He couldn't bear to see the one undeniable reason he knew the wedding shouldn't go ahead. Claire didn't want him, he understood that, but he shouldn't be marrying someone else when every cell in his body still wanted her.

Valda paused. Nobody said a word.

'Wonderful,' she said. 'In that case —'

'I do,' said Nina.

Valda smiled patiently. 'We're not quite up to that part, dear.'

'You're keen, Nina!' someone shouted from the crowd. A collective nervous titter followed.

'No, I mean I know of an impediment to the marriage,' Nina said. She looked up at Scotty. 'You don't love me, Scotty. And I don't love you either.'

The audience gasped in unison as Nina turned to face them. She searched their faces, looking for the one she was sure would be there.

Scotty realised with horror what was about to happen. 'Nina, no,' he whispered. 'Please don't do this.'

But Nina had found her target. 'This is for you, Claire,' she said, her voice loud and clear. 'This is all for you.'

CHAPTER TWENTY

Claire had seen enough movies to know that an objection at a wedding was swiftly followed by pandemonium. There was outrage and accusation. People fainted. Elderly relatives clutched their pearls. Explanations were demanded. Sometimes punches were thrown.

But in the movies it was always the mistress or the jilted lover who interrupted proceedings. It was never the bride objecting to her own wedding.

Maybe that was why, in the moments that followed Nina's declaration, there was nothing but silence. Nobody knew what to make of her announcement that she and the groom were not in love, so nobody said anything.

Except Nina herself. Once she started talking, she couldn't seem to stop.

'I'm so sorry, everyone,' she said, but she was looking directly at Claire. 'Scotty and I – we're not a couple. We never really were. He's just a wonderful friend who offered to help me and didn't want to go back on his word. Even if it meant losing everything.'

Claire waited to feel vindicated. She had been right all along. Scotty and Nina's wedding – the entire relationship – was a farce, and now the bride herself was admitting to it. But all she felt was numb. The shock of it was paralysing.

She turned to Alex. 'What's happening?' she managed to say. She could hardly speak. Her chest tightened as she struggled to make sense of what Nina was saying. She felt two hundred pairs of eyes swivel to stare at her. The weight of their judgement was like an anvil pressing on her heart. They thought she was responsible for this. They thought she was about to ruin Scotty's life – again.

Alex just shook his head, clearly as baffled as she was.

'It should be you standing up here, Claire, not me,' Nina went on. 'This wedding isn't even legal.'

Scotty put his hand on her arm. 'Nina, stop,' he said, his voice forceful. 'Please.'

But Nina wouldn't stop. She gathered up a handful of her chiffon skirt. 'This should be your dress. It looks better on you anyway. Remember how you tried it on? Couldn't you picture yourself wearing it on your wedding day?'

'That's enough!' Scotty snapped.

Claire heard the whispers reverberate through the congregation. *She tried on the dress! Claire Thorne tried to hijack Scotty's wedding! She's crazy!*

Somehow, she got to her feet. 'Is this true, Scotty?' she demanded. 'Does this have something to do with me?'

He stared helplessly at her. She saw a hundred emotions flash across his face, watched a thousand explanations form on his lips, until finally he opened his mouth and said, 'Yes, Claire. This has everything to do with you.'

His words tore her in two. She wrapped her arms around her abdomen as if physically trying to hold herself together. And then she was moving. She forced her way down the row of seats, treading on toes and painfully bashing into knees as she went.

She had to get away from this place, from all of them.

Claire blundered into the aisle and tripped on the hem of her dress. She heard the gossamer fabric tear as she fell to her knees. From the corner of her eye she saw Alex start after her.

'No,' she spat, holding up her palm to him. 'Just leave me alone.'

She scrambled to her feet again and kicked off her thongs. Then she ran, barefoot and blind, into the night.

She fled down the magically lit pathway, past the paddock-cum-car park and onto the gravel drive. She darted past the stable and the main house with its gaudy Christmas tree in the front yard. When she reached the road, Claire kept running. The rough bitumen scraped the soles of her feet, but she didn't care. She would run until her skin was bloody and raw. She would run until she had an answer, until she found peace.

It was completely dark now and for a moment she wished she'd had the foresight to bring her bag, with its handy telephone torch. But a moment later the road ahead of her was illuminated and she heard the roar of an engine approaching from behind.

She moved to the side of the road, praying whoever it was would just drive past her. As if the sight of a desperate woman in an evening dress running barefoot in the dark was nothing unusual.

But the car braked and the engine cut out and she knew it was him even before she heard his voice.

The car door slammed. 'Claire!' Scotty shouted. She didn't turn around when she heard him start running after her. She simply stopped and bent over, trying to catch her breath. He was so much bigger and more powerful than her; he would be next to her in seconds. Trying to outrun him was pointless. Hadn't she learned by now that she couldn't escape him no matter how hard she tried?

She felt his hand on the small of her back. The other grasped her shoulder and eased her into a standing position.

'Are you all right?' Scotty said. He cupped her face in his palms, his anguished eyes boring into hers. He'd shed his suit jacket and tie and stood before her in his shirtsleeves.

She nearly laughed. Was he kidding? 'What do you think?' she hissed. She shook herself free of his grip.

'I'm sorry. I'm so sorry,' he said. 'I can explain.'

'I don't want you to *explain*, Scotty. I'm not interested in more half-truths or alternative facts or lies by omission. I don't want another "version" of reality. Just tell me what's going on.'

He nodded. 'I love you, Claire. That's the truth. That's the truest thing I know.'

She burst into tears of abject fury. 'Don't you dare say that to me!' she shouted. 'You've just left your own *wedding*, for God's sake!'

Scotty made a noise like a wounded animal and hid his face behind his hands.

Minutes passed with the only sounds the shriek of the cicadas and Claire's wrenching sobs.

When her breathing began to calm, Scotty spoke again. 'Nina was never my girlfriend. We had a couple of dates when she moved to Bindy six weeks ago, but there was no spark, so we decided we'd just be friends,' he said. 'Actually, most of the time we spent together Nina had to listen to me go on and on about you.'

He smiled ruefully and to her chagrin Claire felt a flicker of compassion for him.

'You've got no idea how happy I was the night you found me on social media,' he went on. 'It was like Christmas morning, like I'd been holding my breath for eight years and didn't even know it. I fell so hard for you, Claire. Again.' He looked away. 'Actually, not again. I never stopped loving you. I couldn't, no matter how hard I tried.'

'But you never even hinted that you thought of me as anything more than a friend,' she accused him. 'And you waited *eight years* for me to come to you. Why didn't you try to find me?'

'Because you told me not to, remember? When you threw my engagement ring at me and ran off to America,' Scotty said hotly. He caught himself and took a deep breath. 'I learned the hard way then that you need to do things in your own time. When we reconnected, I wanted to tell you every day – every damn *day* – that you should be with me. But I knew that if I was ever going to get another chance with you, it had to be on your terms. And I was willing to wait.'

'Until you weren't,' Claire shot back. 'Getting engaged to someone else is an odd way to demonstrate your undying love.'

Scotty sighed. 'Nina is an incredible vet, Claire. Did I ever tell you that?'

She stared at him. 'So you proposed to her for the discount?'

A smile played at the corners of his mouth. 'She can't practise in Australia until she passes the National Veterinary Exam, but it costs a small fortune. She doesn't want to spend that money if she's not going to be able to stay here and the visa she has now means she'll have to leave in a year,' he said. 'She needs permanent residency, but it's at least three more years until she can apply for it.'

A fragment of a conversation drifted back to Claire. *The sooner I can get my permanent residency the better.* Nina had said as much at the yoga studio last weekend.

'If she's married to an Australian citizen, she can get a two-year provisional spouse visa right away and then permanent residency after that,' Scotty went on. 'She could be practising as a vet within a year.'

Claire's jaw dropped as the enormity of what Scotty was saying hit her. 'You're telling me this was some kind of green-card wedding?' she said.

He didn't reply, but his shame was obvious.

'And I suppose a whirlwind engagement culminating in a romantic Christmas Eve ceremony was supposed to make it seem more realistic? Even though you can't be legally married for another two weeks.'

Scotty stared at her, stunned. 'That's right,' Claire said. 'I'm not as dense as you seem to think I am. I can google.' Well, Jackie could.

'I don't think you're —' he started, only to stop abruptly. 'We'd joked around early on that I should marry Nina and make her a partner in the clinic. The more I thought about it, the more it seemed to make sense.'

Claire couldn't believe what she was hearing. 'For Nina, maybe. But you don't love each other, Scotty. Nina just said as much in front of the whole town. What on earth could be in it for you?' *And what does any of it have to do with me – with us?*

His gaze dropped to his feet. 'I'm not *in love* with Nina, but I thought maybe, in time . . .' He shook his head, as if realising for the first time how ridiculous the whole thing was. 'What's in it for me, aside from gaining a brilliant vet for the clinic, is just helping a friend. And . . . and also . . .'

'What?' Claire pleaded. 'Just *tell me.*'

'When we went out in Sydney that night, I *knew* you still had feelings for me. I could feel it in my bones. But you were so determined to make it clear that you only expected friendship,' he said. 'It was like there was a battle going on in your head between what you wanted and what you thought you deserved.'

Claire felt a painful lump form in her throat. If only Scotty knew how right he was. That was exactly how she'd felt that night – it was how she'd felt every moment since.

'I knew I could never love Nina, not really. Not the way I love you. So I made a decision. A stupid, rash, selfish decision,' he went on. The regret in his voice was palpable. 'I decided I had to try to make you go after what you want. You needed a reason to act. I knew that you'd never see what I see without a little bit of encouragement.'

'And what's that, Scotty?' Claire said. 'What do you see?'

He traced her cheekbone with the pad of his thumb. 'That we belong together,' he said huskily. 'We always have.'

Claire took a deep breath and blew it out slowly. 'That,' she said, 'is the most unbelievably arrogant thing I've heard in my entire life. You don't get to tell me what I want, what I *need*.' She didn't even feel angry. She was just so, so disappointed. The man she believed knew her better than anybody, who always had her best interests at heart, simply had no idea.

'I know,' he replied in a threadbare voice.

'You thought inventing a marriage would bring us back together?' she railed, taken aback by the fire in her tone. Maybe she did feel ever so slightly angry after all. 'How did you imagine that was possibly going to work? How were we going to be together if you were married to Nina? If everyone in Bindallarah thought your marriage was for real, you having a girlfriend might seem a little strange.'

'I wasn't thinking! I was just feeling! I was so scared of losing you again, Claire, and I had so few cards to play.'

'Cards to . . .? Listen to yourself, Scotty. This isn't a game. This is your life. And Nina's. And mine,' she said.

'I know that. I just . . .' He trailed off.

'But hey, if we're going with the cards analogy, then guess what? You had an ace up your sleeve all along. There was one card you could have played and won the whole . . . hand?' Cards were not her forte and the whole thing was absurd.

'What?'

'The truth. All you had to do was just tell me how you felt two weeks ago.' Claire shook her head sadly. 'Or, you know, at any point in the past six months.' Could he really not see that?

Scotty scoffed. 'You would have run a mile. You weren't ready.'

'You don't know that! You don't get to decide how I feel, Scotty,' she exploded. 'You say you learned the hard way not to try to make my decisions for me, but you haven't learned a damn thing. Not really.'

'I didn't want to make your decisions. I wanted *you* to make a decision,' he countered.

'But only if I decided on you, right? You wanted me to choose as long as I chose you.'

He hung his head. 'Yes,' he whispered. 'That's all I've ever wanted.'

Her tears flowed freely now. 'Well, then you should go and get married, Scotty,' she wept. 'Because I've made my decision. I choose me.'

She saw Scotty's shoulders begin to heave as she turned away from him. She broke into a run once more.

She didn't know where she was going. She didn't care, just as long as it was far, far away from Scotty Shannon.

CHAPTER TWENTY-ONE

'Merry Christmas, sweetheart.'

Claire forced her eyelids open as Vanessa's voice came to her as though in a dream. The gloom of her bedroom was suddenly swallowed by bright sunlight as her aunt threw open the curtains. Claire sat up in bed, feeling unsteady and disorientated.

'Is it morning already?' she whispered.

'It's lunchtime,' Vanessa said gently. 'It seems you walked most of the way home last night, so I thought I'd let you sleep. You must be exhausted.'

Claire nodded. She felt like she'd been flattened by a road train and not just because she had run more than a kilometre with bare feet before Alex, who had left the wedding to look for her, picked her up and drove her back to Vanessa's cottage. She must have slept for twelve solid hours, but it had been a black, dreamless slumber. She had never felt more worn out in her life.

'Christmas lunch is ready. Will you join us? I really think you should eat something.'

At the mention of food, Claire's stomach growled loudly. She couldn't remember the last time she'd eaten. She certainly hadn't had anything at the wedding. The memory of helping Scotty plan the menu with Toby Watts suddenly filled her mind; she quickly shook it away. She had felt so close to Scotty that day, but it was make-believe. It was all make-believe.

'Actually, I'm starving,' Claire said. 'I'll just have a quick shower. I shudder to think what kind of state my feet are in. Apologies in advance if these sheets are covered in road grime.'

Vanessa smiled. 'Don't worry about it, honey. It will all come out in the wash.'

Claire went to the bathroom and stood under the stream of hot water until it ran cold. She was physically clean, but her heart and soul still felt stained, sullied by lies and grief.

She wanted to crawl back into her pyjamas, but forced herself to brush her hair and put on a red 1950s-style sundress she'd brought specifically for Christmas Day. She even added a slick of red lipstick.

I choose me. That was what she'd told Scotty the night before, the moment before she had walked out of his life. It was time she started acting like it.

Claire went to the back patio and her heart swelled at the sight of the gorgeous Christmas table Vanessa had prepared. There was holly and tinsel, candles and Christmas crackers. Her napkin was secured with a twist of twine and a candy cane. She had dragged the Christmas tree from the hall to the garden, beautifully wrapped gifts stacked beneath it. Silver bells hung from the branches of the fig trees, tinkling in the gentle breeze.

'Aunty Vee, this looks amazing,' Claire said as she took her seat next to Gus.

Vanessa flushed with pride. 'Well, it's not every year we get to share Christmas with you,' she said warmly.

It was just the kind of Christmas celebration Claire had hoped for when she had decided to come back to Bindy for the first time in so many years. But she had figured it would be a happy occasion. She hadn't banked on the anchor of sadness she was now dragging around with her.

Vanessa gestured for Claire to hand her plate over and when she did her aunt piled it high with cold meats, prawns and an array of salads. Her family had never done the traditional turkey dinner on Christmas Day. It was always too hot in Bindallarah for such a heavy meal.

'So,' Gus said as Claire lifted a heaped forkful to her mouth. 'Scotty was here this morning.'

Claire just about choked on her food.

'Gus!' Vanessa said sharply. 'What did I tell you?'

Gus shrugged. 'What? I thought Claire would want to know. Sorry,' she said, not sounding remorseful in the slightest.

Claire coughed violently and reached for her wineglass. After three deep gulps of chilled chardonnay, she managed to regain some semblance of composure. She knew they would want to talk about it. Everyone in Bindallarah would be talking about it. This was a scandal of epic proportions – it would be discussed and dissected for years to come.

'We don't have to talk about it,' Vanessa said, shooting her daughter a murderous glare. 'Not today. Not until you're ready.'

'It's okay,' Claire spluttered eventually. 'We might as well get it out of the way.'

'Well, he looked like hell,' Gus said. Claire detected a distinct note of satisfaction in her tone.

'He did?' She knew she shouldn't care – Scotty deserved to look every bit as wretched as she felt – but the thought of him suffering still pained her, even after everything he'd done.

'The sun was barely up and he was knocking at the door, Claire,' Vanessa said. 'I don't think he'd slept at all. He wanted me to wake you, but I sent him on his way. I told him you'd gone back to Sydney and that he's not to contact you unless it's to grovel like he's never grovelled before.'

Claire frowned. 'Didn't Scotty go back to Cape Ashe after I left?'

Her aunt appeared stunned by the question. 'Oh, heavens, no. I don't know where he went. Everyone left very quickly after Nina's little display. Poor Mike and Janine looked mortified. Evidently they had no idea it was all a furphy.'

The disapproving way Vanessa said *Nina* made Claire's heart ache. Nina didn't deserve condemnation. She was as much a casualty of the whole debacle as Claire was. All she wanted was a chance to do the work she loved in a place she had come to treasure. Claire didn't blame her for taking Scotty up on his harebrained offer. She was, after all, the one who made him finally tell the truth.

'Don't be too hard on Nina,' she told her aunt. 'This really isn't her fault. I'd hate to think that the community won't continue to support her.'

She gave her aunt and Gus the broad strokes of Scotty and Nina's ruse, leaving out the part about it being a ploy to win Claire's heart. Vanessa pursed her lips, but said nothing more.

Gus, on the other hand, wouldn't be so easily dissuaded. 'Oh my God,' she said. 'So Scotty did all this for you? That is *so* romantic.'

Damn her shrewd eighteen-year-old brain. She should have known her cousin would immediately see the subtext. Gus didn't miss a trick. 'It is not romantic,' Claire said. 'It's deceitful and manipulative and controlling.'

'Who cares?'

Claire's fork hit her plate with a clatter. '*I* care, Augusta. Scotty lied to me.'

She shrugged. 'Only because he knew you wouldn't believe the truth. You were still so hung up on what happened between you eight years ago. If he'd just come right out and told you he loves you, you would have freaked out and run away again. And it's not like you haven't been lying to him too, with all that "we're just friends" nonsense.' Gus stared at her, one eyebrow cocked in a way that said, *You know I'm right.*

The funny thing was, Scotty had said almost the exact same thing to her last night.

'It's not that simple,' Claire said sadly. 'You wouldn't understand.'

'What don't I understand?' Gus said, rolling her eyes. 'Scotty loves you. You love Scotty. Don't' – she held up her hand as Claire opened her mouth to protest – 'try to deny it. It's the most obvious thing ever. A whole bunch of bizarre stuff happened, because the two of you are idiots who won't just admit how you feel, but that's over now. It *is* that simple, Claire.' Gus leaned back in her chair and crossed her arms. 'It's the simplest thing in the world.'

Claire looked to Vanessa, silently pleading for backup. But her aunt's expression was apologetic: she was with Gus on this one.

'He broke my trust,' Claire said, her head swivelling between the two of them. 'Don't you see that? What does *Cosmo* have to say about betrayal, Gus?'

'Yeah, he did,' she replied. 'And I don't need *Cosmo* to know that if he hadn't, you never would have admitted to yourself that you're crazy about him. The question is what are you going to do about it?'

Claire paused, trying to untangle her knotty thoughts. She had to admit that Gus was right in one sense: Claire hadn't exactly been upfront with Scotty about the way she felt or even why she had come back to Bindallarah in the first place. He had made some big mistakes, but Claire knew she was far from blameless. She may not have duped an entire town into believing she was marrying the love of her life in a romantic Christmas Eve ceremony – but she *had* convinced the people of Bindy that Claire Thorne and Scotty Shannon were ancient history and that simply wasn't true.

She'd had good reasons for keeping her cards close to her chest, she reasoned. She was only looking out for Scotty, trying not to burden him with her baggage, while at the same time trying to stop him from making a huge mistake. His happiness meant more to her than her own. All she wanted – all she'd ever wanted – was what was best for him. And . . .

And he wanted the same for her.

She knew that she would be happy with Scotty – had known it all along – but didn't think he wanted her any more. He said she was the only thing that would make him happy, but he'd been afraid to say so because he didn't think *she* wanted *him*.

Oh my God.

They wanted the same thing. The exact same thing.

Each other.

It was so clear, but she'd missed all the signs. Scotty had known all along: Claire had needed to see what she stood to lose before the pieces of the puzzle could fit together. He had hurt her and he had embarrassed her but, damn him, he was right.

And Gus was right, too. It *was* simple. If she loved Scotty, she should be with him. Maybe she didn't have to lose him. Maybe it really was the simplest thing in the world.

Claire wiped her mouth with her napkin, pushed back her chair and stood up. What was she going to do about it? She would show Gus and Vanessa exactly what she was going to do about it.

'I'm going to get my man.'

Gus squealed like the proverbial stuck pig. 'I *knew* it!'

An elated smile lit Vanessa's face, but as Claire watched, her aunt quickly rearranged her features into an expression of familial concern. 'Sweetheart, are you certain?' Vanessa said. 'Everything you've just said makes a lot of sense.'

'Screw sense, Aunty Vee,' Claire replied. 'I've been sensible all my life and it's got me absolutely nowhere. It's time to embrace the crazy.'

Claire watched Bindallarah recede into the distance in her rear-view mirror as she pressed the accelerator flat to the floor and headed for Thorne Hill. The back seat of her hatchback was littered with clothes and shoes. She hadn't even bothered to pack them into her suitcase; she'd just tossed them into the car and hit the road. One way or another, she wasn't planning on sleeping in Vanessa's spare bed tonight.

The sea breeze reached in through the open window and tousled her curls. The car's interior was stifling and she was desperate to cool it down while she waited for the air conditioning to do its job. Now the salty-sweet Bindallarah air drifted in as if to underscore the choice she'd made.

Scotty had wanted her to make a decision and finally she had. He was stuck with her, now and forever.

If he'll still have me.

Who knew Gus was so wise, with her magazine psychology and her black-and-white view of life? There was, of course, nothing remotely simple about any of this – and yet the answer was as clear as the cloudless Christmas Day sky. Her cousin made her think of Scotty at that age. He'd been the same: so decisive, so sure he had all the answers.

Claire watched as the needle on the speedometer crept past 110 kilometres per hour. She knew it was reckless, but she felt consumed by the need to get to Scotty as quickly as possible, to make sure he still existed, that he was still hers. She wasn't sure whether he would even be at Thorne Hill – perhaps he'd be spending Christmas with his family at Cape Ashe. But she had to start somewhere, and if he wasn't at home she would search the entire district until she found him.

The car rounded a sweeping bend and in her peripheral vision Claire saw a flash of movement. Suddenly, an animal darted into the road directly in front of her car.

Not just any animal, she realised with horror.

'Tank!'

Claire stomped the brake pedal with both feet. She felt the wheels lock and the rear of the hatchback lose traction and then she was spinning, fishtailing wildly across the highway. She heard the screeching of tyres on tarmac.

Claire closed her eyes and braced for impact.

Seconds passed with no bang, no crunch of metal on bone. When the acrid stench of burnt rubber filled her nostrils, she opened her eyes.

Her car had come to rest on the dirt shoulder on the other side of the road, facing the wrong direction and surrounded by a thick cloud of dust and smoke. There was no sign of Tank. Claire began to tremble violently.

As she fumbled for the doorhandle, Claire heard a shout. Her heart in her throat, she peered through the driver's side window and saw a black four-wheel drive parked in a rest area a little further down the road. She squinted to read the lettering on the shiny black paint.

Bindallarah Veterinary Hospital.

Scotty.

And then there he was, running towards her car, wrenching the door open, unfastening her seatbelt and dragging her to her feet.

Scotty ran his hands over her face, her arms, through her hair. He checked over every inch of her and when he was satisfied she was still in one piece, he said, 'You always were terrible at parking, Thorne.'

'Tank,' she replied, trying to catch her breath. 'Is he okay?'

'He's fine. I only stopped to let him out for a toilet break and he ran off, cheeky little bugger. He's back in the car.'

Claire's relieved sigh came out in a *whoosh*. 'What is it with that dog and throwing himself in front of your girlfriends?'

Scotty laughed, but the sound was hollow, mirthless. Gus hadn't been exaggerating when she'd said Scotty looked terrible. He was unshaven and his hair was unkempt. His skin looked sallow and his eyes were puffy. He was still in his wedding suit trousers and shirt, though both were as creased as if he'd slept on the beach. Maybe he had.

But he was still beautiful.

'You don't look like you should be behind the wheel yourself, Scotty. Where are you going? It's Christmas Day,' she said gently. 'Shouldn't you be with your family? Or perhaps sleeping?'

Scotty rubbed his face and stretched. Claire felt a telltale heat pool within her as she saw his muscles undulate beneath the thin cotton of his white shirt.

'I'm going to Sydney,' he said.

'Oh,' she said. Something akin to hope flared in her chest. 'Why?'

Scotty turned away from her and gazed down the long, straight stretch of road, as if trying to visualise the city that lay eight hundred kilometres to the south. 'Because you're going to Sydney.'

'Actually, I'm going to Thorne Hill.'

Scotty's eyes widened in surprise. 'But Vanessa said —'

'Vanessa was fibbing,' Claire cut in with a smile. 'She was just looking out for me. That's what she does.' It was what she had always done, Claire could now see, and she loved her aunt for it.

Scotty didn't respond, but regarded her steadily. His

guarded expression made Claire's stomach twist. Not for the first time, she wished she could read his thoughts, to ensure she wasn't about to make a total fool of herself.

'So you're only going to Sydney because my scary aunt told you to apologise?' she continued, trying for a teasing tone.

'No, Claire, I'm going to Sydney because I'm in love with you and I want to be wherever you are,' Scotty said. 'I thought I'd made myself pretty clear about that last night. Why are you going to Thorne Hill?'

There was no trace of fatigue in his gaze now, but there was a challenge in his words. His green eyes were as hungry and penetrating as Claire had ever seen them.

Tell him, her inner voice screamed. *Don't waste another second!*

Interpreting her silence as hesitation, Scotty said, 'I know I've been an idiot. I know I've hurt you and I'm sorry.' His tone was all urgency. He put his hands on Claire's waist and drew her in close. 'But I can't lose you again. I can't just stand by and watch you walk out of my life. I promise I won't ask you to marry me again. I promise I won't try to tell you what you think or how you feel. I'll wait for you forever if you just tell me I've still got a chance.'

With still-trembling fingers, Claire touched the triangle of smooth skin that was visible at the open neck of his shirt. She felt the throb of his pulse beneath her fingertips.

'Well, that depends,' she murmured.

She felt rather than heard his reply. 'On what?'

'On whether there's an opening for another equine special-ist at the Bindallarah Veterinary Hospital.'

Scotty laughed and the sound warmed her to the tips of her toes. 'I'll see what I can do,' he said. 'I know the owner.'

Scotty's arms tightened around her and Claire let her head fall forward to rest on his chest. She remembered how good it felt to be wrapped in his arms, even in the blazing afternoon sun on the side of a dusty highway.

'Just so there're absolutely no misunderstandings this time,' he said, breaking the silence, 'are you saying what I think you're saying? What I *hope* you're saying?'

Claire took a deep breath and looked up at him, so that her gaze locked with his. 'What I'm saying, Scotty Shannon, is that I love you. I've loved you since I was fifteen years old. I choose you. Forever.'

And when Scotty's lips claimed hers, it felt like the first time.

EPILOGUE

'Whose stupid idea was it to have a beach wedding in the middle of winter?' Gus grumbled, pulling her faux fur stole close around her. 'It's freezing.'

'Toughen up, princess. It's not that cold. Only a few more weeks until spring,' Claire replied. She handed her cousin a bouquet of lavender, snowdrops and soft pink hellebores. 'Anyway, isn't the excitement of finally getting to be in a wedding enough to give you a warm glow?'

Gus couldn't help but smile at that. She turned to appraise herself in the full-length mirror in Vanessa's living room, which was doing triple duty as a dressing room, hair salon and makeup studio for the bridal party.

'I do make a pretty spectacular bridesmaid,' Gus said approvingly, smoothing the flowing skirt of her navy blue gown.

'And so modest,' Claire teased, nudging her cousin aside so she could give herself a last-minute onceover. She retied the satin ribbon that secured her own snow-white stole around her shoulders and tucked a stray curl back into her elaborate up-do, wishing she'd opted to leave her hair down. She was inherently uncomfortable in such a formal ensemble, but it was just for one day, after all.

Claire glanced at the clock on the mantel. 'We'd better get a move on,' she said.

'Chill, cuz,' Gus replied. 'It's traditional for the bride to be late.'

'What's the bridesmaids' excuse?' Claire said, planting one hand on her hip and picking up her own bouquet with the other.

'Don't worry, we can go,' came a voice from behind her. 'I'm all set.'

Claire turned and gasped as she saw Nina emerging from the hallway into the living room. She was a vision in a strapless ivory wedding dress with an elaborately beaded bodice and a skirt made of what looked like acres of tulle. A vintage rhinestone necklace glittered on her décolletage and a crown of creamy white roses gave her the dreamy quality of a woodland fairy.

'You look like a princess,' Gus breathed.

Tears pricked at Claire's eyes. 'Nina, you're absolutely breathtaking,' she said, her voice thick with tears.

Nina gave a wry smile. 'The look is a little different from last time, huh?'

Claire giggled. 'If I'd known you better eight months ago I *never* would have believed Scotty's and your wedding was the real deal.'

'Are you saying I'm a bridezilla?' Nina said, pressing her hand to her heart in mock outrage.

Claire laughed again. Her friend was way too easygoing to deserve that label, but Nina had certainly been more pro-active in planning her *real* wedding than she'd ever been in the lead-up to Scotty's and her sham ceremony. From the flowers to the groomsmen's boutonniere, this time around Nina had a clear vision – much to the delight of Gus and her library of bridal magazines.

'Ready, sweetpea?' Nina's eldest brother, Brock, appeared at her side. In his rented tuxedo and shiny dress shoes, the tall Texan cattle rancher looked as uncomfortable as Claire felt in her own fancy garb – but his face radiated love for his little sister.

Nina nodded and took her brother's hand. 'Let's get this show on the road,' she said excitedly.

With Gus, Claire and Nina's sister and Maid of Honour, Claudine, leading the way, the bridal party made the short walk from Vanessa's cottage to the beach. It was a stunning early August day in Bindallarah. Though the afternoon air was chilly, there wasn't a breath of wind and the sky was a brilliant blue. Contrary to Gus's complaint, Claire couldn't imagine a more beautiful setting for the wedding of two people who were so wildly in love with each other.

When they reached the top of the path onto the sand, Nina's younger brother, Doug, who was a groomsman, sig-nalled to the waiting string quartet and they began to play the classic Beach Boys song, 'God Only Knows'.

Claire's heart swelled as she saw Scotty waiting at the altar next to Doug and Callum Jessop, the groom's brother. Scotty looked unbelievably sexy in his slim-cut royal blue suit, chosen by the bride to complement the girls' gowns and the sparkling ocean that was the backdrop for the ceremony.

As she glided down the sandy path towards him, Claire winked at Scotty and saw a familiar expression scud across his face. It was a look she'd seen often since she'd returned to Bindy for good in February: lust. The feeling was mutual. When they weren't working at the vet clinic, looking after Autumn and her foal, January, who had both come to live with them, or tending Thorne Hill's fledgling acai berry plantation, Claire and Scotty couldn't keep their hands off each other. They had eight years of lost time to catch up on, after all.

Claire reached the altar and paused to peck the groom on the cheek. 'Wait 'til you see her, Alex,' she whispered in his ear. 'Your girl is an absolute stunner.'

Alex said nothing, but smiled and squeezed Claire's hand. His palm was clammy and Claire felt a rush of affection as she realised bombastic Alex Jessop, mayor and all-round renaissance man, was as nervous as a little boy on his first day of school.

Or a grown man on his wedding day.

Suddenly, the quartet segued from 'God Only Knows' into Wagner's *Bridal Chorus*. The wedding guests turned to face Nina as she walked down the aisle on her brother's arm, but Claire kept watching Alex. His chin trembled and his eyes shined as he drank in the sight of his stunning bride. Not for the first time, Claire wondered how she could have missed the obvious chemistry between Nina and Alex when she first came back to Bindallarah the previous Christmas.

It wasn't long after Claire's permanent return to Bindy that Nina had confided her crush on Alex. Even while going through the motions of preparing to marry Scotty, Nina had admitted to Claire that she'd been fighting her growing feelings for her boss – but she was certain their professional relationship meant Alex would never entertain the thought of dating her.

Claire knew from torturous personal experience that making assumptions about somebody else's feelings was a recipe for calamity and convinced Nina to ask Alex out for a strictly not-work-related drink, just to test the waters.

They were engaged by Easter.

'What can I say?' a rapturous Nina had said with a laugh when she told Claire the news of her second quickfire engagement. 'I've never been a patient woman.'

Now Valda Chadwick stepped forward and began to speak.

'Good afternoon, everybody. Thank you for joining Nina and Alexander here on Bindallarah Beach on this lovely winter's afternoon,' the celebrant said.

Claire took a deep breath. *This is it.*

'Before we get on with the official stuff, Nina and Alex have asked that we get one little matter out of the way early. We all know what happened last time, so does anyone present know of any impediment that should prevent this marriage today?'

Laughter rippled through the crowd.

It turned into a horrified hubbub when Nina opened her mouth and said, 'I do.'

Claire saw Scotty's jaw drop. Her own heart felt like it was going to burst out of her chest.

'Don't worry, guys,' Nina went on. She held up her hands, appealing for silence. The agitated chatter died down.

'Nothing is going to prevent me and Alex tying the knot today, but there's some business that needs taking care of first. I made a scene at this point in proceedings once before and caused my two best friends a whole lot of pain. So it seems only fair that I fix that today.'

Nina turned to Claire. She reached out her hand, her huge diamond engagement ring sparkling in the sunlight, and took Claire's bouquet. 'Over to you, Claire,' she said with a warm smile. Next to her, Alex beamed.

Claire clasped her trembling hands together and stepped forward. Behind Alex, third in the line of groomsmen, Scotty stared at her, his beautiful face a picture of confusion and more than a hint of concern.

As the entire town watched, Claire went to him.

'Claire, what's —'

'Scotty, nearly nine years ago, you asked me to marry you,' Claire began, cutting him off. Her voice was resolute and she was surprised to find her nerves had vanished. 'I ran away from you then because I was trying to run away from myself. I don't know what I did to deserve it, but somehow you kept loving me through all the years we were apart and you were willing to wait for me to realise that I will never love anybody but you.'

There was a murmured chorus of *awww* from the wedding guests.

'At Christmas you promised you'd never propose to me again,' she went on. 'Do you remember?'

Scotty cocked an eyebrow. 'Vaguely,' he said with a wry smile, prompting laughter from the crowd.

'Well, I've been thinking about it, and I've decided that I can't accept that.'

Claire sank onto one knee.

She reached for Scotty's hands. 'Scotty Shannon, will you make me even happier than I am already and marry me?'

There wasn't a sound bar the crashing of the waves on the sand. At nearly thirty, Scotty still had a terrible poker face. His thoughts splayed out in his expression, just as they had when he was sixteen. Claire watched as he made his decision.

He pulled her to her feet. 'It's about bloody time,' he said. He kissed her fiercely as Gus squealed and all of Bindy clapped and cheered.

'What do you think about a Christmas Eve wedding?' Scotty whispered in Claire's ear as he held her close.

'No need to wait that long,' she replied. 'What are you doing thirty days from now?'

ACKNOWLEDGEMENTS

First and foremost, thanks to my fabulous editor at Penguin, Kimberley Atkins, for uttering those immortal words: 'Want to write a romance about vets?' Why, yes. Yes, I do!

Thanks also to Amanda Martin and Alexandra Nahlous for your spot-on editorial insights and your patience as I clumsily juggled two books at once.

I am a dog person, but Claire inconveniently decided to be a horse person and that left me in a bit of a pickle. Thoroughbred-sized thanks to my old friend Dr Samuel Hurcombe, equine specialist extraordinaire, for giving me a crash-course in horse medicine and answering all my silly questions.

As ever, I could not have written this book without the support of my husband, Mark. Thanks, NP. The contribution of wine and procrastinaps to the writing of this book also cannot be overstated.

And finally, thanks to everyone who loves romance novels as much as I do and who reads them unapologetically. Love is a universal experience and a fundamental human need and we could all use a little more of it. #loveozromance

Also by Laura Greaves

How does a regular Aussie girl win the heart of the most famous man on the planet in the unforgiving glare of the spotlight?

Talented, gorgeous and hopelessly in love, American movie star Mitchell Pyke and Brazilian supermodel Vida Torres were Hollywood's most talked-about couple. They seemed destined for 'happily ever after' – until Vida left Mitchell for his best friend, and Mitchell publicly vowed he would never love again.

Sydney dog trainer Kitty Hayden has never even heard of Mitchell Pyke. When her work takes Kitty to Mitchell's movie set, their worlds spectacularly collide. The chemistry between them is undeniable – and it's not long before Kitty is turning her life upside down to be with her leading man. But as Kitty quickly discovers, when someone as famous as Mitchell Pyke tells the world he'll never love again, the world listens.

Some are born to be great mums, some achieve greatness, and some have motherhood thrust upon them.

Ambitious, independent and happily child-free, Anna Harding isn't worried when her best friend, Helena, unexpectedly falls pregnant. After all, she's living the expat high life in London with her boyfriend, Finn, while Helena is on the other side of the world in sleepy Adelaide. Anna's not even fazed when Helena asks her to be the baby's godmother. How hard can it be from 15,000 km away?

But when a depressed Helena turns up on Anna's doorstep, begging her to look after baby Ivy while she escapes to Scotland to get her head together, the dirty nappies really hit the fan. How can newspaper gossip columnist Anna carry on her A-list lifestyle with a screaming kid in tow – especially when her job is at risk and Finn ups and moves to Ireland in pursuit of his own dream career?

With Helena swept up in her new life in Scotland, Anna fears she'll be left holding the baby for good – until her grumpy neighbour, Luke, unexpectedly emerges as her go-to infant expert. Maybe pseudo-parenthood isn't so bad after all . . .